THE
SWIMMERS

Also by Marian Womack

The Golden Key

THE
SWIMMERS

MARIAN WOMACK

TITAN BOOKS

The Swimmers
Print edition ISBN: 9781789094213
E-book edition ISBN: 9781789095920

Published by Titan Books
A division of Titan Publishing Group Ltd.
144 Southwark Street, London SE1 0UP
www.titanbooks.com

First Titan edition February 2021
10 9 8 7 6 5 4 3 2 1

A CIP catalogue record for this title is available from the British Library.

Printed and bound in the US.

To Anita and Oliver

PART I

THE RING / SURFACE

PEARL

1

This is a white and pristine room, no space for shadows. Soon, the glass vent will slide open over my face, and the music will start. The music is always the same: ethereal women, their voices reverberating, as if the recording had been made in a cave, or else the deepest conservation chamber of the Registry. I think it is music from before the green winter, not connected to us, nothing to do with us. But it is calming, reassuring. I feel this is why it has been chosen for the task of gently bringing me up into the world each morning: I am in the last throes of pregnancy, not meant to survive delivery. I am expendable.

It is possible that today I will not see anyone. It is possible that a group of doctors will come to see me, loom over me and prod me, look inside my belly, the child magically appearing in the hovering monitors that float above my head; I sometimes can get a glimpse of its watery, amorphous form.

It is hard to admit this, but I can't seem to find within me any particular feelings about this creature, neither good nor bad, when I hear her heartbeat mediated by those machines. Perhaps it is not my fault. So much has happened to get here, to this point in time, to this moment, bad things and good; now I can only be a vessel for what will come. Like I said, expendable.

Expendable is a good thing. It means that I will not have to worry beyond some point in time, a date that is clearly marked in the calendar. I am so exhausted at this point; there is so little that can be fixed by an elusive sleep. I just want it to end, to get her out. This suspended state, this waiting, is slowly taking away my will to live, my capacity to decide for myself. It's easier not to question, it's easier not to feel.

I am not special. One more surfacer from the pile. There are many of us up here. But the child surely must be. At least I know she will be kept. It is possible that she will be reallocated to a ringer family, and will live happily ever after. No one has explained these things to me, what the steps are that will be taken, what is usually done. But I can imagine, infer things. I can only hope her skin is fairer than mine, more like her father's, those things count for something up here.

Is life better here, in the ring, than down there on the

surface? How can I know? I haven't really lived that long, I have never 'lived' up here. I have only been kept, prodded, examined. Not the same thing at all.

There is a little table, and a chair, and if I climb onto the table I can look out through a round window. I can then see it, Earth, the surface where I belong. The green advancing, intent on devouring it all. The Three Oceans, brown and orange, home to the leviathans, cetaceans as big as old countries; their babies as big as houses, as big as Gobarí; their shadows sometimes distinguishable from up here… Yet I know that is not possible, not really. But there is a famous one down there, I know that. As big as a continent. A famous one. And I think I have seen it, its back gently pushing up the surface of the debris-covered water, the liquid swelling under its massive form. If I close my eyes, I can see myself swimming among them, exactly as Mother wanted me to. I see him sometimes as well, my father, although we never swam together. Or perhaps it is a *mullo*, a devil with his face.

They say that sometimes the leviathans leave the waters and fly into space, and turn and twirl for a minute until they get bored, and then they go back into the ocean, splashing around, causing tidal waves which erase whole coastlines. When I am looking down onto Earth, my chest contracts sometimes. For a moment I cannot breathe. It is grief, I think.

—

Who am I? I am a child of the surface. I was born and raised in Gobarí. We left after Mother remarried, when I was still no more than a child, changed it for Old Town and the Registry. The earliest years of my life took place in the house, with only sporadic visits to Old Town; but all those happened while my father was still alive, and, try as I might, I do not remember much of those early expeditions. My knowledge of Old Town was punctuated by Father's absence, by the deprivation it brought. Later, after Mother's death, I would enter the Registry; again, I was unmoored. And then came Arlo and hope and disappointment, although perhaps not in that order. But before all that was Gobarí, and the forest, and Savina, and Eli. And swimming in the pond, and swimming in Kon-il; limbs loose, feet kicking, and my eyes avidly taking in all that was old and new inside the water: the dragonflies, the fireflies, a little mouse with its nose just above the oily surface. The greenery, falling languid over the banks, its overgrown leaves forming canopies on which to rest from the heat, and all the creatures visible and invisible—chirping, tweeting, roaring. I imagined myself safe inside the water, always had. It was a whole world to me, contained in a little spot, hardly noticeable from the sky.

The pond was where I liked to play best. I went there often. Muddy water flowed into it, clouding it dark. The stench was unbearable. I grew up imagining it bottomless, and that quality meant it exuded some mystery as well. Some of the beanies believed it to be a holy well, with hidden caves twisting and turning beneath the surface of the water. They said that an *alicanta* lived there, a basilisk, and they swore that some days you could see her about. To me, the pond was no more than a place to pass the time, although that would change. After I met Eli it would start to mean something different: her love for swimming in its cloudy embrace, my made-up tales for her about the trees and the stars, a place that was ours and ours only. The pond was protected by the cool shadow of the pine trees, with their pungent smell at the height of summer. The smell of almond flowers prevailed as well, forever dying under the sun. They always seemed to have bloomed so long ago, that was why the smell made me feel giddy, as if I were about to pass out. But it was also comforting. The heat, heavy and sticky; the solid air condensing around you. I could catch glimpses of the sun through the branches above me, and little white sparks covered my vision. The forest pulsated, you could feel it stirring up in the morning, going to sleep at night; a living thing. You were safer then, when the forest rested. You could almost feel it, breathing regularly, sleeping, perhaps.

Some people called the forest 'the jungle'. After the green winter, it had grown rich in many species previously unknown to the region, the Mediterranean and the tropical mixing in a wild, feverish embrace. The jungle grew more each year, its flora mutating constantly into larger and more impressive exemplars, some deadly if they caught you unawares. A vine could target you and twist itself around your body until you were dead. An oversize leaf could hold a great blob of poisonous sap, ready to drop it on you at the exact moment you passed by. A carnivorous orchid could attack you. And this was only the plants: no one knew which new animals might be encountered each day; they mutated so rapidly that it was impossible to know what was going to emerge from beneath the shrubs and the trees.

Despite all this we rarely went to Old Town. Gobarí was my home, with its crumbling walls and its mouldy porch, and those flowers and bushes and trees, all closing above like a roof. The Venus flytraps as big as a small child, the vines and the tendrils that moved like the living things they were. And those strange days when the sky was green, blue, electric. We did not know it then, what it meant, when the blue surge of light blotted up the sky; most people still don't know. The day would have been atypical, even in a place like the forest. You could sense it: the animals refusing to make an appearance, the odd silent birds. And the greenery twisting and twirling around you, as if it were on edge. Then, at dusk, the sky an ominous purple, followed by the blue light dancing over us, caressing the stars and the constellations when night fell. At the time, I thought the sky was going to collapse upon us, finally devouring all the monstrosities that lived with us in the forest. Now that I know what the light means I can only feel sadness at my past ignorance.

After one of these events, the forest would grow a little, but never engulfing Gobarí. At the beginning of the property, the green stopped abruptly. At night, I closed my eyes and thought of trees and the vines and the branches, advancing towards the house, and I could hear the shrieks of so many creatures, unnamed long-ago-mutated things that now came back to feed on us. But I couldn't have slept anywhere else; the smells and the odd noises and that feeling of oppression, of not being able to breathe... To me, that was home. The forest gave us everything we needed: wood, for fuel and building things, and the cork that furnished the insides of the vessels; plants and flowers and vines and shrubs, and we ate them, we cooked them, or we transformed them into remedies and potions; and wild animals, surreal creatures that changed so quickly that they could never be trapped by any taxonomy, and were wilder than the forest itself, the only meat we consumed. It was fair that they in their turn consumed us, that the forest gobbled up a beanie child now and again, advancing towards a settlement and making it disappear from our world.

At the pond I was surrounded by flowers and plants of many different colours. I could see rabbit's bread and the *sierra* poppy Eli liked to collect in thick bunches. Pale flowers grew on the bank, and close to it some silver sage. Savina would know all their properties. Love-in-a-mist, mournful widow, oleander. It was poisonous. The prettiest flowers usually are: she had taught me that when I was very little. Never, ever, succumb to hunger if you don't know what you are eating. Her first rule of many.

Gobarí wasn't like the wall, not by a long way. It was a late twenty-first-century construction, the vestige of a lost civilisation, brick and sand and mortar. No one understood why it still stood, situated as it was in the middle of the overgrowth. It had survived the green winter that devoured everything in its wake; it had survived floods and extreme cold and extreme heat. It had survived all the darkness that came after. The storms that hit against its walls every rainy season, but which did not seem to erode its crumbling buttresses, as if some kind of unspoken contract mediated between the house and the elements. Gobarí had always belonged to Mother's family: an old family, one with certain rights and a ruin in the middle of nowhere. They had been allowed to keep it.

I spent most of my time in the little meadow by the pond, among the eucalyptus plants. It was rich in wild orchids. I had heard somewhere that they could be literal aliens, fallen from some distant planet. They were odd and beautiful, and their names were odd and beautiful: the bug, the bee, the lizard. Frightening, unreal. Orchids were my favourite plants. Eli hated them. She would look at them, terrified. And then she would say: 'Those horrid things!' Little by little, the story emerged: the orchids in Gobarí were like miniature versions of the flowers that had killed her grandparents.

'How do you know that's true?'

'There were witnesses. They were at the bank of a river, the Guadin. The tendrils surrounded them. They spent ages dying, minutes and hours.'

She explained this with a serious face on, as if she had learnt to live with the horrid knowledge. But I could sense some intense feeling underneath, as if she were trying very hard to remain composed, when in truth she was as horrified as anyone. I knew it then, that there was a hardness inside her.

Me, I could live with the greenery, I could navigate the forest. I could anticipate a sudden change in the landscape, a passing moment of danger. I could sense new noises, interpret the metamorphosing terrain, an intimate knowledge of the space, developed somehow from early childhood. Allowed to roam freely, I had to look after myself from very early on. Animals scared me more than plants. Some of them made me think of demons, crawled scratchily up to the surface of the Earth to torment us. I knew this knowledge was one of the few things that remained from when Father was with us. He would insist on passing this on, books and diagrams and conversations that would always end in this one lesson.

'Never venture somewhere if you hear a call you don't recognise. Never make friends with a small animal: its mother may come after and eat you. Never go into the forest when the birds are not singing; never go when their shrieks are so loud that they are all you can hear.'

And so on. I would be sitting next to him, my childish senses picking up a hidden current, something underneath. I have a clear recollection of my mother asking me to be quiet because my father was around, and I now know that the moods of the house depended on his moods, that he expected us to be cheerful and happy if he was, and to be subdued and out of sight when he was morose. I now wonder if I internalised this fear of animals because he was the one teaching it to me, and I was scared of upsetting him or something worse. Was I scared of animals, or was I scared of him?

Many years later, when my father was already dead and in the ground, one morning I was waiting for Eli at the pond, by the water, and something happened. A hare came out of nowhere. She was so beautiful, orange with streaks of yellow all over her body. But she was also as big as me, and obviously much stronger. The hare got up on her hind legs and heaved her body up, looking at me with curiosity. Her head tilted softly, as if she were asking a question. She stretched her body up even further. I realised she could kill me with a bludgeoning of her powerful front arms. I took a step back, and of course a branch cracked under my feet. The hare did not like the noise.

She opened her mouth, showing me her pointy teeth, and hissed loudly. I knew she was marking her territory. I thought of Father. If I didn't make any sudden moves, I would be safe. Hares can be impressive creatures, but you are usually okay if you treat them with the same caution you would take with the larger centipedes.

Something moved through the eucalyptus trees; a rustling sound of branches and leaves being pulled aside. Someone was approaching the pond.

The hare turned in the direction of the disturbance with another sudden hiss. Her eyes as open and big as her mouth as she prepared to attack the intruder.

I grabbed a branch lying on the floor; it was thick and heavy. I moved swiftly, bludgeoning the hare just before she could attack Eli. Next thing I knew, I was staring at a beautiful pattern of colours I couldn't for a second make sense of. And then it hit me: I was looking at the hare's brain pouring out of her head, mixed together with a dark red liquid.

I stayed where I was, spattered with the warm blood. I was trying to think of anatomy lessons, the circulation of the blood. How to put it all back, all that patchy learning, first aid, basic cures, herbals. Those things all surface children needed to learn, in case we were one day sent up to the sky. How to put it all back? The thought, like a flash: you cannot put it back. The brain would stay there, on the ground. I looked at Eli, her head round, and in place.

The hare jerked horribly. I kneeled down close to her, and beat her until she stopped moving. Perhaps a couple of times, three, four.

I was panting, covered in blood and sweat. I looked up to the hot sky, white dots still clouding my vision.

Eli was staring at me, at the hare, at the branch that I dropped.

'Thank you,' was all she could muster.

But I had an odd flavour in my mouth, as if I were remembering something from long ago. It was the metallic taste of the hare's blood, splattered over my mouth, horribly. I saw my father in my mind, coming towards me. Towards us: me and a little beanie girl. She used to be my friend. She was dead now.

We were playing, my father advancing towards us, a malignant look on his face. Was it my father, or was it a *mullo* with his face, coming up from Hell to take us back there with him?

2

It had all started there, with the hare, dead by the overgrowth. Thinking hard of all the ways in which I could put her brain and her blood back in place, and thinking hard about how I could not. Seeing in my mind the little beanie girl, and knowing that she wasn't there any longer, and knowing that she stopped being there at the same time that Father did, and wondering why. She used to dye her hair blue, and I did as well. What was her name?

Now, in my pod up among the stars, I benefit from all the scientific and technological advances that the Upper Settlement can offer a surfacer like myself. Miracles are performed in the ring; everybody knows that. Would it be possible, here, to put it all back? As soon as I arrived up here, things progressed quickly. We were sorted like cattle, and I am carrying the biggest possible prize. And yet, and yet. I doubt they could do it themselves: put it all back together, bring the dead back to life, prevent from dying that which should not live.

Here, I dream that there is some problem with the delivery, or the child moves to a difficult position. I suspect they will cut me in half to get her out if that happens.

The hare had brought back those images of Father, of the beanie girl and me playing together, scenes perhaps seen in a dream, or that took place many years back. I went back again and again for several weeks to see the corpse, forgotten among the branches, for some reason untouched by the other creatures. Perhaps some of her striking fur possessed an unexpected poisonous quality. No maggots crawled through her orange fur. Instead, a liquid mass of yellow and pink covered the open wound, and the rotten flesh that had somehow gushed over the grass looked sticky.

I felt a strange comfort in her presence. The sweet smell of rot did not displease me, not really. I would pretend to gag at it; otherwise I could imagine the beanie youngsters who worked for us would single me out as 'odd', or 'fancy'. They might laugh at me as they laughed at Mother. But death was as natural as living, I thought. Perhaps there was a bit of swimmer in me.

I was often sent to harvest with them, the beanie youngsters. We collected nuts, leaves, flowers. They were not children, but not fully grown up either. They existed in that indeterminate time of understanding cruelty, of understanding pain. And, after the Delivery Act, of understanding that I was not better than them any longer.

First, there were the elegant techies, then their servants, the beanies, and lastly those on the Upper Settlement, the ringers, lording over us all. The *shuvanies*, like Savina, did not even count. No one mentioned them, worried about them, either their fears or their desires. They occupied a liminal space within our society, at once part of it and outsiders. They kept themselves to themselves, and were only part of a household if they served a family; and they would not serve anyone but the most aristocratic and old ones. Employing one was a mark of high distinction. Hence, they were both inside and outside of our lives, neither believers nor followers of the condoned doctrine.

After the Act was passed and ratified, we were all equal. Or were we? With the new knowledge that we were no better than them, other ideas awoke in the beanie brains of my harvest companions. They knew that our clothes were shabby, that our only vehicle had been repaired a hundred times, and that it didn't hover over the road anymore. It needed to go on its six wheels. This was a problem for us: the roads into Old Town were not accessible at that point. Once the hover system started failing, we were cut off from the world. You would never see another vehicle; you would never see a drone from the ring descending with its annoying buzz, as unwelcome as a queen butterfly; you would never see the ring itself. This absence of the Upper Settlement from our sky made everything more unreal if I was ever taken into town. For I was so little used to seeing the white translucent structure, all lights and shiny colours orbiting around itself in the middle of the night, that I could not quite believe that it was up there. The answer to my childish question would in turn depend on who I was asking:

'Mommy, is the ring real?'

'Of course it's real. Mr Vanlow has lived there.' This was our new neighbour. 'Many people live there. You yourself have some family up there: one of my second cousins managed to emigrate years ago.'

'Savina, is the ring real?'

'Real? What do you mean, real? What is real, child? Is this house real, or the forest, or the ocean that we can never see behind the wall real?'

The truth was that there were many things in our world that were not part of our life, of our existence, up in the *sierra*. It hit Mother hardest. For she was the one who needed to come down to the coast regularly; she was the one who needed contact with the water. They were right to insult her, the beanie children. She had been a swimmer, and a swimmer is always a swimmer. I wondered if she knew the truth: that it was the beanie children themselves who had tampered with our hovering vehicle, so we would be trapped there on purpose. I had caught them doing it, two scruffy girls, no bigger than me, crouching next to it, and a smaller boy keeping lookout. I did not understand what they were doing, so I kept hidden behind some bushes. They had opened some small latch on the side, and were tampering with the mechanism, with a stick of all things. Afterwards, the vehicle did not fly anymore. It was only years later that I understood one thing: those children could not have known by themselves where to find the circuit that needed to be tampered with, so it stands to reason that they were given precise instructions by adults. The realisation sent shivers up my spine.

But that was not all: those children knew cruelty. I saw them often, looking at her, while she sat on the balcony. Mother, lost in her dreams, thinking of the distant ocean. They would call her names, shout at her that she was a swimmer, but I was still made to work with them, for no one should harvest on their own, letting the forest decide whether to come for you or not.

A strange tension surrounded our interactions. They did not miss an opportunity to remind me that my mother could be a techie, but that my father was not, and that therefore I was nothing more than some trash caught in the middle.

On a particularly hot morning, they played their most sophisticated trick on me. I went into the shed to replace my shields. They were not cutting properly, and I was halfway through my task of clearing a bed. The shed we had in Gobarí was round, and white. It had built-in shelves filled with all sorts of tools and bits and pieces: odd bits of rope, opened seed packets, dirty tools put away without any care, bamboo sticks prepared for planting, empty pots. It was always warm in there, but today I found it cool and fresh inside, so I pushed the door a little, to keep the heat out. The little structure could only be locked from the outside. In theory, it was to prevent animals from going inside at night. Sometimes servants, beanies, had been locked in as a punishment. Of course, we could not do that anymore. After the Act, the ones that remained with us expected now to be paid with credit; I wondered how we were going to do it. But I wondered from afar, not really worrying. Not fully grown up yet.

I felt safe there; I didn't want to go back, face them, to have to bend down to pull the wild *randunes*, cut out the leaves from the bed in preparation for planting, all

21

the tiring little tasks I had undertaken that year. I bought myself some time inspecting the tools. There were long spears, hanging from the walls. We used them to cut the upper palm leaves. For other things as well.

Sometimes we got trapped out there, in Gobarí. The hovering vehicles didn't work so well in the forest; the HivePods couldn't find any signals. Sometimes we were cut off, and the spears could clear a path, if needed. We went long periods without using them, but that thought was not reassuring, for it surely meant that the time to do so again was nearly on us.

A bell rang somewhere. It could be that it was time to eat. Was it really time to eat? I remember thinking. I sometimes went into vacant moments, fugue states, when I lost the sense of time. The bell could also be signalling that the forest had moved, ever so slightly, or had swallowed one of us up. Unlikely.

At some point I walked confidently towards the door of the shed to get out, but found it locked. This was unexpected. I moved the handle up and down with all my might. It didn't open magically, of course. And I knew no *shuvani* prayer that would help me. Only then did I notice how small the shed was, how its walls seemed to close over my head, not leaving a lot of space for breathing.

Would I *die* there?

I started panting.

It took a minute, but eventually I recognised what was happening: I was having one of my episodes.

To know this was comforting; at least I knew this was not death, my heart failing. This was simply out-of-control fear. But knowing that did not ease the feeling of dread, did not stop me from actually going through it. I would have to go through it.

This was a battle between my irrational fear and the rational notion of knowing exactly what was happening to me. I couldn't move, I couldn't react. Eventually, I found the willpower to advance a couple of steps and crouch by the wall, under the shelves, folding my body over itself. I hugged my knees. And I sat to wait it out. I was insanely proud of having taken those two steps, of deciding to crouch down and hug my knees, and of being capable of putting my decision into action.

Outside, the dark was growing. Someone would have noticed my absence by now. Or would they think the forest had taken me? If that were the case, then no one would bother looking for me.

I had had similar episodes before, but this one hit me particularly hard. What was I meant to do? I tried to remember. Something about retreating mentally to your 'safe place'. We were encouraged to create those. I had not undergone the formal training, but any of us could in theory be sent in a vessel up to the sky. A 'safe place' was meant to be a useful thing to have. Even after knowing all your life that you were meant to go there, the shock of space could hit you, I could understand that. The episode made my chest feel heavy, clenched; I could not settle on a place of security, a calming idea. I had read the guide to the NEST programme that we kept at home several times, and I had tried to think of a safe place. What would that be for me? Gobarí, perhaps? The forest? The pond? The pond. That was it. I imagined that my two feet advanced down the little shore, advanced until the water reached my waist, and that I took a plunge below the yellowy surface. I would resurface feeling refreshed, clean and new, and all my worries would be gone, and my solitude would be a distant memory.

That did it. Unexpectedly, once I felt calm, another image sprang to mind: the dead hare, her dark orange fur and her yellow gluey brains. Inside the shed, far away from its body, decomposing near the pond, I thought deeply of her, remembered her sickly sweet rotting smell. Willingly, it seemed; quite willingly.

I have felt this, I thought; I have experienced all this, this exact combination of events. A strong sense of déjà vu overtook my brain at that moment, as though I were drowning in memories. I was glad of this, for it numbed the episode a little. The darkness, the closeness of the walls falling over me, the sweet smell of rot… It was like a combination lock. And suddenly I had all the winning numbers.

These elements together managed to do it; they opened the memory like a flower.

Something dormant, something that had happened years before, perhaps when I was very young: four or five years old.

I was looking into the eyes of the bright ocean. The monstrous seagulls wailing above me. If I looked up, I saw nothing, so blinding the white light was. The swimmer travelled methodically, moving away from me. His movements looked precise, automatic. Every couple of strokes his black mouth came out for air. He was moving away from me, away from the rock, where I sat perched like a little bird.

Was that the day that I cut my feet on the rock? The scenes from that outing appeared in my mind mixed up with those from another, one that included Mother and my little brother. Their figures appeared and disappeared from the shore as the memories intertwined. I remembered the sharp pain, and the thin red ribbon of blood in the clear water.

Did I know the swimmer?

The swimmer was my father.

Yes, but did I know him?

I was perched on a rock at the pointy end of the shell-like *coquina* stone.

To my left, the swimmer.

To my right, the coast stretched for fifty kilometres, curving out on a bay: delicate little shores, abrupt rock formations. At the very end of the curve, the isthmus of Old Town.

If I followed the curve of the coast with my eyes, I could see them, sitting at the end: the two vessels.

It was not a clear image, not really. It flickered in and out of my vision, like a mirage; masses of rock, the town at the point, the isthmus, and at the very end the two gigantic structures: all odd, all hazy, as though I were peering at them through a glass vase, or deep water. It was the rising heat that made them look like the ghosts of two mountains, pale and almost translucent.

The vessels sat quietly there, at the end of the known world, abandoned on the staithe, the whitish skeletons of two enormous beetles. The old white marble cathedral, now the Registry, looked dwarfish at their feet. Their vastness imposed itself on everything, producing a kind of vertigo in the onlooker; I imagined them taking flight as they once did, higher and higher, a heavy cloud crossing the blue sky, upwards, always upwards.

I looked at the vessels, stared at them. My father continued taking his exercise, perhaps doing something more sinister. Was he planning to give himself to the Three Oceans? Was he planning to leave me behind?

Where I sat, on the *coquina* rock, fifty kilometres separated me from the vessels; fifty kilometres of yellow sand, darker stone, a flat sea that lapped delicately at the shore. The water was the bluest thing I had ever seen, coming and going, a calm receding tide, leaving behind a shiny mirror of darker sand. So pure, so constant, the water on this side of the wall. I wished that this water might wash everything. I wished it could wash me. I wished for my mother and my brother.

To my left, the swimmer. Even now, I have no words to describe him. I can't say he moved gracefully, or that his huge body splashed water bluntly over the surface as he advanced. I didn't really know my father. I guess I must have known him at some point, but I don't anymore, not really. He was soon going to be out of our lives. Was he a good swimmer, a bad swimmer? A believer in giving yourself to the Three Oceans?

All I remember is that I sat, perched on a rock. To my left, the swimmer. To my right, a little beanie girl, her hair dyed blue and a smile of happiness on her face.

There was blood that day: my feet got cut on the stone,

its porous edges alive with seashells, little barnacles, the pointy soft skeletons of centuries-old dead crabs. I looked at the red ribbon escaping from my skin: little rubies; red pearls, if such a thing could ever exist. And I cried. Two forces pulling at each other, from opposite places. I was meant to be there; I was not meant to be there. There had been an urgency in my father's taking me out of bed in the early hours, putting me inside the hovering vehicle still in my sleeping robe, wrapped up in a travel blanket, wrapping me up like a little animal he had found on the road and needed to bring to life, urgently, in secret. 'Quiet, my little bird,' he said; for that was what he called me. His little bird, his little blue bird.

For some reason, me and the beanie girl had come alone with my father to Kon-il beach. Was this unusual? Again, I cried.

3

The music continues to wake me sweetly each morning. Melancholy sounds that resemble the shrieks of some creatures, down in Gobarí, but that I know are called 'stringed instruments'. They accompany the haunted voice that sings alone, to be united with other voices at the end of the song. I look at the little screen displaying the data: *Melody title: 'Ingen vinner frem til den evige ro'. Class: Traditional. Place: Earth, Northern Hemisphere. Epoch: Unknown (Pre-Winter). Translated as 'No one reaches the eternal calm'.* I marvel at the truths contained within this pristine technology.

The interior of my LivePod is white, immaculate. Blue and grey signs that must mean something to the initiated. Little flickering lights here and there, glass lids that open up to small recesses where extra pouches of water magically appear. I grab one, unscrew the little cap, and press the plastic square hard, until all the liquid has passed from the pouch to my body. I have never been this thirsty before. I have nothing to compare it to, since I have never been pregnant before. The skin on my hands is papery, almost translucent. I can discern all the lines that will break into flakes. I have not seen my face in weeks, and my hair has never been this long. It is intricately plaited, but not by me. Someone must have done it while I was unconscious or drugged or asleep. I should feel safe here. Everything is designed for a particular purpose, with a definitive use in mind, exactly as Arlo explained to me. The carefully plaited hair makes sure I do not get the hair tangled with the small indents and recesses inside my pristine coffin.

The forest, on the other hand, was an uncertain space where we made and remade the rules daily. It was filled with plants that could kill us, animals that bared their pointy teeth before springing on you, and the cries and shrieks of so many new things no one could identify them. Why did I feel safer in Gobarí? Why were we brought up there?

There was no beach in Gobarí, no sea, no ocean. The little beach at Kon-il was half a day's walk away. There was only the pond, where the *alicanta* lived in his underwater caves. Every week down by the water, Savina left cut-out pieces of fruit, hand-woven baskets filled with gigantic petals, and the petals filled in their turn with miniature sculptures, woven from flowers, mimicking people, trees, and a little house. Tiny decorated pebbles, delicate bone carvings, exquisite quartzite. Dainty offerings, for the basilisk was meant to have a face that resembled a human being, and Savina was scared of it.

But no, no ocean. And Mother loved the ocean.

I was ill when I came out of the shed, dehydrated. It turned out that the coolness inside had been a miscalculation on my part, and the little white thing, baking under the daylight, had got so hot I had passed out when they found me. I almost died of sunstroke that day. My mother was furious at me. I was old enough to know better, she said. It was true.

After that day, Savina brought Eli. She was the daughter of one of her friends. We would go and sit by the pond together. This was my favourite place in the whole world, and I took her there immediately. Now I would not be on my own anymore. Now I had someone to be with, no need to mix with the beanie youngsters who locked me up on purpose, who were merciless and cruel. They knew things. They called my father a *mullo*, a tainted one; and I had nightmares of my father waking up in his tomb and coming to get me, the way *mullos* do. For my father had a bad death, the worst possible.

So Savina brought Eli, and now I had a friend. A friend to bathe with in the pond. I did not know what friendship was, not really, but I was a fast learner.

Savina and I spent the afternoons sitting around the kitchen table where we did most things, from peeling potatoes to skinning rodents, and eating the delicacies that she knew a growing child needed: mango-spread, *rumbatán*, green milky *milbao*. I had always known that other things went on in Savina's kitchen. I knew this was where Savina sometimes practised her *shuvaní* magiks. She would say little prayers while skinning the rodents or dicing the *rumbatán*. Sometimes other women were there with her, helping with the incantations; or perhaps, I thought, being helped by her. One of them was Eli's mother.

One day, at noon, I walked into the kitchen as I did every day, and she was there, a woman I didn't know, helping Savina throw things into the fire. Their faces were rigid, concentrated on the task. I knew they were performing some *shuvaní* ritual, and I looked on, fascinated. Perched on a chair was a sulky teenager who needed a wash, devouring some fried bananas. Eli looked at me furtively, as if I were the intruder, when Gobarí was my house, and Savina's kitchen my kitchen. She continued staring at me oddly, as if willing me to leave, but saying nothing. I stood where I was.

Later, we were sent out to entertain ourselves. It was so hot that day we couldn't go anywhere, so we sat on the porch, sucking melon slices and spitting the black seeds out. Eli suggested that we go to the pond the next time she visited.

After that Eli came back to see me often. We mostly sat around, eating mango that we had picked ourselves and chatting. I would invent stories to amuse her: those days I was reading about our shared constellations, the ones all children of the surface knew by heart. I would tell her stories about the fox, the three sisters, and Alira, the little bird ascending. When I didn't remember exactly what the story said, I invented their endings, or mixed them with others. I could have spoken with her about other things, as friends are meant to do. I could have shared with her incidents from my life, our family. But I wasn't as good a friend as I thought; I was selfish, wanted to keep some things private, only for me. I carefully avoided some subjects. My father's death by his own hand, inside a NEST prison; my brother's illness. Mother's melancholia that was doubtless linked to them both. And how unhelpful, what a useless daughter I was to her. I was scared of being asked anything about those topics, so I kept us busy with the imaginary telling of the stars.

Eli, on the other hand, was capable of sharing things

with me, and I took it as a sign of our developing friendship. She spoke about her family often, had many brothers and sisters. The woman who had been with her in the kitchen that morning wasn't her mother after all, but her older sister, who had looked after her since she was very little. I asked where her mother was.

'Dead.'

I should have known. We were looking after a patch of herbs that she grew on purpose to help her family earnings. Everyone collected wild specimens, but Eli had a knack for growing things, and introduced me to some new species. Eli would grow everything except flowers. She hated animals as well. Eventually, she shared the story of her mother's death with me. Her family, she explained, had kept two stoats as pets. This had happened when I was very little, I hardly remember the incident. But as soon as she mentioned this I knew what would come next; the story returned fresh into my mind. The stoats had grown as big as the children, and attacked and eaten the smallest one, a newborn, barely a month old.

I had even been in Eli's house, and had a vague recollection of going with Savina to visit her mother when she was pregnant with the baby in their shack on the outskirts of Gobarí, and she had lain on her back, Savina letting her pendant drop over her full belly. If it moved in circles: a baby girl. If it moved like a pendulum, right and left, right and left, it would be a little boy. The pendant had predicted a girl.

How cruel, to be born to that fate.

Savina had said nothing when she heard about the stoats eating the child, I did remember that. She left the bread she was kneading on the table, and went out of the kitchen in silence. This had impressed me a great deal. The woman, Eli's mother, killed herself shortly after. She walked into the forest one morning on her own, and that was that.

Even if I knew the story, I let Eli tell it to me, from beginning to end. There was something in her inflexion, in how she shared the knowledge, that made me realise that she needed to tell it, to share it at that point in time and with her new friend, and so I let her. Eli and I had this in common: her mother and my father had both killed themselves. The knowledge made me feel closer to her; warmed my heart a little. Finally, I had found someone who might understand. But I said nothing, even then.

We took to bathing in the pond that winter, Eli and me, normally after eating. One morning she suggested that we do so naked; it had been difficult to dry our clothes after each bath, even in the hottest autumn weather. We started swimming next to each other, and soon were embracing each other in the water, our legs interlocked, and I felt a strange passion. We kissed often after that, long and hard kisses. I liked kissing Eli; but one day she stopped it all abruptly. We were hiding among the eucalyptus trees. Our kissing practices, as Eli called them, had increased in intensity quite quickly. She got up suddenly, took my shirt and put it on, and she left me there alone, hiding between the bushes. I just could not stop thinking of her little breasts, of the unexpected wetness. I did not know what was happening, as I started to pant, and I felt such jolt of guilt and pain and sweetness and joy, all together and at once. All I knew was that I didn't want that feeling to stop.

The stone hit me hard, and when I looked up Eli was back and, from the way she was looking at me, I knew that she wanted to kiss me again. But she also had that stubborn look on, like that first day in the kitchen, and I knew that she wasn't going to move any closer. She threw another stone, the perfect parabola floating in mid-air until it hit me, again, drawing blood this time.

'What are you doing?'

She bent down to pick up another stone.

'Eli! Stop that!'

I dodged the stone.

That's when it happened. When I realised she had

always known it all; all of them, all the beanies, had probably always known. For she started calling me names, saying my mother was insane, and that my dad was *mullo*, that he had killed a little girl and was in Hell now; and that he was going to come for me one day and drag me deep into the forest, deep into the jungle.

That he was going to come for me, for his little blue bird. I could not believe she knew that my dad had called me that. And I realised: they all knew everything.

I bent down and took a stone myself, but she was already leaving, taking my clothes with her.

Eli did not give me back my clothes, but that didn't bother me. Fabric wasn't particularly abundant, but somehow I put together a grown-up outfit. It all came out of trunks, boxes, suitcases; things that had been packed perhaps even before I was born. Rummaging in those trunks wasn't exactly like rummaging in family memories, scenes and stories once cherished, now half-forgotten. My life did not need those; my life needed rules, certainties, knowledge, in order to survive. But this particular puzzle I had willingly avoided. Was Eli right, when she said that Father had killed my little beanie friend, the blue-haired girl? I knew I would not dare ask anyone, neither Savina nor Mother.

I knew I would not ask because I knew it was the truth. Of course it was. It had been a scandal. He had killed a little girl, and then he had kidnapped me, presumably trying to dispose of me as well. But why had he done those things? What did he expect to achieve?

I was thinking about my new outfit, matching faded garments from a previous life, but the story from the past was threatening to burst to the forefront of my consciousness. I started to cry, and the tears were warm upon my cheeks.

Among the discarded, packed up things, I found other mementoes. Old-fashioned ImagePods where we all smiled and danced and talked to one another. My parents with a couple older than them, I think it might have been neighbours of ours, here in the *sierra*, and some images stranger still, of Mother accompanied by this very lady, dancing on the shore. It looked like Kon-il.

When she was younger, my mother had been a swimmer. The remnants of an old, pre-Winter religion, or so it was thought, the swimmers gave themselves to the embrace of the Three Oceans. As with many other doctrines, they had been persecuted for centuries, and now operated underground, in secret. Their act of defiance was directed against all ringers, all techies, against those who had believed in techno-fixes to solve our predicament, against the people who lived outside of the planet, against those who had built the Barrier. The Barrier protected us from the Three Oceans, and even looking on the other side was forbidden by our lords and masters, orbiting above in the sky: not only illegal, but also a heresy. The swimmers believed humanity did not deserve to separate itself from the destruction it had created. Swimming away, to die among the waves, was the highest form of protest they enacted. To die for their beliefs, to atone for humankind's transgression in destroying the planet, to offer themselves in return.

A swimmer could be a normal, even prominent, member of society. One day they would be gone, leaving a note behind, or simply their sign somewhere: a crude image of a fish drawn in one single line, and which resembled the mathematical sign for infinity. And then their family would know. Their sudden absences, the space they left behind, would be all their families were left with.

My beanie friend had disappeared from my life suddenly, so had my deceitful father. Now, Eli was gone from my life in equally sudden fashion, but I told myself that I didn't need her. I felt as if my childhood had ended, and I was a grown-up now. I started despising our recent secret encounters in the bushes after our swims, when only a few days before I had looked forward to them expectantly. It was something intimate, private, ours. But now I felt older, wiser. I suddenly remembered that I had a family, people to care about and protect. People who needed me.

With my new outfit on I went to look for my mother. I had not been inside her drawing room for weeks, but I knew that people came and went from there sometimes. Somehow, even trapped here, Urania's allure meant that people gravitated towards her, and at least a couple of times a week there was some sort of courtesy visit.

That was how I found out we had new neighbours. There was another house, near Gobarí. It had a bad reputation, and no one talked about it. I knew why: its previous owner, my mother's friend from the ImagePod, was a swimmer, but one who had gone all the way, who had offered herself, and never returned from the ocean's dark embrace. Sadly, the abandoned house had been set on fire by some delivered beanies after the Act freed them, and the property stood for a time like a dead thing crawling over the *sierra*, with shut windows like shut eyes. They called it Benguele, the demon-house.

'Pearl! What in the Three Oceans could you possibly be wearing?'

I looked around me at the group that sat quietly with

Mother, sipping cool *milbao* drinks: juicy, sweet fruits liquidised by hand, usually by servants. They were a mark of distinction, but a fake one in our case: we had no servants anymore to make them for us. We had Savina, to help us pretend. I saw the visitors all wore the ordnance white country-issue outfits, with tight neat pockets and compartments, zips and Velcro openings. Their white boots were miraculously clean, although the outside of our house was a long stretch of mud because we had no one to keep it in check.

Who were those people? What were they doing in our house?

Mr Vanlow had taken the neighbour's house, it seemed. He explained this while laughing at its nickname. *Benguele, Benguele!* he repeated, sipping his *milbao* and smiling at Mother. He was explaining all the repairs that he was doing after the fire: the roof and the walls, and how he planned to use the dug-up orchards. He was an elegant man, wearing ringer outfits, although he did not look at all like a ringer. He was tall and imposing, with an easy laugh and short cropped hair going grey at the temples. His outfit was as white and shiny as those of his blond companions, friends from the Settlement whom he was entertaining in his new house.

'You should come and shoot pheasants with us!'

Alarmed, I realised he was talking to me. I shook my head, murmured my thanks; but I was feeling ridiculous at that moment. I looked at myself. I had been proud until the second I entered that room of my makeshift adult clothing, which I had arranged on purpose as if I was going to do a Jump: the sacrificial long skirt, which I imagined white, and knew now to be yellowish; the dark shirt and the flower crown sitting on my head. I had plaited it myself, and I wasn't good at plaiting flowers. I felt suddenly embarrassed.

But Mr Vanlow smiled at me, not unkindly.

In the middle of this neat, hygienic group of people sat Urania, my strange, beautiful mother, striking as a rare bird. Even with her shabby clothing and long, oily hair, she was the most elegant thing in that room.

He came often to visit us, this new neighbour. He grew fond of Mother, of course, concerned himself with her well-being and enquired about Aster, my little brother. Mother was always talking about sending him to a doctor in Old Town, and she confided this to Mr Vanlow; but we all knew there were no cures for him there, that the kind of genetic treatment he needed was only available in one place: the ring.

Mr Vanlow had connections with the stratosphere settlement. He wasn't a true starborn but had spent time up there. His father had served under a well-known politician, and they had been among the lucky ones who emigrated. He had been back down sometimes, moving at ease between the Upper Settlement and the planet's surface. And now he was back for good, he said to make his fortune.

Over the months that followed, he often spoke about his contacts up in the ring, and how they could help the child. How he would send him up there to be cured.

'Will we all go, Papa?'

By that time I called him Papa, because Mr Vanlow and Mother had married. It happened shortly after that first visit. It couldn't have been more than a few weeks later. He had been very taken with the beautiful woman, marooned in Gobarí, a crumbling island in the middle of the extreme green. He won her over quickly. First, he lent her a hovering vehicle that worked properly, and Mother flew every evening to parties and picnics and what-nots. She often went to Old Town, and to the wall, and to the ocean. She thought we didn't know, but we did. And every time she left, I was scared that she would not come back. I stayed behind, alone with Aster, without Mother, without Eli. Only Savina to keep me company.

Savina took pity on me, and let me spend the long afternoons with her in the kitchen, helping with her *shuvaní* recipes. I would powder the spices, mix the herbs, and throw them inside the enormous pot.

When had Savina come to live with us? It was impossible to know. She seemed to have been there forever, since I was a baby. My dad gave her to my mother as a present, many years before the Delivery Act was passed. But even after the Act's passage she had decided to stay with us, or rather with Mother. She had been taken from her village when she was a child, taken to Old Town to serve with a family of techies, that much I knew. It had been a hard life for a child. The mother of the techie family had been a cruel sort of woman, and Savina had hardly been fed. She explained all this to me as if she were telling a fairy story.

'They had a compound on the wall itself; the father was an engineer. And one day, I saw the ocean on the other side from there. There were no windows on that side of the construction, no way of looking over that side of the Barrier back then! But I was lucky.'

She had found herself up on the roof one day. Mere chance; some technician needed something fetched, and she was the closest servant around to take it to him.

'So, there I was, on the highest point of the wall!' It was

difficult to imagine Savina atop the massive structure that protected us, defined our existence. She had taken a peek, of course; only one, though it was forbidden in those days. I would never forget what she said to me: 'There was no ocean, not really, but a sort of mushy pulp, stretching as far as my eyes would go.'

'A mushy pulp?'

'Yes, millions of shiny things floating over the surface of the water, covering it all, like dead brown crabs, the corpses of millions of them.'

'What colour *was* the ocean?'

'Ah, I'm not very sure, child. Brown, yes, a dull brownish colour, on account of those dead crabs I guess.'

Many years later, during my apprenticeship, I would learn the reason for this indeterminate brownish colour: a collection of soft translucent debris that glimmered prettily under the sun. It was the plastic that we had been trying to keep out with the Barrier, which had come to serve this primary purpose, although it had been conceived to do something very different, to protect us from the waves generated by the leviathans. So, it was the plastic, and not the corpses of crabs as Savina had said.

I had thought plastic was colourful. I was misinformed.

She had started showing me a few secret *shuvani* recipes. She would never call them potions. She explained that Mother and Mr Vanlow had known each other as children, and that was why they were marrying so soon, for he had loved her for many years, in secret. Afterwards, some malicious people started talking about those evenings in the kitchen. Had Savina and I cast a spell to trap Mr Vanlow? Had he married Mother because of our *shuvani* ministrations? Even now, I cannot answer the question, for I am not sure what concoction we were putting together, Savina and I.

Shortly after the wedding, Eli came back to Gobarí once more. Mr Vanlow was determined to bring the house back to its former splendour; he seemed happy to abandon Benguele (a farm, and therefore a much less aristocratic place), and he hired people to do repairs around the balcony, the crumbling porch, the land and the gardens. This took me by surprise. Did we have gardens? Until then, I had not known. Everything was overgrown with wild vegetation. Everything seemed to be infused with the stagnant smell of the leaves and the thicket and the flowers. Passion fruit rotted on their branches. The bats flew chaotically over the canopy of the trees, their shrieks the last thing you heard before allowing sleep to overcome you.

I had been back to the pond often on my own. The truth was that I was always hoping to see Eli again, moving the branches, joining me in the water. But she had never came back after that last afternoon. In my head I talked with the basilisk, and sometimes would feel something moving between my feet. But there was nothing there. My swimming sessions were a joy, even without her, or perhaps, precisely, because they were only mine. I was foolish to think that, as would soon become apparent.

I was glad to see Eli back in the kitchen with her sister. I still was angry with her, at the things she had said by the pond. My family and I were leaving. We were going to spend some time in Old Town during the refurbishment of the house. Savina would come with us, and Eli's sister would stay back in her place, feeding the men who were going to set our house straight. I was glad Eli had seen me with my new city outfit. She was still wearing the shirt she had taken from me months ago. It looked like rags. It was much darker and I could see it had been mended repeatedly. I felt pity; but the cruel sort of pity. At last I mounted the hovering vehicle, and Mother, Savina, my brother Aster, Mr Vanlow and I glided over the land, following the missing road into Old Town.

I can see now that I was behaving like a petulant child; but something else nagged at me, I had other reasons to feel betrayed by Eli. A couple of weeks before leaving, something happened. I had been collecting yarrow and violet, on Savina's orders, and I decided to have a swim; but this time the pond wasn't enough, I wanted to taste the flavour of the ocean in my mouth. So I walked to Kon-il. It was a long walk, half a day in good weather, to reach the coast. It was the same place where I had seen my father swimming, all those years back.

Little blue bird, little blue bird. Where are you going, little blue bird?

There were some people standing there, on the beach, my beach, the last thing I had expected, and I hid among the rocks. When I looked again, it surprised me to see my mother with another woman, much older than her, and another one, younger. They were chanting something, and they had drawn a spiral with shells and other offerings at the edge of the tide. The ocean was receding, and the water touched the shells lightly. Some kind of intuition awoke within me, and I understood that I was witnessing an initiation. The younger woman entered the water, and swam. I did not move from where I was hiding; I was sure I was not meant to be there. When the younger woman returned to shore, I could see her face, Eli's face.

I thought many times of Eli after that, and she appeared in my dreams. In one of them, we were next to the vessels, and she was scared to be put in one and sent up to the sky, up and up we go. But I made her do it. This was a good way of killing her, for it would be a slow death no doubt. I knew she would die up there, everybody knew that; they were just too scared to admit it. What I dreamed was that she was sent in my place, that this was her punishment. And I knew the dream would come to be true, as all my dreams did eventually.

I had seen a Jump, only once, when I was little more than a toddler. It was the last one. It took place many years ago, but some things have stayed with me, some images that were difficult to shake. The procession celebrating the heroes, who were paraded around the streets, their faces stuck in manic smiles, although their eyes looked sad to me. Their beautiful white robes, their ceremonial flower crowns. Their constellations, drawn on the floor in thousands of coloured petals. The rest of the streets completely covered with green leaves.

Eventually, the time came, and the vast structure was sent up from the staithe built into the sea. People were frantic, excited; I looked at my parents for reassurance, for I could not understand the electricity in the air. As I've grown up, learnt about the Jumps, I have also come to realise that sometimes they were followed by rioting crowds, social unrest; as if the same society that promoted and encouraged them intuitively knew that they were sending those children to their deaths. I remember how the vessel could be seen for a long time, a small star in the middle of the day, a pale dot that never really disappeared. At night, it was possible to follow its ascent, if one knew where to look, confused among the stars.

Up, further up, the massive ring of the Upper Settlement was also lightly visible. I always found it difficult to imagine that human beings lived up there, perched like birds over the planet's atmosphere. But there they were, enjoying their pure air, domesticated gardens; away from the forest that swallowed us up and spat us out raw, day after day after day. Safe, protected. A privileged balcony from which to observe the vessels' ascent, jumping up into the dark embrace of the sky; those people sent to find a better world for us all.

Did I fear that the Jump was the fate that awaited me? I cannot be sure of when that knowledge entered my consciousness. The Jumps, the selection of beanie and techie children, the NEST project, were no more than remote ideas, strange words on adult lips. But I was, I am, I will forever be, scared of the vessels. The massive structures had always produced a falling sensation in the pit of my stomach. As if I instinctively knew that something so gigantic could not really hold itself up there, would eventually fall from the sky, crushing us all. As if they were nothing more than a mirage to keep us going, to help us pretend we could escape this green inferno, touch the sky if needed; an illusion as unreal as the Upper Settlement itself. Now I know better, for I made it up here eventually, to the ring, and let it trap me in its orderly prison.

4

We are on the move. One white corridor followed by another white corridor followed by another white corridor. My LivePod hovers over the floor, advances smoothly. The rocking motion could send me to sleep if I am not careful. I would like to be awake, I need to be awake, fully aware of what they do to me.

I wanted so badly to come up to the ring. It was what I had always wanted. This used to surprise my friends from the Registry, especially Laurel.

'Aren't you scared to go up there? I thought you didn't like enclosed spaces,' she would say. I would explain that the installations inside the ring were so extensive, filled with gardens and avenues and boulevards, storytelling theatres, public-curated collections, sports installations... Inside, it was as big as two or three of our towns, more perhaps. It was impossible to feel trapped. This was all second-hand knowledge, of course, from my stepfather.

Now, I am here, inside a white, vast chamber, oblong shaped. The ceiling sends me back my own image with its metallic reflections; it reminds me of me, looking at my own reflection over the pond. At one end there is an oval window. Through it, I can see one of the many green spaces here. There is hardly any furniture. My Health-issued LivePod. Some monitors hovering about it, moving around madly as they check on me. Far away, at the other end, a red sofa in front of the window. The system checks every morning, decides if it can open the glass lid for me to get up or not. So far, it has opened every morning. That means that she is healthy, doing well. Food appears in pouches at regular intervals, so does water. I am visited by the health professionals, or at least that's what I think they are, who talk among themselves and don't really share much of what is going on with me. But I catch their conversations, and know that all is well. At least, I imagine it, allow myself to imagine it.

They are all wearing masks and plastic goggles and gloves and other protective gear, so I've never seen their faces. But I recognise them by their voices, and there is one who is obviously the leader, instructs the others, and the little drone machines that hover around me, tells them what the next steps are.

I cannot tell if they are wearing protective gear because

they want to protect the baby, or because they are protecting themselves from me. Everyone who comes from the surface needs to spend a minimum of a fortnight in quarantine as soon as they alight from the transport. You present your credentials, a tattooed barcode on your inner wrist, and then you move on to the decontamination chamber. It is more tedious than anything else. Once you are given the go-ahead, you exit into a plastic corridor that takes you directly into the quarantine facility. There is no way of escaping this. I do not remember my fourteen days of quarantine; they all blur into each other in my mind.

I do remember the trip skywards in the second-class transport, how badly the straps adjusted, too big and no one around to help me fix them, and the sudden horizontal ascent, much more shaky than the smooth hovering vehicles I was used to down on Earth, and the smell of sweat and unwashed clothes and fear. We were around fifty people in several rows, closely sat next to one another, no space to move a leg, and having to fight for the hard armrest. They were mostly beanies, probably going up to serve some family, or destined for the farming levels. The few techies were distinguishable, mostly because they looked with disdain at the others around them, hoping to make clear that they were made of different stock. But even these techies were heading for minor positions as clerical hands, or low-level engineers. These kinds of individuals were always needed up there. I felt sorry for them. They tried very hard to look as if they were used to coming and going between the two places, while obviously trying to hold themselves back from vomiting.

I tried to hold myself back as well. I didn't know what had been done to procure the ticket for me; it would be better not to ask. They did not fly easily into your hand out of nowhere, they were a once-in-a-lifetime affair. I worried somebody had gone short; someone had lost their life-changing opportunity.

A loud crack announced the departure, and, for a few minutes, the pressure of my stomach against my throat. Holding on to my ill-fitting straps for sheer life. And then, shooting up, up and up we go, into the unknown. Our imagined landscape of uncertainties left behind, a gigantic planet with a blotch of green and the uncertain golden and maroon ocean so loved and mourned by Mother.

I remember arriving at the receiving station, presenting my tattoo, and being ushered through quickly, as even a low-level curator has more status up here. Although this only meant that I was transferred to another, faster queue. This queue was to take my temperature, receive a state-of-the-art health scan. I walked into the machine, placed my feet where the signs were, elevated my arms as instructed. And all my secrets were revealed. Even to myself. That was all. I had condemned myself to this LivePod.

And, this morning, an emergency in my little white world. A red light flashing somewhere, little rubies of a warning. I panic. The interior of the LivePod is ample; but the idea of staying here all day, lying on my back or on my side, cannot be considered for a second. Despite my condition, my episodes, I believe that I have not feared this since I got here. I wonder why this might be. I have not reached a special kind of wisdom, or *ulalé*, that moment in which you swim away and the ocean waters and the sky become one, and you ascend. No, nothing as impressive as that. The truth is that, in recent days, perhaps weeks, I have had no energy for anything, even for worrying. I am simply so tired, and in constant pain in any position, that nothing else matters.

In response to the red lights, the warnings, for the first time the lid over my face does not move. My anxiety starts to spark up. Not only about staying put, and whether I would survive hours, perhaps days, inside the pod, where I can hardly move, but also about other more prosaic ailments that might make this waiting impossible.

Every day now I wake up with back pain, particularly severe on the right side. I spend the night changing position, moving between lying on my back or lying on my left side; this is what I have been told to do, in order to send more of my blood to the placenta. But no position is comfortable. I have an oversized pillow which I use to support my back, put my legs up, rest my arms and my head. But it is not enough. Nothing seems to be. I also seem to have permanent cramps in my legs, and I suddenly long to jump out of the pod and walk a bit towards the window, hopefully sucking a *milbao* pouch dry. The lid continues to not move; but I should not have worried, for a group of people enter immediately—I have never seen so many— and hover over the machine, a circle of unknown eyes behind pristine white facemasks.

And then it strikes me.

She hasn't moved as much recently, has she?

It is difficult to estimate; I've not been keeping tabs. Perhaps I should have? No idea. But the truth is, now that I think about it, that the last few weeks she was moving all the time... and now? It is difficult to tell. Definitely less. Is that why they are here now?

So they press a few buttons, and my LivePod starts moving towards the door, and out we go... Where?

One white corridor after another white corridor after

another white corridor. I stretch my neck as far as it will go. I want to see. I need to see. People, places. Those strange bio-engineered animals Arlo was always talking about. Those polished, pristinely dressed brave new people. The little drones that carry things and bring messages and play sweet music to make you forget you are in Hell. Nothing.

There is a larger ward at the end of our short journey. My LivePod hovers and hovers, and soon I am reaching the white ceiling, pushed against the white ceiling. I do not understand what is happening, why they had let it go like a balloon, up and up we go.

It comes now, all of a sudden. I can only see the ceiling through the glass lid. Suddenly I cannot breathe. I have to say nothing, communicate nothing. The Health-issued LivePod picks it all up. My heart rate, I guess, my muscles contracting. It descends to floor level. It opens up like a flower. I breathe then, the dear, stale, purified air of the Upper Settlement.

'Calm down, you have to calm down,' someone says.

They monitor her movements for twenty minutes, half an hour, one hour, two hours. I am plucked and prodded, and the monitors are sending a curve up and down madly. She is fine, it is all fine…

I doze. Finally.

I am in an underwater cavity, and I know that I must swim to the other end. So I swim and I swim and I swim. What is there at the other end? I only know that I need to get there. The cave gets smaller and tighter, it is more and more difficult to move, and I cannot spread my arms to advance. Luckily, I realise that I can get hold of protuberances in the rock to propel me forward. At some point, I decide that I do not need to breathe down here. There is no hurry, I can take all the time in the world. I guess that now I am an underwater thing, as simple as that. I reach the other side at last.

I am in a garden.

I am in a forest.

I am in a jungle.

The jungle has been made especially for me with some kind of terraforming technology.

The hare by my feet is dead. She has a purple-rotting hue in her orange fur, and her eyes are lost and unmoving, like the dirty amber water that simmers in the pond, back in Gobarí. Underneath it sit the orbs, two pebbles in the centre, dark and deep. What does she remind me of? A doll, perhaps, fallen from the sky. It looks as if she is looking at me through her two dead eyes.

'Can you help me, please?' I say to the hare. 'I need to find my husband.'

'Why do you think I know where he is?'

The hare's voice is eerie, distant and rusty, and she speaks without moving her thin hare lips or her limbs or her face or her eyes.

'Don't you think you owe me?' is all I answer. 'You asked me to kill you, and I killed you.'

'Look, even if I did want to help you, I probably couldn't.'

'Why?'

'Because you'll have to be prepared to Jump, all the way into the sky. Up and up we go… Up where the dead children are.'

I wake up.

I learnt early to pay attention to my dreams. I once had a really vivid dream, and my life seemed to align with its essence in uncanny ways, as if my subconscious were sending me a message.

It was Savina who interpreted the dream for me the next morning, and that was when she explained that Mother had been taken with the fashion of giving yourself, of swimming as far as possible, not knowing if you were going to be able to come back. It was risky, as the believers had to find places to jump into the water at the other side of the wall, and sometimes they got shot at. She had always survived; not just the illicit throwing herself into the forbidden deep, but the swimming itself. The offering. She always came back, and I truly could not tell if that made her relieved or angry. I can imagine her, turning back towards the town. The strenuous effort of her legs kicking, of keeping her eyes and mouth over the water and the plastic debris. Swimming back had to be a conscious act; she had to decide upon it, turn the other way, already exhausted, and kick and kick with all her might, push the water with her arms as much as possible, and consciously try to make shore again. Why? Why set off, and why come back?

Some days, the sky was radiant with a fluorescent blue, which sent rays of light down even during the small hours. We did not know where the light came from, why the sky was tainted that colour. Some people said it was connected to something they did from the ring, some explosion, or energy surge. For the believers, this was their preferred moment to swim away, under the uncertain blue lights dancing on the horizon. And one such night she almost did.

That very scene was the one that came to me in a dream. Its hypnotic quality meant that I had experienced it all, and seen myself far away from the shore, heavy with a full belly, desperately trying to move away, panicking, and then desperately trying to swim back. And, as soon as her feet, my feet, touched the wall again, regretting my weakness.

The dream confirmed a thing that perhaps I had known and forgotten, or that perhaps I had always known somehow: my mother had tried to swim away in this manner when she was pregnant with me, imagining her offering to the ocean would be doubled. Now, looking back, I can see that Mother was not proud of that weakness, regretted it deeply, and it tainted her life. In that case, what was I for her? Nothing more than a sacrifice, expendable? This generated more questions than ever; about my parents, their union, my strange childhood, my distant and beautiful mother.

'You are right to believe in your dreams, child,' Savina said. 'For you yourself have a little *shuvani* blood in you, from your mother's side.'

Was this possible? Were we like Savina, if only a little? Mother's family was old and aristocratic; having mixed *shuvani* blood did not tally with what I had been told about them. And then she explained further: that one of our ancestors had owned hundreds of *shuvani* souls, and that among them was one young woman, so beautiful that he could not help but marry her. And so she had passed us this curse.

So now I knew for certain: Savina's story was true and my mother had been a swimmer in her youth.

And a swimmer is always a swimmer.

Had my father found out that this had happened, and got angry at her; was that why he tried to take me away with him, with no intention of harming me? But, even if that were the case, why had he murdered a beanie child?

This was before the swimmers put bombs in the wall, before they killed people. This was when they only offered themselves to the Three Oceans to atone for humanity's sin of destroying the planet. But in time things would become confused in people's heads, the way things do: my mother would be dead long before they decided to up their fight; and still, still... The storytellers would have done their work by then, and people would have been told what to think, and how to think it.

Swimming was different from what they said, from what they thought. Even I, in my little pond, would feel like I was doing something a little bit subversive, forbidden. Between the shore and the Barrier everyone could enjoy a few hundred yards of clean water, unspoiled half-moon sandy beaches, like the cove in Kon-il, like in Old Town. But elegant techies did not swim; there was something polluted in the very idea of submerging yourself.

I, however, loved my swimming sessions. Every time

I entered the yellow-green water of the pond, I felt as if a secret boundary had been crossed. I was one with the little flies, the fallen leaves and other pieces of nature that floated away as I rehearsed my weak strokes. In communion with the water, I was reborn into a different realm. The world seemed more silent from inside there. The forest and its creatures did not stop their jittering; it simply was that, once in the water, my senses seemed to mutate, and I stopped paying attention to them, my attention diverted to other things that were more pressing, more real: the light brush of the carp at my feet, the change in the light, the new perspective of my vision, which for once made the overgrown seaweed found in places more dangerous than the trees above, the flickering of something unknown to me, possibly dangerous, that always seemed about to reveal itself beneath the surface. Afterwards I would lie on my back and look at the canopy, some light managing to reach me through the leaves and the branches. I felt as if I was hanging from the sky that was only dimly visible.

In those moments, I belonged to the water entirely, and could feel its pull.

It was a mirage from their reality, from what the swimmers were trying to do. There were no real dangers on my pond, secret undercurrents that swirl you from left to right, or suck you down. For starters, the swimmers would throw themselves naked, and receive wave after wave over each bit of their body, abandoning themselves to its capricious movements. They would tread water, or swim, or simply let themselves be guided until that point, that moment, in which the ocean and the sky would touch. And this could only happen on the other side of the Barrier, where cetaceans wailed and monstrous creatures lurked, where survival was almost impossible. How many had ascended in this way? I had no way to know; to my knowledge, their beliefs were not recorded.

This is what I knew: they would happily walk the three or four miles until the weakest point on the wall for a pre-swim within its clean contained waters, and, perhaps, they would consider what they were about to do, they would reflect. I wondered if they had prayers and superstitions, like the little *shuvani* beliefs enacted by Savina. There was no way to know: theirs was a world of secretive rites, unknown meanings. Why had Mother initiated Eli and not me? I tried not to think about it, as I did not think about so many other things, but a furious rage simmered under my orderly surface whenever I remembered the scene. It tainted everything I did, everywhere I went.

Afterwards, they would defy the militias that guarded the wall, and cross at some point to the other side. This action may have only got easier as time went by, as the military presence in our settlements had gradually decreased. I wondered if there was a liminal moment in which the water on the other side felt like the water on the protected side, to suddenly change into the unknown; or whether they threw themselves directly into the long vista of brown debris. I had no way to know, I had never looked on the other side of the wall.

Now, I was in Old Town. But I still dreamt of my pond, and thought often about the ocean, so clean and pure on this side of the Barrier, and of what it meant to Urania.

'What are you doing here?'

I was startled by the question and the unknown voice, a distinctive tone of anger hanging in the air. I looked up. The little patio where I had taken my reveries to was a communal area for several compounds. I had gone there following the animated sound of water, and had sat in front of a little fountain dripping golden reflections. A techie boy of about my age, perhaps a little younger, was looking at me from between the eucalyptus plants.

'I live here,' I replied.

'Here? In this compound?'

Disbelief was evident in his clear blue eyes.

I knew at once what was happening. I recognised the scene far too well.

If he looked at me, he was bound to misinterpret it. I was wearing expensive clothes, but my skin was not entirely white, my eyes darker than his. My accent a bit off-kilter. There is no other way to put it: I looked, I look, a bit wrong, not altogether techie, not altogether beanie, not altogether right. I waited for it. At last, it came:

'Do you mean to say you are part of the help here? You are not allowed to use this space.'

My first impulse was to get up, walk the small distance between us, and hit him hard in the face. I contained that impulse. Instinctively, I knew it even then, before I had grown enough to understand it: it was important that I kept to an even higher degree of decorum than the boy in front of me... precisely because I sounded wrong, I looked wrong. He could say everything he wanted to me, but I could not answer back, defend myself. Only he and he alone had the privilege to hurt others.

'Okay, I will leave now.'

'Good.'

'My stepfather will hear about this. Which one is your compound?'

'Your stepfather?'

Now he looked confused.

'Anmal Vanlow.' My stepfather was one of the richest members of the community. The boy looked alarmed.

'I'm sorry, I...'

Despite the glee with which I got up and left, I was sad, for that was the moment when I knew it: I would never make a friend in Old Town.

5

Mother had always become more absent the longer she spent without seeing the water. All her jubilant dreams and sumptuous desires were situated in the short space of the offing. Did Mr Vanlow take us to Old Town because my mother was going mad in Gobarí? I never dared ask that question.

I had my own secret desires back then, other worries to occupy my teenage brain with: would we ever go up to the Upper Settlement with Mr Vanlow? The ring, perched over the atmosphere, the place where all the dos and don'ts were decided. It was not surprising that the servants thought so little of us, for they knew well that we did not make any decisions that mattered. We too were also forced to stay on a dying planet. Nothing of what they were doing up there was ever explained to us. From time to time we woke to the news that the forest had swallowed up this or that settlement. I grew up imagining the forest like a huge living thing, dormant until we did something to upset it. And then it would slowly stir all limbs as trees and mountains and those gigantic flowers, and the ever-changing vines, and the man-size leaves, moving as if it were one uncanny thing. A monster that destroyed and consumed everything in its wake. I didn't know it then, but my imaginings weren't very far away from the reality. I just didn't know the reasons behind what had happened; I did not completely understand about the vessels either, about sending people up, to get lost in all eternity. To swim among the stars.

Back in Gobarí, when I was little, Savina had shown me Old Town in one of our books—our household boasted a collection of twenty, a mark of distinction. The drawings in them depicted round stone buildings, domed stylised gardens, and elongated rockets which were meant to be the vessels, although the vessels were a bit different, I think; perhaps the book was outdated, and those were previous models. From them, the children of the beanies and the techies—never ringers—waved goodbye to their proud parents, big smiles on their faces. There were more drawings than words, no more than three or four sentences per page, printed in thick, round letters. You were meant to infer all the meaning through the drawings. I knew this was made on purpose, so the book could be used by people with different degrees of learning.

Savina had been taught to read by the first techie family she had served, and now she taught me. The Registry merited its own chapter, and the book alluded to its many treasures, kept from ancient times, times before the green winter caught up with us. It was difficult to imagine a world that had not been mostly green, composed of long, empty stretches of naked earth ('desertic', as it was called); but this was how things had been for a long time before me and my parents and grandparents had been born. It was difficult to imagine a world where something known as 'balance' existed. We were the children of excess. The Registry, for example, was said to contain all of it, the ancient and the new knowledge, to preserve it all, exactly as all the other Registries scattered across the planet. I remember looking at the chapter in awe. It was one of my favourites, together with the book about animals, which showed how animals used to be, before time accelerated: to survive, most species mutated rapidly afterwards, and were still mutating.

Some people thought that the mutated creatures had come from above, discarded experiments from up in the ring. But Savina did not believe that. She said that, as time had stopped at some point, and humanity thought itself eternal, time had decided to go quicker. I was not sure I knew what she meant. But it had to do with that idea of some Earth 'balance', and with the loss of it. One thing was certain: if the animals had accelerated quickly, but we hadn't, this ought to mean that they had been forced to mutate into beasts by an external force. By what force? By whom? When had this happened? I had no answer to those questions.

The ring, the Upper Settlement, also merited its own chapter. The interior scenes depicted long corridors and citizens dressed in their approved white clothing, talking to each other, watering plants—strangely small specimens kept in white containers—or playing with small children. Of all of them, I was always impressed the most by the lady in white. She was overlooking these amiable scenes from a huge balcony, and she was said to be the scientist who had initiated it all. To me, more than scientist I thought she was a magician, perhaps even a witch. She also smiled benevolently over her neat, beautiful subjects; but I could sense something off in her countenance, as a child I was instinctively afraid of her and her power.

It was because of the book that I had dreamt of Old Town as a white city, immaculate streets and elegant citizens, perhaps a bit aloof, not looking exactly where they were going, but charming and beautiful nonetheless. I was modelling them on Urania, my mother. Unexpectedly, after our arrival in Old Town she had been more absent than ever, lost in her thoughts and her memories. I knew she went every day to walk by the ocean. I knew it because her mood would be more cheerful when she returned. She never ate anything in the morning, but would accept a little glass of *milbao* from Savina, and next thing she would don a shawl full of peacocks and flamingos, would kiss the air next to my face, and would leave our luxurious compound. Her cheerfulness let me know she was going directly to the water for her morning walk. We would not see her again until lunchtime, and sometimes she did not return at all until my brother and I were in bed. Some nights she would come to see me, and she would bend over me, and look at me with her big, odd eyes. She would say nothing, and I would pretend to be asleep if I could. She would smell of the ocean then, of the salt and the air and the sun.

I hardly saw Mr Vanlow. While we were in Old Town, he was busy most of the time. There were lots of opportunities, he claimed.

'There are fortunes to be made now that the Delivery Act has decreed that all human beings remaining on the planet's surface are equal. Fortunes! And I intend to make one of them.'

'I don't understand; how is the Act going to help you make money, Papa?' I would ask. He always took all my questions seriously, and so he would reply:

'It is very simple, Pearl. The old servant caste is going to need things, want things. And believe me when I say that I will be only too happy to help them get them.'

With Mother visiting her beloved shore, and Papa occupied in his business dealings, I was left to my own devices.

'Child, go out and fetch me sage from the market. Here, take the credit purse.'

The coins would feel heavy in my hand. At Gobarí, I had never handled money, as there was no need for it. But I knew that most of the freedom that Mr Vanlow had procured for us was bought with it.

Savina had good intentions: she liked seeing me useful, and also getting as much fresh air as possible. But I was a little scared of the city, of how it aligned and at the same time did not with my bookish ideas. I had gone from roaming wildly in Gobarí to not leaving the interior of our new dwelling here.

I left the compound, but I was too scared of the water to venture beyond the winding streets that I knew would take me to the market square. I did not want to see the ocean, even our tamed version before the Barrier. And I did not want to see the horrid structure, either: it was imposed on me from Mr Vanlow's elegant compound every day anyway.

'Hello.'

It was the techie child. I had taken a turn, and had almost crashed against him. I swallowed my apology.

'Hello,' I replied, and moved around him to continue on my way.

'Wait!' Was that an imploring sound? I turned to face him.

'What do you want?'

'I… I'm sorry about the other day.'

'Don't lose sleep over it,' I replied, and made a further motion to go.

'Have you told your stepdad?'

I had to feel sorry for him. Was he worried about the possible repercussions of his rudeness? What did that say about my stepfather? I held my breath for a second, let out a long sigh. Gave him a moment to reflect on things. Eventually, I said:

'No. Don't worry.' Once more I turned to go.

'Where are you going now? Would you like some company?'

He was called Ariel, although he was no starborn, so

it was a mere affectation. He and his sister Laurel lived in the compound with an aunt. Their parents were dead.

'Have you guys noticed? The city is not white, not at all.'

They looked at me as if I were mad.

'What do you mean, white?'

I could not explain it, not really. I was still holding to my bookish ideas about things, about how neat and pristine things ought to be here. Everything, however, seemed to be made of that light brownish, porous stone; every single road was cemented, covered by beautiful ceramic *loza* forming coloured patterns. I marvelled at the abundance of colour, all the rich patterns. They were drawn in such a way that the tiles, next to each other, looked like a continuous geometric design. We ate lunch at a little market stall, fried fish and baby squid. There was a fish named like me: little pearls. It was a sort of baby fish that was deep-fried in batches, damped on a cauldron of boiling oil as they were caught, their small size meaning you couldn't remove their tails or their heads. You fried them like that and ate them like that, eyes and all. They were delicious. After lunch, the streets were emptied and there wasn't anyone around. The squares and alleyways were deserted, and filled with a curious smell, a little like fish rotting, but not unbearable. People would flood the streets later, when it cooled down. From far away, the monotonous tolling descended punctually every hour from the Registry's bronze bells—towers shot up into the sky inside whitewashed domes. They were painted like this in order to reflect the overreaching moon, and the Upper Settlement, the ring, slowly turning around itself. I had never been so physically close to the vessels, either. Even the ring seemed to be perched right above us, impossibly high in the sky. But I knew this to be deceptive, a mirage of sorts. We were not much closer than we had been in the *sierra*, but the angle of orbit appeared in closer proximity to us from Old Town; and of course, the ring could not be seen from the jungle.

'I want to get closer to the vessels,' I said.

'Why?' This was Laurel. I needed to touch the massive structures, to feel their solidity under my hand, but I did not know how to explain this. For the first time, I didn't feel scared of travelling inside them into the unknown, but instead a strange lightness; I imagined that they could help me ascend to the ring, somehow. I knew that they had escape pods inside, enough for at least half their passengers. I would fantasise about stealing one of these mid-ascent, and making my way to the ring, where I would make my fortune, exactly as Mr Vanlow was doing here.

I was daydreaming too much, and I was too old for daydreaming. After so many years in the jungle, not setting foot in Old Town since I was little more than a toddler, it was strange to find myself among the certainty of the *coquina* stone buildings, to the fabled marble cathedral, walking those strange streets every day at all hours. The cathedral itself was beyond my wildest imaginings. A religious building in the old days, it housed the Registry now. I knew it as the place where things were collected, interpreted, and explained back to us by the storytellers, the place from which all known taxonomies emerged. Little did I know it would become my home in a few months' time, and that I would spend the next few years of my life inside its stone walls, that I would share it with Laurel. She mentioned that her aunt was trying to get her a place to study there.

'Is it very difficult?' I asked.

'My grandfather, he sacrificed himself to the ocean.'

I could not form a reply but could not help opening my eyes wide in recognition and awe.

'It was terrible for my family. My father lost his job, we were really poor for a very long time, while I was growing up. Eventually, my parents had to go and work in another town. Getting there, they had an accident in their hovering vehicle.'

'I'm really sorry.' I winced at my own inadequacy; could I really have nothing better to say after such a revelation?

Their life must have been very difficult indeed, they must have suffered terribly, been really ostracised.

After I heard this, I felt sorry for Ariel as well. I could now interpret his attack when he first saw me as a survival reaction: eat before you are eaten.

Getting to the vessels wasn't difficult. They sat in an old, disused port, but entry to that section wasn't restricted. There were youngsters around, playing with hovering cycles, racing each other. They were scruffy techies, as if they were wrong versions, or copied versions of techie kids. Everything about them felt posed. I would later learn that it was the richest kids, the ones who had this studied, uncaring air. Their presence there, ignoring the gigantic structures that sat indifferently behind them, like white beetles, was unexpected; although the vessels weren't white, and being so close to them now I could see they were not translucent either, that was a visual effect when I looked at them from Kon-il cove. In fact, they looked brownish, dirty, and somehow abandoned. I knew the NEST project had been discontinued now, and that those vessels in Old Town were left to rot. What I did not know is how pitiful they would look up close, reminding me of two dying, beautiful birds.

That was what the city reminded me of, precisely: a rare bird, an unexpected mutated animal or place, exactly like our overgrown 'garden' in Gobarí, or like my mother, Urania. I had so few models to make sense of it all. I felt dizzy, looking it all avidly; hearing its citizens' conversations; finding the squares and the alleys from which I could see the ring; discovering two ancient trees, meant to be thousands of years old, thick and solid and magical, their many branches and profusion of roots a climbing frame for Old Town children. They were known as the *draco-milenario*, so my surprise was acute when I learnt that they had only been there for a few hundred years. Nevertheless, I was obsessed with them. Everything in Old Town possessed that same capacity to fascinate me, including the siblings who had accompanied me on my illicit walk. Old Town was not excessive like Gobarí, but suspended in time somehow, awaiting its yet-to-come fate.

'How is it?' I asked Ariel and Laurel, my chin pointing up towards the Upper Settlement. 'How is it, living so close to it?'

'We are not close. Not as much as you think, anyhow.'

'Exactly. We are as close as you are up in the *sierra*.'

I smiled. They hadn't got my meaning, poorly expressed as it was: they were much closer than I would ever be to the ring, even with their problematic family past, for unlike me they were techies through and through. I was a strange mixture of beanie, from my father; techie, from my mother; with a little *shuvaní* blood intermixed. I would never own up to this, but they, of course, could read it in my looks. Despite everything, they could jump on the twice-daily flights up, if so they wanted, in one of the many daily exchanges between the town and up above, in which people like them came and went constantly. But other people, not me. Surely nobody like me. I imagined their lives had been determined by it; perhaps even more than my own, I reflected, since I had enjoyed a certain freedom in Gobarí. I imagined them constantly looking up to their benign gods in the sky. I already knew that some people, mostly beanies, made offerings to the ring regularly.

One thing that puzzled me about Old Town, though: where were the people like Savina? I could not see anyone that looked like they were of *shuvaní* blood; apparently, the compounds inside the Barrier were full of them. They were known as the best servants, and the richer techie families had been able to keep them after the Delivery Act, paying them formidable salaries to look after their houses and their children. However, they hardly ever ventured outside the wall.

From time to time I would see a *shuvaní* girl looking after some expensively dressed children as they busied themselves climbing the roots of the *dracos*. She would invariably be dressed in colourful garments that reminded me of Savina's, but which possessed a different quality, somehow; they were much dearer versions of her ample skirts, and it was obvious that the fabrics came from exclusive manufacturers.

Most things in Old Town looked like that, improved or better versions of things we had in Gobarí, made to last longer. Everything was a little bit different. Everything had a different flavour, was surprising to some degree, while at the same time being recognisable.

Time also felt odd in the city. Things felt so solid, so certain. I could not comprehend these many certainties around me—the stone buildings, the garments and objects made to last—not after so many years in the forest, an uneasy space, but nevertheless my home.

One thing: the first few nights in Old Town I did not know how I would manage to sleep, deprived of all the living things that sang their lullaby, the sweet rush of the waving branches in the dark, each and every one of the million living things a conduit for my childhood emotions. The shock of the stone buildings had numbed me. I understood it, that I had been a child until that point, and this unmoored feeling was growing up.

Eventually, I got to see it. I had gone alone with Laurel this time. She had guided me through some secret alley-ways.

It was raining, a light summer rain. Laurel guided me across a patio covered in puddles. On both sides, similar walls of very similar buildings: the same humidity stains, the same flaking paint right and left, the same empty, boarded-up shops, partly covered by the ocean mist. It was very early in the morning. A wild cat appeared from around a corner, and crossed ahead of me. I followed it with my eyes. Its flexible body found an impossible space between the buildings, and it disappeared.

'There,' said Laurel. I looked up.

The ocean behind the Barrier felt like a vast monster. Even if the Barrier—we did not call it the wall, for that was the beanie word for it—was so close; and yet, it was also at a great distance, a curved, gigantic smile, laughing at us. What did it protect us from? What exactly was this debris, plastic, that we had been told could kill us? This was not true, of course. It may have been a poisonous material, for it had help precipitate the green winter; but Mother had been a swimmer, and I knew that she had moved inside the water, deep within its embrace. And she had survived. That lie was like all the other lies that floated down from the ring, lingering like a bad smell, designed to bend us into submission. We perched on some rocks, put there centuries before to stop the ocean from breaking against the old medieval wall; a useless endeavour. I had never been so close to the thing. It didn't feel like protection, but like the wall of a cell in a prison.

That day, looking at the ocean, the clean bit on our side of the Barrier, sensing its pull, I felt that I understood Mother for the first time. Perhaps it was my *shuvani* blood, perhaps it was that I missed the forest. Or perhaps it was that I was my mother's daughter after all, and I understood the power of dying well and on your own terms.

'We should dye your hair blue, like when you were little,' Mother said. She had not spoken directly to me in weeks; or if she had, it had been without seeing me—the way she did those days—looking over me while imparting this or that instruction. A smile formed on my face. It hurt.

The oddest thing about Old Town: there were hardly any animals. A few birds, the town's beloved flamingos. But that was it. A peaceful, managed scene.

'Laurel, where are the animals here?'

'Animals?'

'I haven't seen anything, except those pink things.'

'Ah! Well, I guess we have hundreds, thousands of specimens; but they are down there instead of up here...' She said this pointing with her finger to the floor, and

I knew she meant the vaults of the Registry, where she longed to go one day.

'What do you mean?' I was envisioning an underground zoo.

'They are preserved down there, everything they can get their hands on, from the olden days as well.'

'Preserved? Alive?'

She laughed at my ignorance.

'Of course not! *Mummified*.'

'Whatever for?'

'For us, so we can study them, learn what happened.'

This made some sort of horrid sense; although, eventually, I would also learn that things were never that simple. Learn what, exactly? All I had ever learnt about animals was to fear them. My father had impressed on me early the fear for the creatures that now shared this world with us. Perhaps that was why there were so few in town, and it was said that the ones in the ring were bio-engineered to behave in a tame fashion. The animal that I feared most when I was little was the arrow snake. It opened the skin around its neck as it glided towards its victim. It didn't fly, not exactly, but it looked as if it did. It was called 'arrow' because the beanies thought it could cross through people's hearts while in mid-flight, and kill them on the spot. Thankfully, I never saw any; only its constellation, it seemed, had followed me to Old Town. I think I feared it because it looked like the basilisk, back in our pond.

Sometimes, when I was little, Savina called me feral. When I asked what that meant, she said that I was an unruly, stubborn sort of child. Wild. That was a bad thing to say; I used to rat her out when she called me that, saying she had said something 'unkind' to me. It was my childish way of protesting. Being compared to animals was the worst possible insult.

But in the city, I felt it: we were wilder, untamed; our nature differed from those who surrounded us, those elegant people. Mother could mingle easily among them; she came from a true techie family. But Father didn't, and that made me and my brother suspicious in people's eyes. Could we be refined, perhaps? Was there any hope for us? My stepfather started mentioning the Sisters as a possibility. Perhaps they could do something for me. Would I not like to be a curator, one day, perhaps? Study those objects and palimpsests from the olden days? That would mean going to live inside the Registry, leaving my family behind for many years.

One day, Mr Vanlow took all of us, including Laurel and Ariel, to a storytelling observance. It took place in a round room built for that purpose, adjacent to the main

Registry building. We sat on wooden benches surrounding a little podium, quite insignificant, on which eventually a young man perched. He started declaiming. The words were alien to me. But something was happening, inside my head, underneath my eyelids, which I could close and still see it all.

I have since understood how storytelling works, what it does with your senses. It was as if they somehow became entangled. The meaning of the story presents itself, sensation on top of sensation, all of them building together to create one woven pattern, one in which no one element is primary, the story a single perfect whole made of fragments and patches, moments of understanding, smells, vision.

Several figures appeared, and they changed shape, and they changed colour. They were yellow, and blue, and red. And they told the story of some benevolent masters who looked kindly from above, and it made me feel safe somehow, contented. The lights danced, and mutated into something else, and I knew they had always meant to be that and that only. Colours around them exploded, and there was a fire in my heart. I had no words to explain what had happened to me, I was overcome by feeling. Some of the words danced in my mouth with sparkling tastes, some ideas lurked in my mind far too long with colours that saddened me. I looked around me, and saw Laurel clapping and smiling wildly, repeating some of the tinkering sounds of the recital, bits of the performance that she seemed to know by heart. When it all ended, I knew that I understood more things now, and that the world, our world, and my place in it, made sense somehow, exactly as it was. This knowledge set me at peace, although I could not have explained the specifics of why it made sense, why it was good. The storyteller had placed the knowledge directly inside me.

The next time my stepfather asked about the Sisters and the school at the Registry and learning to be a curator, I said that no, I didn't want to be a curator, but a storyteller. He laughed at this, saying that I was too wild for something so delicate and precious. Why did he call me wild? What had he been told about me?

Was I wild, feral, like the hare from my nightmares, the stoats that ate Eli's little sister? Or was there some hope for me? There was only one way to find out: I agreed to go into the Registry and learn the curator's trade, a lesser form of knowledge, as soon as I was of age. I had to wait until I was thirteen to start my apprenticeship.

Eventually, as a new routine established itself, I only

saw Mother and Mr Vanlow at mealtimes. Savina looked after my brother Aster most of the time. My wanderings around the city, mostly with Laurel, sometimes with her and Ariel, went unchallenged by any adult. I revelled in my new surroundings, strange and intoxicating, but now we had started to walk often in the direction of the Registry, the huge domed building overlooking the ocean; I was curious about my future home. Mr Vanlow was adamant that I would attend the school, and Laurel often looked at me admiringly, perhaps with a certain sadness. We sat in front of the entry building, the old cathedral, sucking our frozen *milbao* pouches dry, the way oldtowners preferred to eat it. The whiteness of the domes reflected the yellow light pouring from the lamps, shining with eerie reflections. The ocean mist, the dusty street in the odd crepuscular light, the tedious monotonous sound of those rotten bells calling. A strange feeling of void overtook me on those occasions, as if I were falling into an abyss—the ocean, perhaps; or maybe swimming in space, among the stars. I hadn't had a fugue moment in a long time. But thinking about my future always gave me some vertigo.

'Can you imagine, Laurel? These buildings have seen it all happening. The Registry was exactly there, standing in the same place, centuries before the green winter happened.'

'Wow. It's true! And the Barrier and the Settlement were there too, all those centuries back.'

'No, they weren't. We built them.'

But she was adamant. The Barrier at least, she said, came from the olden days, as it had been put there to protect the shores from the advancing water. It must have first been built hundreds of years ago, perhaps thousands. Perhaps she was right. What did I know about anything? The notion was enough to set anyone's head spinning. All those walls around us, all those cobbled labyrinthine streets, connected us to a remote time; or, rather, their existence challenged the very notion of time itself. If I touched them, I could feel as if time had stopped, or as if the last thousand years were part of the same thing: a straight line that started with our forefathers, or even before they existed, past the green winter, stretching into our present, and that it would surely carry on well into the darkness of the future.

I felt that if the building was standing there, in front of me, and I could use it, the same as it had been used by humans pre-Winter, then one thousand years meant nothing. The debris in the ocean would not dissolve for another five or six centuries at least; if it ever disappeared at all. We were all part of the same thing, of the same life; space and time didn't matter so much, not really. The rules, the laws, the dos and don'ts that trickled down from the Upper Settlement, all the way to us little people, were a useless attempt at domestication, for the world had lost its human scale. We were like ants, at the mercy of the forest, of the elements.

Had the Barrier survived old storms as well? Who knew. They could be ferocious. The pattern was recognisable, at least by those of us who had experienced the jungle outside of those streets: long periods of heat, followed by torrential rain; long periods of heat, followed by torrential rain; and repeat. Old Town enjoyed milder weather; however, it seemed that we had brought some of the horrid circular pattern with us. We were enduring our sixth day in a row of impossible heat. We had eaten so many frozen *milbao* that my throat was dying; we carefully avoided being sent on errands by adults in the middle of the day— unsurprisingly, most oldtowners had no idea of how to behave in these mini-heatwaves—and Ariel had taken to sleeping in the internal patio, next to the fountain, where we had first met.

'The heat will break, I promise,' I said to reassure my friends. But I knew what that would entail; and, after seeing mothers allowing their children to play, climbing the *dracos* in the middle hours of the day, the hottest, when all exercise ought to be avoided, or letting their toddlers' skins burn until they peeled, I doubted Old Town would know what to do once the storms arrived. Not all of the science or the *shuvani* magiks would be enough to protect them.

6

Although Mr Vanlow did not belong to the most affluent caste of citizens, he had enough money to pay for his own private view of the ocean, and this is where his white square mansion-compound decorated with silver ornaments and fake flickering lights, apparently in imitation of the ring's interiors, sat. You could usually find him, if he was around, in his favourite spot, overlooking the clean-filtered ocean water, gazing languidly out of his vast glass walls, while sipping expensive drinks and eating forbidden food: fried baby fish, pigeons, sometimes even more exotic species. At the limit of his vision was the Barrier, that gigantic protective structure, all whiteness, the little windows of the abodes it contained glimmering in the distance, the sharp flickering of their security systems— red, green—reassuringly shining here and there. Over its roof, the hovering vehicles glided elegantly until they found their docking places. Sometimes, flamingos flew in this direction from the neighbouring marshes, and all the humans gathered politely on the other side of their glass walls, pointing at them in awe, marvelling at their existence. They ought to be extinct, those birds. But the marshes had been miraculously spared generations back, and the flamingos had thrived accordingly. Now they were the symbol of the city, their image attached to everything imaginable.

You could tell he was a contented man, happy with the position he had attained. He treated Mother with respect, although he had clearly married her for her status and her beauty. He tried to give her everything she wanted: an array of doctors paraded into our compound to see Aster; Mother had the exclusive use of her own little hovering vehicle. Our table was always brimming with exotic and expensive edibles. The one thing that Urania laughed at was her husband's fondness for a 'view' of the ocean. She preferred to walk there, to remove her silk slippers and dip her feet in the water. I think he was a bit hurt by her light mockery, and this made me even fonder of him.

I was also happy in Old Town. At home, our inter-actions as a family had resembled the movements of a structure that needs constant oiling but is left to rot. I had almost made my life with Eli, with Savina. It hadn't helped that Mother had been so overprotective of my brother as to jealously guard him—for herself, that is. Here, with Urania leaving for the shore most mornings, I sometimes ventured into his tiny room. Savina, or one of her helpers, would be reading to him, giving him a sponge bath. Some other times he would be sleeping on his own.

My brother was a mystery. Nobody knew what was wrong with him, except that one day he had decided to stop interacting with us. He had never learnt to speak or to walk. Now, once Mother left the compound, I would walk into his room and sit with him. I didn't fancy the idea of reading him the constellation children's books that he always had around, but I tried sometimes. He seemed to like the fable of Alira, the flying girl. I also started telling him about my adventures with Laurel and her brother, and I think that he reacted similarly to when he heard a story he favoured, as if he enjoyed my little outings—could that be possible?—and that his eyes glinted in a mischievous way when I told him of my escapades: climbing the rocks to touch the Barrier, catching a furtive glimpse of the ocean, devouring the pouches of frozen *milbào*. During a particularly hot day, I brought him one of them, and I patiently helped him eat it, lying in his bed. I swear he almost smiled in my direction that day.

But just when I was getting used to Old Town, enjoying the new, fragile connection it was helping form between me and my little brother, Mr Vanlow announced that all renovations were finished, and that we would be returning to Gobarí. Mother received the news with vacant eyes, and moved towards the view, following the flight of the flamingos. As much as the coast pulled my mother, Gobarí called to Mr Vanlow. He was eager to see the changes and improvements done to the property, and to start playing at being the owner of a historical house with aristocratic connections. He might have brought the money to the marriage, but Mother's old family line of techies, rotten and half mad as it was, had certainly brought the distinction.

Urania did not want to go back, and her refusal didn't have anything to do with missing the ocean. She had a single reason: the weather was about to break.

It was difficult to pick this up if you had not lived through it. Almost none of the oldtowners, not even Mr Vanlow, it seemed, with his short stay in Benguele, could understand what the storm could mean. But we knew; oh yes, we knew. Savina claimed that she could smell it in the air, and Mr Vanlow laughed at her for being superstitious.

'Oh well, I wonder how much you will laugh soon, *jeré*,' she said darkly, and left the living room and went into the kitchen. I followed her. She had made the neat kitchen her own in the time we had been there, and bunches of dried herbs hung from the ceiling. I sat and she put a plate of green chickpeas in front of me, and I started peeling them, taking them from their shells and pushing them out with my thumb. Like a child, I didn't want to see my mother and Mr Vanlow arguing.

The signs were clear: it would be the storm to end all storms. The moorhens abandoned Genovese Park, venturing into the streets; the wall received little electrical discharges during the day, anticipating the large ones coming. And the heat was like we had never experienced, utterly unbearable. The change in the weather would be equally dramatic. If a storm of these proportions was about to break, and if it would bring torrential rains that might last days, it would be safer to stay in Old Town, not to risk the wilderness of Gobarí, cut off from civilisation. We had not experienced fast floods in years, but it had always felt like a lucky escape. Now, there was something ominous hanging over all of us.

Mr Vanlow would not listen to reason. He called Mother frivolous for not wanting to miss parties, and dances, and soirées. Mother pointed out that she did not want to be cut off from the doctors. She was thinking of Aster. Mr Vanlow claimed that with the new gliding vehicles, capable of hovering over anything, the rains could not maroon us. Mother reminded him that even hovering vehicles had to land sometimes, and that they could not do so over the forest, or in the roads if the roads were rivers.

But Mr Vanlow was determined. We packed. I said goodbye to Laurel and Ariel. There was no reasoning with him. 'There is no reasoning with stubborn men, that has not changed,' chanted Savina, half laughing. Was she laughing at Mother, at me?

Nothing happened on the way back, of course. Mr Vanlow had been right about that. The rain had not picked up, although Savina had explained to me that it could increase in strength suddenly, as if someone had pulled a plug up in the ring without warning, letting the water flow in full force. She had lived through fast floods. But we managed to arrive shortly before the rain gave way to a much worse scenario. It was raining, of course, and with some force, and so we could not see the extent of the repairs and marvel at the vision of the many improvements that Mr Vanlow had kept us apprised of in the city.

Instead, we went in quickly, and Savina entered the big house with us, when she should have taken the back path into her kitchen shack, an external construction where she also lived. This was odd. But she was helping my mother carry my brother into his room at the back of the house, to put him in bed. He was exhausted from the journey. The odd, heavy rain had made him cry a little.

The odd rain, I call it, for we had just arrived at the door when it changed in force, becoming a mad downpour. For that was what happened, there is no other way of explaining it: the heavy drops were suddenly collapsing from the sky like thick buckets of rain, forcefully trashing everything in their way. I saw leaves and branches and trunks and whole trees falling; I saw what remained of the external shacks rushing into our porch, and branches and animals and children and objects, floating indistinctly on the surface of the brown water; I saw a mighty eagle, the kind that could carry a grown man, crashing from the sky, breaking our porch roof. And then I knew we were in trouble. Our new, shiny, repaired house was collapsing. Not all of it, but some bits, here and there: the porch, the balcony, the adjacent shacks of kitchen and bathhouse; and the back of the house, where our sleeping quarters were—carried away by the force of the water. Before we could prevent it, before we could take him to safety, beds and walls and little brother and all.

7

They used to fish for pearls at the depths of the ocean, in the olden days. And now, we try to fish for pearls at the end of space. Nobody knows what is out there, and how could we? All those children gone, lambs to slaughter. Nobody ever returns, or sends a message of hope. And if they did, would it have got to us?

The swimmers also gave their lives. They also did it for us, in a way. Their desire, to get to the point where water and sky touched; there, they would ascend, *ulalé*, no need for vessels. Urania used to say that if you managed to reach the line of the horizon, the place where the ocean and the sky met, you would continue swimming among the stars.

I knew it was only a tale, the line of the horizon a hallucination, our planet a sphere that would never really, truly, touch the ether. But sometimes, at night, when the ocean and the sky were the same colour, and the constellations appeared reflected over its mirrored surface; on those nights of waters as calm as the space above us, I could almost believe her.

The Fox. Alira, the Little Bird Ascending. My own star sign, the Kingfisher. The Three Sisters, each of them given a special task, a special power to look after us all. I was capable of recognising some of them up in the sky, the ones all the beanie children learnt. The line of the horizon was the threshold, the place where the boundaries blurred. Which boundaries? What were they keeping apart? That, no one remembered.

Whenever I couldn't sleep properly, I would wake in the small hours of the night and would go out onto the balcony that ran all round the first floor at Gobarí. The constellations appeared then. If I believed Savina, followed my *shuvani* blood, I would think that all known history was there, all the lore; and then there was the future as well, written in capricious formations, the stars showing us the path we must wander, heavy with meaning. To believe that, you ought to accept that there was only one possible future, not many. To believe that, you ought to accept that there would be a future at all. And I wanted to believe it, that was what I had always wanted: to trap this future, this thing, and make sure it did not escape between my fingers like sand from the ocean shore.

I have never seen constellations so clear as I see them now—I can almost touch them from my window in the Upper Settlement. Only back in Gobarí they had been so bright; in those sleepless, endless nights of my childhood. At dawn, after interpreting their auguries, I would leave the house quietly and run to the pond, and wash in its waters. Savina insisted that I learnt the histories of some of the constellations at least. Just in case, she said. Just in case time stopped once more, or even worse, just in case it accelerated all of a sudden, and more monstrous creatures were spat out at our feet for us to deal with, eat or be eaten. Just in case I needed to find my way back home.

After the flooding I found myself back in Old Town, alone now. Something else had happened in Gobarí, something I did not know how to interpret. I was a child after all, and my world was collapsing. The flood was receding slowly, painfully. Some of the fields were still half-filled with water. There was debris and destruction all over the place. The forest, which had always seemed shiny to me, the purest green, seemed off colour somehow, midway between green and brown. It was a tired forest, an exhausted forest.

Everywhere we found the cadavers of animals, and they were even more fantastical than we remembered. The flood had overturned a nest of giant centipedes, and there they were, in the middle of the road, a little mountain of them, piled atop each other, all their purples and yellows and reds, the colours that indicated their capacity to poison us, utterly gone. They looked grey now, a dull colour. The beanies danced and partied around them, and set fire to the little promontory. I could understand them: we had all been terrified of finding one when we collected *rambután* or performed any of our daily tasks in the jungle. They were perhaps the most dangerous creatures we knew.

At least these centipedes had been spat out by the water; we could admire their demise or not, pity them or not, but their fate was a certainty, and there was consolation in that. My brother was still missing; his body had not been recovered. Urania was more aloof than ever now, a shadow of her former self. I have patchy memories from those days: I hid a great deal from people, did not want to be found. Everybody was so busy that they did not miss me. I wandered alone among the destruction, without thinking where I was going. I was lost, perhaps; I felt lost. I could not stop thinking about him. Where could he have ended up? Something broke inside me, something that could never be repaired again. My only consolation was to hope that it must have been quick. He surely could not have tried to swim against the current to save himself, as he had never learnt how, like the fishermen who ventured the Three Oceans to bring us food, who never learn to swim in order not to prolong their agony if a leviathan wrecked their ship: falling into the abyss quickly is a much better fate than an agonising and long demise.

The pond had overflowed as well. The little shore around it had disappeared. The plants around it were destroyed. I still walked there every day to be safely on my own. Nobody else went there. The beanie children never swam in it, scared as they were of the basilisk. And I myself started seeing the place through their eyes for the first time. It was a ghastly place, that was the truth. Now, this was easier to perceive as well. Its murky waters were now brown, almost black, with dirt and upset. It was a curiously altered scene, as if a cataclysm, something precise and unavoidable, had toyed with the little civilisations that camped around its humble shores. The hawkbit, the water-mint, the calendula: all gone, destroyed. The shores were thick with debris, its glistening sands all disarranged. There was a strange wave-like movement to the water, reanimated as if from the dead, which I had never seen before.

These animated waters gave me an idea I had never thought of. They were imbued with a certain energy, that much was clear. I had an idea.

Firstly, I gathered my tools; then, I thought of the words. I imagined the ceremony as a ritual bath. I would feel clean, refreshed, purified, even among the debris, perhaps precisely because I was communing with that chaos, alluding to it, petitioning to it. I brought incenses, fragrant oils belonging to my mother, *shuvani* staples: rosemary, lavender, valerian. Pine cones, seashells. The most important thing: my brother's sponge. I could see as if from afar: distant memories of baths when I was little, Mother above me, her happy face dipping a small cup in the bath water, and repeatedly bathing my head with the liquid, small gestures of the old, forbidden religion the swimmers had sprouted from; after all, the symbol of their deity, of he who died for our sins, had been a fish.

I did my ceremony, hoping that I had managed to raise the required energy from me, and from the place, and feeling that the ritual would be heeded precisely because I had chosen the broken pond of all places. I tried to imagine it all unfolding, my petition heard, my brother found.

I had cleaned myself; I had cleaned the pond; I had cleaned the past.

There was no reason to think it would not work, and work it did.

One morning I walked to the pond, as per usual, and what I found inside its waters was Urania herself.

Her eyes were lost up above, towards a sky that could not be seen due to the thick canopy over the pond, even after some of the trees and the branches and the lianas had been washed away. I stayed where I was; I did not want to disturb her. She emerged slowly, and I could see that she was dressed in an expensive techie robe from Old Town, now ruined after her swim. A branch must have broken beneath my slippers, and she looked in my direction for a moment; thankfully, she did not see me. Her eyes were vacant, strangely white, and her look was lost and uncomprehending. I saw there and then that my mother had transcended this world at last. She had finally accomplished her swim, albeit not where she would have wanted. But she looked dead somehow.

She wasn't dead, of course. But her vacant expression scared me a little. She ignored the noise and moved towards some bushes, and there, after much moving of branches and breaking leaves, she uncovered what I later learnt was my brother's corpse, bloated and rotten and as grey as the centipedes after its time in the water. She kissed it lightly on the forehead, and rocked him gently in her lap.

I had done it. My first magiks had worked perfectly.

I turned around and ran as fast as I could towards the only security I knew: Savina. Papa wasn't around, of course.

When Urania was found, she could not speak a word. She was unresponsive; beyond death now, but also beyond life. Nothing mattered to her any longer.

Mother was ill, that was all they were saying to me; no one would tell me where she was being sent. Perhaps they thought I would have no interest in seeing her, and would prefer to forget her. Mr Vanlow flew up again to the Upper Settlement. Eventually, Savina left to live with her son, and that was it, I was alone. She came to see me before leaving, put something in my hand, saying a little prayer as she did: later on, I would find out that it was a little pouch of herbs. I looked at her quizzically.

'Keep them under your pillow,' she said, and she hugged me. 'It is time, the time is now,' she said, caressing my blue locks with her open palm.

'Time for what?'

'Time for being brave, as brave as you can be.'

I felt something break inside me. When I looked at

her face again, her eyes were slightly watery, but she didn't cry. She was smiling. I smiled back.

'We will see each other again.'

'When?'

'Sooner than you think, my little bird.'

That was the hardest, to see Savina go. I have never lived through a night like that night, and I hope that I never will again. Gobarí, or what was left of it, was deserted; only a skeleton team of servers had been deemed necessary to keep things in order in our absence. The last night, alone in the house with only a handful of servants, was one of the strangest I can remember. A sadness so deep that it crushed my chest. I went through the empty rooms, now clouded in the darkness of dusk, and felt as if something had finally broken, something I could never put back together again. I walked from one room to the next, from Urania's to Savina's abandoned space, to the place at the back where a few struts now gave strength to the part of the house where my brother's room had been. The loneliness weighed heavy upon me; I could not breathe: it wasn't an episode this time, but something oddly different. I felt as if a hole had opened inside of me, a hole I could never fill. First my father, then my mother, then my brother. There were only a couple of books left from our collection, and I went to find them. I could still see my father, going over them with me, before he disappeared and Savina took over. I could see him, swimming away, while I was perched on the rock. And the urgency of those days was mixed now with the belief, deep within me, of his innocence. Could it be possible? I had always felt that he was trying to protect me when he took me away. I decided I would do what I could to find out.

The next morning I started my journey to stay with the Sisters, and that meant going back to Old Town. I promised myself I would not stay in Old Town forever; that, if I could not go back to Gobarí, I would go up to the ring as soon as I could. Even then I knew many years would have to pass for that to happen.

The Sisters had made an exception for me, for I was still two months away from my thirteenth birthday. They changed my date of birth on the admission screen, and that was that. I felt odd when I saw them do that, alarmed; as if that little lie had the power to set off a chain of events of cataclysmic proportions, that would at some point erase my whole existence.

8

The sorting of accumulated knowledge, that was the Sisters' business. And it turned out I had a gift for it, for organising, cataloguing, thinking of those who would come after us, who would need to make sense of it. I started training to work in the Registry, a vast, unending collection of knowledge from past days, dating from long before the green winter itself, everything that remained of a lost world, and the foundations of all our beliefs. Whether I wanted it or not, it seemed that I would become a curator.

I spent the first month with a group of six other girls undertaking some basic training, and learning the history of the place. We took our meals together at a round table, and slept in a dormitory which contained ten beds, three of them empty. They were all from techie families, and hardly looked in my direction. All except one of them. A nice surprise awaited me in the Registry: Laurel was starting as well, and we were in the same little cohort.

'Your stepfather arranged it.'

'Mr Vanlow?'

I could hardly believe it. My stepfather, perhaps sensing that I would be lonely, had brought Laurel there to be with me. I was ecstatic.

'I am so, so thankful,' she said. But I did not want her to feel any sense of debt towards me, so I hastened to say:

'Laurel, I am really glad that you are here! But I did not do anything. You owe me nothing.'

As soon as the words left my mouth, I winced. But Laurel, good old Laurel, did not seem to mind. She chuckled, and explained:

'Our fortunes changed, thank the Three Oceans!'

I smiled, and we hugged. I was conscious at that moment of how lucky I was to have been accepted into the school as well, and wondered how many strings Mr Vanlow had to pull to make it all happen. Now, I would train for a few years, and emerge on the other side with a profession. He would not need to look after me, or think of me. I would not be a burden.

Once the first month was over, the seven of us were taken for the first time into the Registry itself. A Sister directed us there. She was mostly dressed in black: long black skirt, white shirt and, over it, the black *manto* falling on her shoulders. But she was young, and low-ranking, so we could see her face, unlike the higher-ranking *cobijadas* who covered their faces completely with the *manto*, only allowing one of their eyes to shine out with its vast knowledge. The entry room exhibited examples of what could be found inside, a melange of artefacts and relics. It was haphazardly put together, or so it seemed to my uneducated eye; in truth, everything there was meticulously placed and labelled. That entry section was opened to the public, and all of us would work there in turn during the first year of our apprenticeship, looking after these less important objects.

The profusion of cabinets formed a maze of wood and plastic and glass; each turn a thousand new discoveries, so packed they were. It never seemed to end, object after object superimposed, mingled, one overlapping another. There were also some religious objects in view: from the ceiling hung the astrolabes and the compasses and the clocks; from the corners, sextants and quadrants, some of them made decorative by twisting over themselves into infinite spirals, with complicated calculations painted on their surfaces. Behind these objects the vaulted ceiling was painted black; and in that ominous representation of the sky shone the constellations, composed star by star with shiny silver paint. At one end of the room, a massive Totem; around the chamber the walls were covered from floor to ceiling with bookcases, where the papers and the scrolls and the bound volumes competed for space. We were facing a never-ending profusion of objects and books and manuscripts, even though these were dearer, and people could only gaze at them from behind triple glass and at a great distance. But what the room also contained, which fascinated me from the beginning, was the cadavers of the long-past 'digital' times that had marked the last epoch of humanity before the green winter itself. There were pods for looking at digital archives, as well as artistic interactions. All of these were, of course, mixed up with *shuvaní* recipes for sale in little glass jars, and storytelling merchandise. In other words: things and things and more things.

I could hear admiring noises coming from behind me— the other youngsters of my cohort—but I was suddenly overcome by the impossibility of it all, by the notion that making sense of those things and of that place would be beyond human capabilities. I felt one of my episodes coming on. I looked for a quiet corner, and hid myself between the monstrous glass things, keepers of hundreds of items, from the minuscule to the enormous, dreading the taxonomies that I would be forced to understand to make sense of it all. It was an excess very similar to the excess of the forest; but this was man-made, which surprised me greatly. I could do a number of things: I could force myself to calm down by retreating to my safe space; but now I could only see my brother, Aster, bloated in the pond, my mad mother, and Savina, leaving me behind. And, if I concentrated on ignoring them, all I could see, what my mind stubbornly returned to, was the dead hare, the liquid and the brains and the skin melting out, and her sweet rotten smell. In order to push away all these images, I sprang into the pond in my mind, instead of thinking about the landscape, trying to recreate in my mind the feeling of first submersion in the water. That did it, and at last I felt calm, reassured.

I knew that the Registry was the place where we studied the past, venerated it, certain in the knowledge that our survival depended on avoiding its repetition; but I had no idea of the vastness of its collections. And this was only the entry chamber. The real collection was kept behind the large wooden doors I could see at the end: stack after stack of items to catalogue, study, describe.

This was one of the first things that I learnt and marvelled at: the real proportions of the Registry. It did not restrain itself to occupying the old temple of a lost religion that used to be called a 'cathedral', but connected underground with many other buildings around the city which the curators had assimilated. The archives and repositories went on for miles. I became particularly interested in the past digital culture, and learnt that the visual and digital pods served to inspect their old version of what was their own HiveMind: a primitive thing called a 'web', inspired, it seemed, by the overreaching webbing of arachnids; but oddly without understanding the basic principle of the insects' netting technique. Instead, this 'web' resorted to chaos and an apparent desire for data-profusion of which only some faded remnants had survived. Other sections were occupied by papers and books and manuscripts and scrolls, carefully looked after. Some of those were indeed so old that it was forbidden to touch them, breathe on them; a knowledge of the past so fragile, it seemed, that it could crumble from the weight of your gaze on it.

At home, in Gobarí, everyone had been welcome to our collection of books, around twenty tomes at some point; here, I could, in the performance of my training duties—carrying a message from a curator to another, changing the water for the instant *milbao* machine—traverse rooms and chambers that contained thousands of them. The first time I was faced with this reality, with so many books that I would not be able to read them in my short lifespan, I had to force myself not to feel dizzy, for the notion was enough to send my head spinning. The high-ceilinged rooms in the Registry tended to overlook another alien vision after the jungle of my childhood: the quaint hidden patches of garden, large, green quads of tamed nature, where the younger storytellers relaxed by hitting a ball with a stick. I was as mistrustful of a 'managed' patch of green as I was of a 'managed' collection of things: I expected that both would eventually rebel.

I had been in the Registry for one year when I was finally given the most basic tools of my trade: a white apron and gloves, and my own set of protective masks against the dust and mildew. It was my responsibility to look after these, make sure they were kept in pristine condition. We were taken into a round, high-ceilinged chamber, with different recovering stations. Each of us had a high stool, a table with the basic HivePro apps installed into an oval machine, and a conservation pod of our own. The automated trolleys would bring us little objects— unimportant tomes, little stuffed animals from the past —each of them a test of sorts, all part of the same dusty menagerie of rot and decay. We would put these *memento mori* inside our portable conservation pods, where their mould would be eaten away, their corners unbent. Inside the machine, the stuffed little birds we used for practice acquired an odd shine, as if a little bit of life were infused into them from the sterile insides of the white oval, making me expect that they would take flight when I passed my hand over the glass lid to slide it open. It never happened, of course.

One morning my automated trolley delivered one such stuffed specimen, a young osprey. I performed my duties and took it back. But it had taken me longer than usual, as the little test had become several tests: for while preparing it, I had noticed something else had been stuffed with the animal, all those centuries back—two centuries, three? Its parasites. I found myself performing this strange exercise in assemblage; everything had its place, its meaning, its reason for existing: the nest, the eggs, the bird, the parasites… Everything was taken apart, and put together again, as if I was making a puzzle. Everything… except the parasites themselves; for I suddenly had the intuition that this *was* the test I had been given, and that I was meant to do something else with those. There was a section in the Registry dedicated to processing all lost entomology, and it was there I took them. I was right: that had been the test.

The remains of the assemblage exercise needed to be delivered to the cabinets that would contain the artefact until someone required it for teaching, or to weave a storyteller lyric. The ones connected to the old natural world were called pastorals, and they had become my favourites. An item such as this could feature in one of them. I reached the repository, with its cabinets of treasure, and endless rows of moving shelves; you needed to turn a wheel to open a gap between them, and find the place where the little box should be kept.

It was then that I was overcome by the dizziness again. I simply could not understand what I was seeing, and therefore I could not understand what we were doing: one thing that had been impressed on us during our early training was the lack of space, the eternal, never-ending problem with space. But in front of me what I saw was not one, or two, or even three, but what looked like hundreds of repeated copies of the stuffed bird I was carrying, osprey after osprey after osprey. I took out one of the boxes: the exercise in assemblage had been repeated by curators before me, dozens of times, it seemed, perhaps hundreds. And they had all also kept the nest, or nests, of that and of several other specimens; they had kept the eggs; they had kept the things it ate. The cabinets where all these were stored went on underground for what looked like kilometres; and, in that section, I could not in truth say that I had seen anything other than extinct bird after extinct bird, in dead, dusty profusion.

I had reasons to be confused. For this theoretical

problem with space did not tally with what I was seeing, with how the space was being used in practice: the Registry had been collecting more than could be kept, a problem possibly inherited from times that predated the green winter. But those never-ending rows also pointed at a lack of focus, a lack of clarity. I could now understand why our instructors, seasoned curators, complained that they could not accession new things. There was simply nowhere to put them.

But, equally, I knew by heart the theory that, whatever we did, we could not de-accession. To de-accession, it was necessary for objects to go through a tedious protocol, a formal Un-Significance Assessment evaluating their historical, scientific, aesthetic, artistic, social and spiritual uselessness. And, providing the object passed it, then it was paramount that it was offered to another Registry, before anything else was done with it. Ultimately, de-accessioning, these disposal exercises, was a fantasy. Disposal was pretty much a heresy in the Registry, its protocol too complex. It was also, some argued, morally wrong.

Is that what we were being trained to be, passive curators, occupying ourselves with interpreting what other people had collected generations ago, instead of collecting now?

Millions of items in storage had yet to be interpreted,

and therefore could not be made accessible, or story-sized, which conspired to make the collections dead weight, not useful for any purpose. All that dead knowledge, too much to make sense of, so much so that our collections explained nothing, taught nothing. Hundreds, thousands of curators were needed simply to interpret these colossal repositories of the past, conservators to look after their materiality, and storytellers to narrate them, to help us understand their meaning. This meant that huge provisions of money were needed. Collecting less actively was the only possible solution to manage this inherited profusion. We had problems of space, problems of documentation, problems of conservation, and problems of storytelling. The latest ones seemed to me the riskier. For, as it had been impressed on us from our very first day in the Registry, the main reason to perform this endless interpretation of the past was so as not to repeat it. Ever.

I had not seen Urania in nearly three years. I had not seen Mr Vanlow either. Savina visited me sometimes, and brought me news of the world.

I knew something was amiss the moment I saw Savina's face as she sat, or rather perched, on the chair where she always waited for me, in the middle of the vast marble chamber where we received our family visits. Her face was slightly green, there was no other way to put it. She looked as if she was about to throw up. She saw me advancing towards her, and did not get up at once, as she used to do, but stayed where she was, averting her eyes.

'Savina, whatever is the matter?' I asked, incapable of containing myself, of starting with the little niceties that always punctuated those visits. I suddenly understood. 'Mother?'

She looked up then, and there was such sadness in her face that I felt sorry for her, sorry that it had fallen on her of all people to come and deliver the news I now expected, my stomach contracting inside me as if someone had punched it hard.

'Child,' she said. Nothing else. It was clear then: Urania was dead.

'When? How?'

It turned out that the beanies who had been looking after her had left her alone, sometimes for days at a stretch, tied up to a chair. On one of these occasions, she had managed to loosen the ropes. And then she had gone directly there.

'The pond?'

Savina did not need to answer my question. It was obvious.

Urania had gone swimming, in one of her fabulous robes. No one could tell if she had become entangled in the many layers of fabric, and had drowned unwillingly, or if she had committed suicide.

'We may never know,' Savina said. 'And, child, listen to me. I do not want you to go thinking of the worst, to imagine the worst. Your mother was very ill. She had been very ill for a very long time.'

We said a *shuvaní* prayer together, and Savina left, until the next time she had a free afternoon from her many chores. It would be weeks, not months, she promised.

I am not proud of what happened, but something was pulling at me, a restlessness mixed up with an acute anxiety I started to develop. I told myself the news had made it worse, of course, but there was nothing I could do for Urania, whereas in the Registry everything was being managed so badly, so badly... I became obsessed with imagining that things could change, if only someone worked to change them. If there was no time or space to collect our own present, then there was no time or space to interpret or communicate it to our fellow man. The day-to-day performance of our tasks did not let us see our present, plan our future.

Mother had always been fond of one extinct bird from the past. It was called a robin. I came across the stuffed specimen, an insubstantial collection of faded feathers, multiplied *ad nauseam*; furtively, without thinking, I placed it in the pocket of my white gown. It was so tiny, almost weightless, as if it did not really exist. I did not know then what I would do with it.

Every week, on my free afternoon, I used my Registry pass to walk on top of the Barrier, something that was now permitted. Other people did it in order to see and be seen, as the ocean view with all its centuries-old debris was only available to those with a certain status. My reasons were different: all I wanted to do was to honour her, to see what should have been Mother's last resting place, not some dirty pond filled with muck.

I had finally decided what to do with the robin. It would happen on my free afternoon, when I was allowed to take these walks on the wall. I made sure to leave the Registry by the staff entrance, so as not to be inspected by the X-ray machines. Atop the Barrier, on the other side, the ocean was the same pulpy mush of remnant plastic imported from the past that it always was: it would still last, most of it, another six hundred years or so. It shone with its spectral glint, a faded brown, as if our ancestors had just vomited it.

I took out the stuffed robin from my purse and threw it into the water, saying a *shuvaní* prayer for my dead mother as I did it. With that simple action, I had just committed the highest of treasons. All around us the ocean was the same mixture of maroon debris, an oily surface that did not let you see what lay beneath. I knew that great leviathans lived down below, and I hoped that my offering would make its way to them. I imagined that the cetaceans wailed in recognition of my gesture, and that the sound reached to me across the water. It was said that they simply lay on the ocean bed with their mouths open, and all sort of creatures climbed into them. But that was down below. Up here, the ring was visible, and I wondered if their satellites or their nosy drones could see what I had just done. Behind the ring's structure, all around it, the sky flickered on and off with its fluorescent blue hue, the indigo surge suddenly blotting out the sky. But I didn't care about my fate at that moment. I felt elated, as if a great weight had been removed from me at last.

9

Urania's ghost is sitting on the windowsill, as she is every morning, observing the flamingos flying up and down. They perch themselves all along the Barrier, a little pink line of monstrously large birds. All I can see from the dormitory is the never-ending wall, the bit of ocean before it, and a line of tall palm trees waving with the wind.

And then I realise: I am not in the dormitory, or in the Registry. Laurel is not sleeping in the bed next to mine, and I am alone. The shadows resolve themselves into my chamber in the Upper Ring, and I have woken up inside my LivePod, same as every morning.

Inside me, my daughter is twisting and swirling and kicking. There is not as much space as a few weeks ago, and some of her little movements are painful now. At the moment, I feel as if my ribcage is about to explode. I am in pain if I lie on my left side. I am in pain if I lie on my right side. I am in pain if I move a leg to try to leave the pod. As a result, I stay inside the pod most of the morning.

When we fixed books in the Registry, we worked with very advanced pod models, the most advanced I have ever seen on the surface. It was obvious they were sent directly down from above. The technology was very similar, the look of the machine was very similar to what they have here. I would be given a book that had survived for centuries, perhaps. Some time and effort and credit would be spent in bringing it back to good shape and storing it. Books in particular worried me, for no one had assessed their usefulness. We mostly accepted that they were all important, no matter the subject, no matter if there was someone alive who could decipher their writing or not. The process forced me to place it inside the conservation pod, opening it page by page; I would be there for some time. The process was as follows: after being delivered a book, I placed it inside the white oval, and kept it open with old-fashioned paperweights. The blue laser light started moving up and down across the width of the page. I saw the parchment unbending, cleaning up. I would have called it magiks if I hadn't known that it was science.

So, I would place it inside the machine, wait until

the blue laser light made it look like new, then I would open the machine, take the book out, turn a page, and start again. The little glass door opened up, the machine whirred away noisily, and I would see what they were about, mementos from a past that was now useless: why did we need those things?

Not everyone was trusted with paper artefacts, and my distrust of the objects was accompanied by pride at their being delivered to me.

After a few hours, the book was like new, and could be put back to use. The automated trolley from the curators— the real ones, not students like us—came by punctually, and I would deposit the book inside it.

In Gobarí, our collection of twenty books made our household special, but all the books had a faint smell of mildew, were filled with orange humidity stains that grew like flowers; their covers were slightly rotten, their corners soft and slightly bent at the tips. But they showed us things, they taught us things. I adored each and every one of them. I could never have considered them a waste of space, a waste of resources. My first images of Old Town, or the Upper Settlement, or the inside of the vessels: they all came from those books, Savina's favourite tools for teaching. Basic survival instructions, skills for when we would be up there, first aid teachings. The known taxonomies, flora and fauna. And the constellations, of course, all in one place.

Everyone in the Registry had a different story of how precociously they had learnt to read. Some had taught themselves, as if that were possible, or had learnt how to do it at ridiculously early ages. The conversation also gave the opportunity to assert that your family was a book-owning one. It was considered inelegant to have learnt with screen-based methods: everyone knew that the true mark of distinction was to possess some of these little objects, the majority of which were being destroyed before our eyes. I normally said nothing. I had learnt to read with them and, at twenty, my family had probably owned more books than theirs. But my story was different. I did not learn to read aged three, or alone following a page with the audio version from a HousePod being played at the same time. I did not amaze our helpers or break a record in being the youngest. In fact, I did not learn to read properly until I was eight years old, and Savina would have to force me to do it. She would sit with me patiently, I would lose heart, and would want to stop. But she persevered. No one else in my household had realised I could not read, and therefore they did nothing to fix this, only Savina. She was the only one who did not give up on me. But there was something more back then that I only understood during my time in the Registry: the books had other connotations for me, of things that were not quite right, thoughts that darkened a room in the heat of the midday sun.

During the nights in the Registry, I would lie in my bed and try to remember the night noises back in the Gobarí house just before going to sleep. Once, before the arrival of my stepfather, I had been so frightened that I slept with a tree branch, a makeshift weapon. What was I frightened of? I could not say, not really. I felt an episode coming, and I would go out onto the balcony and look at those constellations, shining in the sky: The Fox. Alira, the Little Bird Ascending. The Kingfisher. The Stoat. The Snake. The Three Sisters. The Lady in White. By then I could read, had read all about them, all the stories, in our twenty books.

But the books didn't belong to Gobarí, they had come to us from my father. It was the only thing that remained from him in our life. The tales of the constellations were his favourites, and I think he had read to me from that book when I was very little; or at least I hope that happened, that it is not something that I have created somehow, to fill the gap he left. He felt a special predilection for those fables, the earlier recorded document of our beliefs, and he had impressed on me, on Savina, the need to know their real versions, not the sugary ones that normally are read to children. Hence his readings, and later hers. From very early on I would hear about poisonings, beheadings, premature burials, beasts that killed and devoured other beasts, or even children, who survived inside the belly of some gigantic hare until the hero came and freed them with her axe, or perhaps flutes made from the bones of a corpse, which, once you held them to your lips, retold the gruesome circumstances of their previous owner's demise. When Savina read to me, some images formed themselves in my head, very much as happened during the storyteller observances.

Thanks to these tales, I learnt about humanity's selfishness; moreover, I learnt something that deeply impressed itself in my conscience: the worst cruelty is sometimes committed between members of the same family. In those fantastic stories, brothers killed brothers, poor parents were forced by hunger to abandon their children in the middle of deserts, or parents too jealous of their daughters' pallid beauty built them coffin-like underground chambers.

Eventually, father was not there anymore, and it was only Savina. It is thanks to her that I can read, for she and only she persevered. Once I could, I was then left to my own devices among the books, allowed access to the precious objects for a while, mostly because no one kept check of my behaviour. They were kept on a shelf on top of a desk in one of the smaller sitting rooms that we hardly used. The windows were always open there, and moths and other creatures came and went from the balcony to their heart's content. Over my head, an air cooler languidly moved its four blades. It was the middle of the day, when people slept, that I knew I could be alone with the tomes in that room. This happiness that I felt around them made me feel guilty, as if I were somehow betraying Mother. For, as I grew up, I realised that perhaps the books had been part of our mysterious ruin. My father hadn't brought more than ten with him when they married, and he had used my mother's fortune to acquire another ten in the successive years.

My mother did not dispose of the books immediately. Years later, when she was married to Mr Vanlow, and we had not left Gobarí to be refurbished yet, one evening I entered the sitting room to find both of them sipping *milbao* with an unknown man, dressed in the religious robes of the NEST compound, the organisation responsible for sending children up in the vessels. I was told to keep away, and no introduction was forthcoming, although I wasn't exactly a small child anymore and would normally engage in conversation with visiting adults. It became apparent in successive visits that the man in question had been procured by Mr Vanlow to dispose of our library.

This was unexpected, unfair. The mere idea of disposing of them had sent me to the realms of despair, and I did not speak to Mr Vanlow or Urania for days. I had the strange, wrong idea that the books were mine somehow, that I would inherit them one day. Only a couple were left, the rest were gone. I realised they had always been on loan in my life. I could not lay claim to something so precious. I never saw them again until, years later, by mere chance, I came across something surprising in the Registry.

I had been sent to fetch some object. The way into the stacks was narrow and dark, and the stacks themselves were no better. Corridor after corridor of movable shelves, the sections only kept illuminated by a light on a timer: it was very possible to end up in those catacombs completely in the dark. The place was like a maze, but by then I knew my way around it. I had more problems deciding which section of the building, or rather which catacomb, corridor, extension or outer building, an item was kept in. The vastness of the collection meant that a guide had needed to be produced, which first told you which gallery to direct your steps to. Once in the right section, the search started. Laurel helped me determine the right catacomb, and I was happy: it was so distant from the main curatorial chamber that they would not expect me back for at least twenty minutes. Of course, I had developed my own method of making the most of this situation: I was able to get to the place in question in a maximum of five minutes by walking briskly—no running was allowed within the building, of course—and then I would quickly find my object. Depending on how quickly I found the required object, I would have enough time left for me to grab any book I wanted and read from it for a few precious moments.

That evening I was in shock, reading about something called 'horses' that had existed in the days pre-green winter. There were pictures of men and woman atop these horrible, huge creatures, pictures I could not make sense of. What were these animals, as big as hares, on four legs, and apparently with the capacity of pulling ancient vehicles filled to the brim with people and goods? They must have been fantastically strong. As always, whenever I came across this kind of ancient knowledge, I felt the strange implausibility of it all. I realised that time must be passing quickly and put the book back in its place, but something caught my eye. Two books along, I recognised a spine… That could not be. With the same care I used to handle everything, I pulled out the object. It was our book about animals, no question about it. It had the same marks of use I recognised so well, as well as some light pencil marks where Savina had patiently pointed at names for me to read them, syllable by syllable, perhaps fifteen years before.

That night I thought of all the books I had treated in my pod, of how I had contributed to one more thing that weighed us down. And, for the first time, I wasn't sorry. I also thought of my father for the first time in a long while.

My father had died what was known as a 'bad death': he hanged himself inside the military compound where he was sent after the militia took him. He had killed a beanie girl, that was the accusation. But there was something else. The militia was sure he had intended to kill me as well, his own daughter. I was four years old.

I have never believed it to be true.

No one had been able to explain to me satisfactorily how they reached that conclusion, or perhaps I should say that no one bothered to talk to me about it. And yet. I have wondered about it all my life, not only his apparent kidnapping of me, but also how undisputed the first charge could be.

So I found out where the documents from the case

were archived, and I went looking for them as soon as I was able. This was a digital quest: everything had been uploaded to one hard-to-access digital repository, militia-level security systems. On my third year of apprenticeship I was given access to some of the upper digital layers, and then I suddenly realised: I could read exactly what my father had done, the investigation against him, and what exactly he had been accused of.

No one knew what I was up to. I had not talked to anyone about my past, not even Laurel.

I found there had been no real investigation. And he never confessed to killing the girl. He confessed to kidnapping me—now, this was surprising. Were my parents separated, divorced? I had no idea; but, otherwise, it could not be interpreted as such. My father, or so he repeated, was trying to 'protect' me. From what?

He took me from Old Town, where we had been staying. We arrived at Kon-il. The water looked beautiful—and how, why, can I remember it so clearly? Translucent, almost white. My father perched me on a rock, and went for a swim. And I remember, even now, my fear then, as clear as that water. Somehow instinctively, without having heard about the swimmers, without knowing anything about their heretic beliefs, four-year-old me saw her father swim away, and thought that he was going to swim forever, to disappear among the waves. That he was going to leave me alone on that rock. I remember that, in fear, I pressed my feet roughly against its surface, clumsily trying to get up and run to him. In my eagerness I cut my feet on the rock. I remember the pain. But it was nothing compared to the pain of losing my father.

These images I remember; but sometimes I remember them with other people in them: Mother, Aster or Verity, my small beanie friend. Were they there, or was I mixing different outings?

Eventually, he came out of the water, and came to me. I was in tears. He then took me to an unknown compound, the coast visible through the window, and he left me. This was first time he had done that, leaving me alone somewhere; it would also turn out to be the last time. He took erratic leave of me, in fact, with the urgency of someone who has an important task ahead of him. Something to do. Something to do that cannot wait. Something to do now and now only.

Time passed.

And that task, my own task, of sitting on the sofa, an uncomfortable sofa at that, started to weigh a great deal. My father's instructions had not been clear at all: 'Stay here.' There, in the compound? There, sitting on the sofa? Terrified, I choose not to move from it.

Time passed hard.

My father was gone a long time. Outside, the sky over the sea, over the wall out on the sea, went black. I lay down, exactly where I was sitting. The beds were unmade anyway, as Savina should be the one making them. And she was not with us. So exactly where I was sitting I lay down.

When I woke, my father was back. He looked, smelled, as if he had just washed. But there was also a lingering smell of fresh earth around him.

Or was it? Is my knowledge of the fact tainted by what he was accused of later, by what I know now? And what exactly is it that I know?

I did not know my father, not really. I was too little to know him or understand him. But I loved him, and he loved me. I recognised that unspoken bond between us.

Again, he took me, this time from the compound, and he wrapped me tight in a travel blanket. And then he put me again in the boot of the hovering vehicle, and he asked me to be quiet again, as he closed the lid over me.

I could see nothing; I could hardly move. Soon, I had difficulty breathing. Until I breathed it all in, that overpowering sweet smell that I could not place. My dad, it would later be claimed, had rehearsed what he was about to do with the beanie child, more or less my height, more or less my age. My friend Verity who, indisputably, had been with us in the cove. Her hair was dyed the colour the ocean used to be in the olden days, like I wore it.

I have no idea how long I was there, and can't remember if we moved, if I felt the hovering vehicle ascending.

Eventually, someone found me, and I was saved; or so I am told. An unknown face wearing a khaki bodysuit, militia issue, opened the lid and took me out. I must have been there a long while, for I was in so much pain, my legs and my arms and my neck and my back, all needed restretching, readjustment. So much pain from bending inside there.

Nothing about this story made any sense. What was he protecting me from? And why did he kill Verity? But also, had he really killed her, if he had never admitted to it? But then, why kill himself? Was that also untrue?

The documents had helped fill some gaps in the story, but I still had the same questions. And his absence, as sudden as if the Three Oceans had swallowed him up, meant I could never answer them.

10

I had not seen Savina for a long time, and my stepfather spent large stretches of time, months on end, up in the ring. But I should not have been so ungrateful, for the Registry was also my refuge. I felt lonely, yet also safe. Apart from Laurel, I spoke to almost nobody. Everyone kept to themselves, lost in the endless day-to-day work. I had finished my apprenticeship, and I was now a junior worker. I assumed this would be my life from now on.

One day, Mr Vanlow, Papa, reappeared. I had not seen him in eighteen months, the longest stretch he had left me. The last time he had been in Old Town, he had come to see me by surprise, and took me to a storyteller observance. He was coming from the ring, he said, and was going straight back the next day. This time was different. This time the first thing he said when he saw me was that he was planning to stay down on the surface for a long time, perhaps forever. I did not answer. I did not know what to say to him.

'You have grown,' he said. He also said he had missed me. I had also missed him; he was my only connection to the past now. We partook of some of the luxurious edibles that he always ordered whenever he came to see me. I had not mentioned Urania's death; he had not mentioned her at all. 'How would you like to live in the Upper Settlement?'

I was speechless. I had the stupid notion that, as everything was old, dusty and false down here, up in the ring everything was shiny and new. I suspected that they forced us to preserve this past so as not to let us see into the future. I feared we were failing to see the here and now, what was happening right before our very eyes. Going up there, I thought, could help dispel the clouds.

'Up in the ring?'

'If you want. I would like you to be happy, Pearl. To be secure and happy.'

I had taken off my uniform for the first time in months, to see him. My newest civil dress did not fit me so well any longer. Laurel had hurriedly helped me mend it. I had felt strange when I put it on, as if I were trying to hold on to a past that didn't exist anymore; my own past.

As we spoke, I thought of Alira, the school's very own

Santa Incorrupta. As her name indicated, she was starborn, a true daughter of the Upper Settlement. Hundreds of years ago she had suffered a mutation. Her sin: flying, and reading minds. She had been part of a group of people that had started to mutate, developing fantastical new skills. Needless to say, they had been heavily persecuted, for the good of humanity. Alira's statue had beautiful wings representing her power, and she was poised in a complicated position, as if she were about to take flight.

Alira's statue was smiling. Alira always smiled.

Swimming is like flying, mother used to say. So I do not know if Alira's story is a metaphor, or if her mutation was real. Other students have told me that the corpse has no wings. But little girls should not fly, wings or no wings. They got jealous of her. Little girls should not fly, read the inside of a man's mind, or walk on water.

The Sisters taught us to think of Alira when we needed to give ourselves strength. Alira, the pious girl who went to her death with a smile on her face. We were taught to smile whenever we did not know what to say, or how to interact, especially with starborns. Papa wasn't one of them, really; I smiled anyway.

I would often pause by Alira's statue. With time, I learnt to read outside of the sanctioned story. I could see there was something frightening about her smile, something

141

unwholesome. Was it possible that only I could see it? It was her eyes. They were wide open in terror. And discovering this fact suddenly transformed that same, pious smile into a twisted mouth crying for help.

Now, I was the one who was going to fly away, it seemed.

After my stepfather's visit, everything became a frenzied gathering: getting my things together, preparing myself to get out of the Registry. Some of the junior curators were jealous of me. Jealous of what? I did not know what happened outside those walls, what the world was really like. I seemed to have forgotten it all. I was an adult, but also, in many ways, I was a child, about to be sacrificed.

I had not met Arlo, my chosen partner. A starborn, he was descending all the way from the Upper Settlement to claim his bride. I was scared of leaving the school, scared of this person I did not know, this Arlo. Scared of going up. I had never wanted to live in the ring, not really, I must have been mistaken when I thought I did. I realised that now.

The designated date arrived, and my stepfather collected me from the school. Inside the hovering vehicle sat Arlo; I had never seen such pure blue eyes anywhere. Blue eyes and lighter skin were more common up in the ring than down here. His short-cropped hair and beard were the colour of dune grass.

We were hovering back to the outskirts of town when everything changed once more, with strange finality, and we woke up as if from a dream; that morning was the morning when the Barrier suffered its first attack, and nearly two thousand people were killed in a explosion. Their bodies flew into the ocean among the debris, and I would never forget this image, seen from above, as our vehicle surged into the sky: the ocean reconquering the beach furiously, a further wave that had also killed hundreds of others, an unholy mixing of water, translucent until the moment that the ocean brought back in its wake the brown debris, rubber and plastic and century-old things, and my little offerings, which would surely be washed up onto the shore as well. And all that the Barrier had managed to keep out. At least for those lucky enough not to see it, for those who had managed not to see, and for those who had not wanted to see it.

It had been the swimmers, they said, and everyone repeated it everywhere. *The swimmers, the swimmers…*

We glided over the city. Were we going back to Gobarí, perhaps? No, we were just going back to our compound in Old Town. But I would soon see Gobarí again. The old house would be waiting for us, for our return. And I knew what would happen next: for I had dreamt of Alira's fate. And in my dream, I remembered it now, all the constellations had been out of shape.

I looked back at the Registry from above; we were very high up. The vehicle was a newer model, it could climb as high as the ring if we wanted, apparently. My stepfather said this to reassure me; but the notion made me feel as if my breath was dying inside my body. My fear must have been painted on my face, for Arlo took my hand in his and squeezed it to give me strength, or as if to say, I am here.

Oh, yes, he was there, and he would be there the next day.

And we wouldn't go up to the ring that morning.

But soon, so soon, one day...

We left the Registry behind and approached our old compound, and I started to feel an unmistakable sensation: as if I could not breathe, as if I were dying. An episode, then. But I knew what it was, and I could be calm, restful. I thought of the pond, of swimming in it. It did not work. Aster and Mother were waiting for me there, both dead. I thought of the ocean, and saw myself swimming in its embrace. I felt calm almost at once. Soon, I thought then, I would be back home again.

It seems all that happened so long ago; it hasn't been even a year, but it feels like aeons. As if we had moved smoothly into another epoch, another time. It is easy for me to feel this way, for I am up here now, up here at last. I flew voluntarily: up and up we go, up and up into the sky. No need for a vessel.

The child inside me moves and twists and wriggles and kicks, until it doesn't do any of these things anymore. And then come the masked men in protective gear, plastic covers for their faces and hands, as if I were contagious, or still in quarantine. And they check measurements in the LivePod, and they prod me as well, and they do not say anything, do not look at me. Even when I ask them directly what is wrong, what could possibly be wrong. And then the LivePod starts moving, and I am taken into another section of the chamber, and the walls open and suddenly my room transforms itself into an operation chamber. And they place a mask over my face and instruct me to count backwards, and to close my eyes, and I know what is coming, and I know that when I wake she will be out of me, and gone.

And then, then, then is when I truly come to love her.

The Fable of Alira

She was so tired she thought that she would die. Her body would slowly shut down, bit by escaping bit, until there would be nothing left of herself, nothing more than an empty carcass of rotten, useless flesh. She would go to sleep and never wake up; or maybe she would sleep for a hundred years, until the next realignment. She was called Alira. Her sin: she was capable of flying, of other things as well. A portrait had been painted of her. It had beautiful wings, and she was poised in a complicated position, as though about to take flight. Of course, she had no wings. All she had to do was will herself to go up and up and up.

They had arrived the previous night. The streets were a maze, mirror images of each other held together by the fog. They had arrived in their velvet coats, their feet in leather boots, expecting nothing but darkness. What received them was the torrid late November sun, scorching every corner of the city. They had travelled light. The people they encountered had all directed them so far away from home, south-and-west, always south-and-west. Here, there were the books, and the books meant healing. And so they had endured the horrid inns, brief stays in hellish flea-infested rooms, walls smeared with brown stains, dust-covered furniture.

At the hour of the crows they were called into the chamber. They saw row after row of wooden tables stretching out the entire length of the place, young men sat on long benches, eating their soup. The old men were sitting at a table in the back, facing all the others, on an area of floor raised one metre higher than the rest. They wore purple and crimson robes, their heads covered with square hats, their hands thickly jewelled, shining crimson and blue, sending tiny, playful reflections all over the room, like some old-fashioned visual shuvaní spell.

'Is this the child?' one of them asked.

Someone gave her a gentle push.

Alira, Alira.

You are named after the old ballad.

And how will we know if you are the one?

'How do you know my name? I don't know yours,' the child blurted out before she could stop herself, turning in the direction of the decrepit old man who had entertained the thought.

The elders looked curiously in his direction and he nodded very lightly.

And then they all knew that she had read his mind.

She had shown herself to be worthy. In the next realignment she would be given to the stars, would travel billions of years, only to be consumed by the cosmos before being returned once more, transmuted into a beautiful constellation. She would be transformed into pure meaning. The ones given to the stars burnt themselves out in the sun's descending flames. The highest possible honour known.

The next realignment was about to happen, a week of festivities ending in the healing—a sacrifice. Sleep brought odd dreams, strange images. Alira saw herself over a large expanse of water that seemed to never end. In it, leviathan creatures swam under the stars. The water was as dark as the sky; it was impossible to know where one ended and the other started. The constellations reflected themselves on it. The Hare, hiding between the twisted roots in her forest of the nearest galaxy. The Librarian, handling an object that could be an old satellite.

Alira woke up tired, feverish. She was imagining how it would feel to swim in those eternal waters, accompanied by the gigantic creatures that dwelt in them. She imagined flying out of them, giving a huge jump that would propel her from the waters into the sky, and she imagined how it would be to soar up and up and up, finding her way among the constellations.

And she knew this to be good and proper, and she felt ready to accept her fate.

There was another dream that never left her for long. The boy was over her, and he was older. His face was red and puffed up and sweaty, his eyes two points of yellow dirt impregnated with blood. She could distinguish the pores of his skin, each translucent pearl of white sweat. His face became blurred, and she could almost imagine that she was somewhere else. Was that the time she had been lost in the forest, her forest? The world donned a light mask of unreality. She remembered running, crying, brown stains. She must have fallen and cut herself with the scattered branches, dark and pointed, which inflicted a pain she had not known before. She was found at last, caked in mud and dirt and blood and sweat. She was ill for a long time afterwards, and could hear her parents crying inside their heads, forced smiles painted on their faces, so nobody knew what exactly had happened to her. That's when she knew she was different, by reading their thoughts about how upset they had truly been because their silly little girl had got lost.

The next time she encountered youngsters, who tried to surround her when she was filling a bucket with water, she started panting and panting, and she jumped, and she soared into the sky.

She had marked herself out for sacrifice with those actions;

but she had never felt freer. Alira, Alira. Oh, Alira, how free you were!

The day is finally here. Spring has proved to be never-ending, infinitely cruel in its vastness, but the day has arrived at last. The flames of the sun almost reach the domes and the turrets and the minarets, drying the mossy walls. The old men work fast to solve the riddle. Healing approaches. At the appointed hour, a promenade of elders in their crimson robes crosses the town at twilight. On the mantelpiece the clock ticks away with stubborn persistence. One, two three. Soon, it will be time. The procession is quietly approaching to claim her.

All Alira's excitement burns itself out and she feels cold and sweaty, as fear replaces it. The bells ring the quarters with their usual restlessness, and she knows, with a frightful certainty, that nothing will change, that everything will remain the same after her ascent. She knows there is no knowledge beyond the stars, no new beginnings. The sun will continue torturing them all in the city; in her village, the twilight will forever cover it all like a shroud, the house and the garden and the dunes and the forest, as it has always done. The constellations will offer no explanation, no resolution.

Understanding this upsets her more than she can explain.

Outside, the oranges and purples are transformed in a violet vista that covers the world as far as she can see. The sun is a white condensed orb, waiting to be fed. The crows circle the town. The old men are finally here. They have found the answer just in time. Healing will be performed.

Alira is taken down to the street.

Eyes up to the sky, she could see everything that had already happened—the famines, the extinction of animals, the men hunting men, the vastness of the waters that flooded it all, and then receded, and then once more flooded, crowded this time by leviathan-like creatures, and the old towns covered in water, their treasures forever lost—and she saw what was happening now, the old men desperately trying to harness whichever power was available, purging all mutations they encountered, purging progress. And then she saw as well what was going to come.

She breaks into a run. Before rounding the corner, and soaring up in a mighty jump, she turns to look back once more to the procession, to the square filled with the old, decrepit men, to make sure they are not following her. And there she goes, to find another world among the stars.

ARLO

11

I was so tired that I thought I could sleep forever, perhaps die in my sleep. Lie down on the dark hammock and never wake up. My body would shut down slowly, bit by bit, until there was nothing left, nothing more than an empty carcass of rotten, useless flesh. All the strange colours and the odd noises would cover me up, until I was one with the forest.

We had arrived the previous evening, me and my bride, invisible hands carrying our belongings inside one of the buildings. We had travelled light. I gather that some of her childish treasures had been left behind, and this was the first time I saw my strange new companion cry—I imagine this to be the cause of her tears—a furtive tear, pushed away by a small hand. She was a feral child from the surface, with strange, wide eyes, alien and unreal. And we were now heading towards her childhood home, crossing a stretch of the forest. The smells and the colours, everything conspired to make me think I was in a dream, perhaps conjured by the strange girl I now called wife. I was finally here, at the end of the known world.

'How far away are we?'

'Not far, now.'

'What is this settlement called?' That was all I had become down here: question after question after question. She hesitated before replying:

'Matanza.'

Matanza, massacre.

'What *happened* here?' I sounded more judgemental than I had intended.

'Nothing, nothing happened.'

And she went on to explain: the arcane tradition of fattening your pig, and inviting all your friends and relatives to a feast that includes its killing, preservation and eating. Carefully organised proceedings, with no living part of the animal left untouched, everything becoming edible or usable. At my question of why a place was called after such a thing, she simply answered that the custom predated an event—that they call the 'green winter' for some reason— and therefore predated modern times. In other words, it was called this because it had always been called this; and that seemed a sufficient explanation. Eventually, I remembered reading something about the bloody tradition in my early days as a bio-anthropology student. I couldn't help but notice how she had left some parts out, deliberately no doubt: the animal's cries of fear from the early morning onwards, the knowledge of what was coming deep within him already.

Some children came to look at us enquiringly; no, not to look at her. They came to look at me. There were half-naked, unsmiling children. They brought us *milbao*; not my favourite thing, but Pearl made me drink it. She said it was so difficult to make, they would be offended if we didn't. And so I drank it: a slimy juice, sticky, that smelt like vomit.

We got back on my rented HoveLight300, what people down here called a 'hovering' vehicle, but we were not flying. For some reason I could not fathom, Pearl had asked if we could go to her house by road. The contact of the HoveLight300 with it made an unpleasant crushing sound. It would also delay us greatly, but I could not deny her this, not after what had happened right before the wedding. It was such a little ask, so easy to comply with. Our advance, therefore, was painfully slow. Travelling like this included a lot of stops. The road became obstructed by the plants often; the hired hands walked ahead then, cutting with machetes the lianas and the leaves and the branches that had appeared overnight over the path. Soon, she repeated, so soon now. But to me it felt as if we were entering the mouth of a beast, all those green branches a cavity full of teeth that could crunch us beneath its force. Everything was extreme. I felt as if I was drowning in smells. Orange, cinnamon, and that vast flower, lady of the night.

We arrived eventually at a place falling to pieces, but her whole expression metamorphosed. I understood: this is how my blue-haired companion looks when she is happy.

A group of sombre-looking servants appeared on the steps, unreadable expressions on their faces. We are home, she announced.

We had survived, crossing the uncertain space of the forest, changing it for the certainty of a place, but I could not shake an odd anxiety.

The strange indeterminacy of the wild, empty zone, composed of millions and trillions of varieties of flora and fauna that we did not understand yet; a vast extension of non-cartographic space, where my things did not work: the HivePod, the HiveCam, some of the hovering tech, including my HoveLight300, no doubt, would prove faulty here. And still, this place where we had arrived was no refuge either. For Pearl thought it hers when it was not. It belonged to them and them only.

There was an old man, and a young girl smiling through white teeth, a slight gap between the two at the front. And then there was Savina, the old family servant, the saviour who had kept it all going, all those years back. Or that was what Pearl explained to me.

'You have to like Savina; I want you to like her.'

'Why?'

'Because she is like my own mother.'

The woman was looking through a sneer, there was no other way to put it, as if she was laughing at us.

But Pearl would say no more than that. We were sitting on the porch. You could not hear the ocean from the house; although, in truth, we could not be so far away from it. In the HoveLight300 we would reach the coast in around forty minutes. Walking it would take a morning to get there. But the whole place felt noisy, its shapes and forms complaining under the cracking sun. Those shapes and forms felt odd and strange: I had seen them on our screens up above, studied them in our digital repositories. But now, facing them directly, the oversize leaves and those eternal trunks, shooting up, covering the sky in most places, made me feel a bit giddy. Perhaps it was the heat, which made everything heavy and my own skin clammy to the touch.

I had an idea of where we were, if I thought of a map, but at the same time it was difficult for me to understand our position, to place myself. I blamed the topography of the place: all you could see was the profusion at the entrance of the forest, and behind it, over its canopy, a glimpse of the rocky mountains of the *sierra*. And then nothing, a white sky, cloudless. It was strange not to see the Upper Settlement. It made me feel strangely unsettled, and the place where we were felt somehow unreal, the drawing of a child. I said this out loud, and Pearl answered:

'Perhaps it is the ring that is a dream.'

'The ring? How could the ring be a dream, Pearl? It is solid, man-made.'

'This is also solid, as solid as it is possible to be,' she said, pointing at the mountains. 'What if it is all a mirage, an illusion they tell us about? There are more of us down here, you know.'

I told her she was wrong: more people now lived among the stars than down on the surface of the planet. She looked troubled. She had not known, realised, or been told: only the remnants of civilisation had been left behind now, most of what mattered was up there already.

She went very quiet after this. I continued looking at the *sierra*, and said, to make her feel better, that she was right, that mountains could not be unreal. But she did not reply.

Later on, I was inside the house. There was a room prepared for us with a couple of books and papers and ink. I could not see any connections for my HivePod, and despaired for a moment. I would have to write on paper, like in the olden days. When I was a youngster, I had used paper for a time: an affectation, also designed to show everyone that I had access to it. Here, it didn't seem to be valued; I saw every day how they discarded perfectly reusable pieces, or how they wrote menus or lists of things to do on them, instead of committing those things to memory. They made a crude version of paper themselves, so they did not see it as something scarce. But their laziness made me sick. I tried to tell the young servant girl to be careful of wasting paper, and she laughed at my face.

What could I do with the paper? Write to my father? I imagined how this may be received, and flinched. I did not know what my father expected from me, what his dealings with Mr Vanlow actually were.

Despite the impossibility of communication with the outside world, I did not write to anyone. How would I send letters up to the Settlement? It all seemed so useless then: my aborted letter writing, this strange place, Gobarí, my recent union. My thoughts were interrupted by the young servant girl, who came in at that moment, carrying something or other. Or perhaps she had been sent to spy on me. She saw that I had spread out the paper and other writing tools on the table and laughed once more, who knows why, and said something I did not catch; I hardly ever made sense of their talk, although it is also true that I did not try very hard to understand them. All the servants did the same, all the time, coming and going in and out of rooms as if they owned the place, and Pearl did not seem to mind.

Instead of the letter, I started writing my first impressions of the place. I could see Pearl from the window, and, now and again, I could hear snippets of her conversation with the old man. The house, the garden, and general maintenance questions were the matters that occupied their discussion. But it did not seem by her tone that Pearl was asserting her place as the rightful owner of Gobarí, it rather seemed that they were talking as equals.

I wondered what this might mean, and resolved to mention it later to her. That was a dangerous slippery slope. I had already noted to my dismay that she did not refer to them as 'servants'; indeed, avoided naming them such.

As if on cue, a voice interrupted my reasoning.

'What are you doing?'

Startled, I turn to find the strange woman, Savina, looking furiously at me from the threshold.

'I beg your pardon?'

She seemed to think my answer an invitation to enter the room, which she did. Instinctively, I got up from the desk. She was glaring at it.

'What are you doing with the paper?'

I did not understand her worry, and I simply could not abide her tone. This created the perfect opportunity to reassert our position.

'I do not need to answer such an impertinent question.' She flinched, her eyes fluttering in disbelief. What was happening here? Had she never been admonished by a superior? 'In fact, this paper is rather inadequate, I trust there is one of better quality for my writing.'

'Your writing?' she chuckled. 'Let me tell you, that paper there is not to be spent so quickly, it takes us a whole afternoon to make it!'

So I had misunderstood, partly, their usage of the thing. Still, behaviour like this could not be tolerated. If this woman needed to be reminded of her place, so be it.

'In that case, you should have procured more quantity before our arrival. I will use all the paper that I need while I am here,' I said with finality. Truth be told, if my HivePod did not work in that place, paper was the only other option to do the work I was expected to do. But I would be damned if I was going to explain myself to her. 'And now, please leave me. I am sure you can find something to do.'

I dismissed her with a wave of my hand, and she turned furiously towards the corridor. I did not even look at her, concentrating instead on the task in front of me; but I could tell she had glared in my direction before leaving, as her two eyes had pierced the back of my neck, as if they were on fire.

12

I did not feel safe in Gobarí. Perhaps it wasn't the forest, after all. For I hadn't felt safe in Old Town either. Mr Vanlow had been very attentive while we were there, and she, the strange girl I was going to be bonded with for life, was infused with a rare intelligence as well. She was trained as a curator, and that was far more than I had been led to expect. The actual ceremony was brief and beautiful. It took place before we started on our honeymoon to her old house in the forest. As may perhaps be understandable, I was wary of the future. For our bond did not follow the rules among the stars, but was earthly made.

I was in Old Town for less than a week, and knew Pearl for a few days before we married. There were not many preparations to make, as her stepfather had arranged everything for us, and there weren't many guests to invite. Pearl and I spent as much time together as we could, sometimes with Mr Vanlow, sometimes with her friend, Laurel, less often on our own. She had few possessions and not much to pack, as apparently the life of junior curators was rather monastic; but still there were some decisions to make, little things to discuss and consider. I could not help noticing, during these conversations, that she looked much more excited at the prospect of returning to her childhood home, Gobarí, than about the actual ceremony itself. I hoped she had no doubts about me. I did not want to displease my father, or Mr Vanlow, and this arrangement suited me as well, for different reasons. Still, the morning before the ceremony was meant to take place, I was told that Pearl did not want to go through with it.

I was speechless, a bit shocked. Was it possible that she was going to reject me? Mr Vanlow could not tell me the reason, so I decided to take matters into my own hands: I got dressed and went out onto the hot promenade. Once in the street, I realised I did not know in which compound they lived, square mansions arranged in huge fortresses, housing several families around a cool patio, and overlooking the cleaner parts of the ocean. My HiveApp helped with that, and soon I was knocking on her door, panting and worried. I am not sure I had grown fond of her, not so soon; I am embarrassed to say that I was ashamed of the possibility of having to return empty-handed, jilted by this half-caste child from the surface. She opened the door angrily.

'Pearl, what is going on? Your stepfather says you don't want us to be united. Please, tell me, what I have done?'

'I know what goes on up there.'

'What? What goes on up where?'

'In the ring. I know why you come down here to find your brides.'

And then she told me, although I wished she had not spoken: how in the Registry school she had learnt from other feral children about what went on in the Upper Settlement, that we had to come down to find our brides because up there we could not have children anymore.

I could not deny all of it; but I deflected, and told her that if she wanted to be a storyteller, there was no better place to train than up in the Settlement: the best teachers were there.

'You will be able to do anything you want, my love, once we are up. Together.'

She considered this a moment, and slowly advanced in my direction with little birdlike steps, and she hugged me. I could smell her hair. She smelled like flowers, and fresh-cut grass, and the ocean, smells we bottled up and artificially reproduced often in our home among the stars.

But hers were the real thing, and I felt it for the first time: a surge of love. And then she said, still holding me, without looking into my eyes:

'They also said that the forest does not eat settlements; that you say that when you expel some people from their homes to steal from them.'

'What, Pearl? What can we possibly need to steal from down here?'

'Please, tell me it isn't true.'

So I told her: it wasn't true. And I repeated: once we were up, she could do anything she wanted. I didn't tell her other things, of course: my certainty of her success in what she called the 'ring' wasn't entirely true. I had seen people emigrating from down below, and rarely did they fulfil their promise, their dreams. They worked for us: served at our tables, cooked our food, had our children, looked after our elders. But they never entered a relevant profession. They all were educated, intelligent people; more so than us, perhaps. The reasons were different. They sounded wrong, looked wrong, not like we imagined real human beings ought to look and sound. They had strong accents, all of them, accents which made us perceive them as uneducated, even those with more knowledge than us.

Pearl and I married by the shore on the outskirts of the broken town, the attack on the Barrier barely a week old, so recent still in all our worried minds. The world had exploded on the same morning that we picked Pearl up from the Registry, and I can understand that her whole world had shattered somehow, become an unsure thing, whichever sense of feeling secure she had must have slipped from under her feet. But I had hoped, perhaps naively, that our union might help her find firm ground once more, would make her feel secure again.

The ocean and the Barrier, which down here they called the 'wall', and Mr Vanlow and a few others, they were the only witnesses of our union. Those few guests were waiting for us on the shore, as tradition imposes. Earlier that morning, Laurel and other girls from the Registry had gone down there, and had drawn a round maze with stones and seashells. I met Pearl a stretch away, and we arrived together, holding hands. She was wearing a loose white dress and a flower crown; I matched her with my white gymnasium uniform, and a bunch of flowers in my hand matching hers. Together, we walked the round maze to its centre, where the officiant, a well-known storyteller, pronounced us united in flesh and spirit, alluding to the lady in white, the Star Explorers, and all the creatures around us.

At the precise moment when she tied us, her ornamental rope decorated with more shells that pricked my hand, a huge, unknown sound behind the Barrier startled us, as if God had blown an oversized trumpet.

'What on Earth...?' Mr Vanlow chuckled. Everyone had retreated from the shore, although the Barrier protected us. A gust of air accompanying the demonic sound had made us waver, and some of our few guests had fallen. I hurried to help.

'It is them, the Behemoths.' This was Ariel, Laurel's brother. I had hardly had the chance to speak with him during the preceding days, but he seemed a reasonable enough young man.

'What do you mean?' I asked. I noticed that Pearl was holding my hand, or perhaps I was holding hers.

'The Leviathans, the Mighty Whales!' I could have sworn there was a glint of madness in his eyes.

I had no idea if this means our union was blessed, or doomed, but the circle of shells was destroyed with the sudden gust of wind brought by the wailing, as well as the small white flowers that covered the sand. I had felt sorry for that destruction of the natural world, so precious it was, up at home; but Pearl had told me the day before, as we collected them, not to worry: those little flowers that I had pitied so much only lived for one day.

13

And so it was that I found myself in that beautiful place, wild, untouched. But without any of the freshness of how Pearl's hair had smelled that morning, the morning of our union. Here, everything was too much, everything was dying a little in its extravagance. Everything was provisional as well, things made of other, older things, handed down, repaired a thousand times: a piece of string, dark with dirt, that I would pull to summon the servant girl. I would follow its progress, rudely nailed at the angle between the wall and the ceiling. Everything was exactly like that, felt reused, made up of discarded things. Up in the Settlement everything was built with a specific use in mind, a finality. Everything was clean, neat, hygienic, and took up the least possible space.

Here, there seemed to be an overabundance of purpose, a surplus, an extravagance of time. I asked Pearl about it. She said she did not understand what I meant; surely reusing was a good thing, not a bad thing. We never had that problem; we would send down what we didn't want any longer, and produce a new, improved version. She laughed at this, and her laughter reminded me of the servant girl's.

I wanted to explain how we did things up there, but I was sure she would laugh some more. I knew that she had already made up her mind about how life in the Upper Settlement was, fixed ideas that had already stuck inside her head. She did ask questions sometimes, and I always tried to answer her as well as I could. But I could see that nothing I said had any effect on her. She was surprised that we could live without animals.

'You once told me that animals are the thing you are most scared of,' I replied.

'Yes, it is true. My father taught me to fear them.'

'Why?'

'You could not understand.'

'But we have animals up there!' I protested.

'Yes, but your animals are domesticated, engineered to be easily tamed. Our animals are not like that. Do you know what some people say?'

'What?' And there it was, as with most of our conversations: for they always tended to end in some kind of reproach to those above, some mismanagement or unfair thing that we had done. I was not disappointed.

'That there are some that could never have mutated like they did; and that they are experiments, creatures that you have tried to put together. And when they didn't work, or they didn't fulfil your purpose, or even if you just didn't like how they turned out, you set them loose on us down here.'

'You are intelligent, Pearl, and educated. It is not possible that you believe such nonsense.'

'Is it, Arlo? Is it all nonsense?'

'You can't possibly believe that we experiment with animals and send the ones we don't like down here.'

'So what do you do with them?'

'With what?'

'With the ones that turn out badly. Because if you bio-engineer species all the time, there must be some experiments that don't work.'

'Who knows.' I was getting agitated. 'Perhaps we eat them!'

I had spoken without thinking, but my reply hung in the air between us, both of us aware that it made sense, for she didn't form a reply this time.

'Very well,' she said eventually. 'Isn't it possible that some experiments have managed to escape down here, perhaps in some of the dozens of transport shuttles that you send down every day?'

'Pearl, you probably don't know this because you have

never travelled to the Upper Settlement, but there are many protocols that would make this impossible. Even for the smallest living organisms: everyone who gets onto one of the flights needs, by law, to go through a thorough process of decontamination—'

She stopped me right there.

'Oh… I see. You don't want to get our diseases, is that right?'

I didn't know what to say. But she was right. I had received a large number of vaccines before coming down here, and still it was possible that I would contract some kind of unknown fever. I had to sign a disclosure agreement with the shuttle company, to the effect that I was the only person responsible for the decision to come down; and that if something went wrong, or I was maimed, or if I died as a result of my trip to the surface, my family would not hold them responsible.

'Come,' she said, getting up from the chair she was occupying, and moving towards the door with determination. 'I want to show you something.'

As always in recent days, grabbing her hand sent an electric current up my body. It was true that I sought her more often now, that I got up and went to her room to find her, that I wanted to spend long hours listening to her voice and looking in her eyes.

But I also felt a strange danger when I was around her, as if she knew something I didn't, and I could die for that reason. As if my life was in her hands.

I felt like this now, as she took me deep into the forest. From time to time, she would look back at me, smiling. And that was oddly scarier, for I did not know her intentions. I felt danger now, and pushed the feeling away.

'Where are we going?'

'To the pond. I would like you to meet an old friend.'

She had told me that a basilisk had been said to roam these waters from time immemorial, long before the green winter.

We saw nothing, of course, although at some point she threw a stone into the cool, inviting water, claiming to have seen him. We were sitting on the deceptive little shore, and I looked at her. Her upper lip was covered in little pearls of sweat, and her chest was heaving, her eyes closed.

'What are you thinking about?'

'I had a friend once.'

'Where is she now?'

'I used to meet her here, she would sit there, exactly where you are. I wanted to kill her once.'

'Why? What had she done to you?'

She looked up; her sad smile was reflected in her eyes.

'She knew things… She must have known all along. And she never told me.'

'What did she know?'

'She knew about my father.'

She looked at me defensively, almost angrily, and I knew she was trying to parse whether I had heard the stories.

Of course I had, for Mr Vanlow had filled me in before our union: it was only appropriate that he did. Her father, accused of murder; the subsequent debacle of the family fortune, and also the lack of evidence available at the time. It had almost finished them. I don't think Vanlow's intention was to present himself as the family's saviour, but it was clear that his intervention had been critical.

She could see straight away, almost as if she were reading my mind, that I had been told the tale. She chuckled, and started singing. *Little Death, little Death, what have you done to me…*

'Pearl, you are safe now, you are safe with me.'

At this, she laughed more openly, and I felt stupid; down on the surface I needed her protection more than the other way around. She turned in my direction, she was not laughing anymore. Instead, she seemed to be examining me, looking deeply into my eyes, looking for a lie, perhaps, to catch me somehow red-handed. And then she spoke.

'Do you know what the beanies call this place?'

'The pond? No, I don't.' I assumed she wasn't referring to the cartographic names we gave to everything up in the Settlement, when we looked from above. The name for a place like this would be something like TR-2486492.

'Dead Woman's Pool.'

I sensed a shiver down my spine.

'My brother was found here,' she continued. 'And my mother's heart broke here. She was the one who found him, you see.' I still said nothing. Something was painfully moving along my throat, and I swallowed hard. 'Look,' she continued, 'I have no idea of what my stepfather has told you, but he killed them both.' She was furious now.

I also knew a bit about that, for I had had to be filled in about the destroyed southern wing of the house, apparently lost to a flood. I knew what had happened here.

'Pearl, I'm so sorry.'

She looked deep into my eyes, perhaps also furious with me. But she must have been happy with what she found, for with a swift movement she straddled me, and began to kiss me. We had not kissed since the ceremony, and that kiss had been different. Now, her tongue went deep into my mouth, and mine into hers, as our hands started pulling away clothes, only some, for we ended up half-dressed, only our pants and the upper sides of our vests hiding our skin.

At some point we lay on the grass, and there we finished, each on our side, hands interlocked and eyes looking deep into the other's.

We stopped moving and only then did I hear the noises of the forest again, the rippling of the water. I looked in its direction, and I thought I could see some odd creature losing itself beneath its rippling surface.

14

Until now, I had looked at this part of the planet only from above, for after studying bio-anthropology I had trained as a cartographer, following the progress of the forest's edge on our vast illuminated screens. We had noticed it long ago: a stretch of land that was always left untouched. The jungle, marked in a violent green, advanced and retreated, capriciously waving itself over the planet's surface like a snake. But some parts of this *sierra*, including Gobarí and the area around it, were always, for reasons unknown, passed over. We had been greatly puzzled by this phenomenon, and it was expected that I would write a full report while I was here to take back to my superiors, a report which would be added to the repository of data we possessed about this strange region.

This was the end of the known world, and our Settlement sat right on top of it. There were five other Settlements, scattered above the atmosphere. Ours reigned over what had been the most southern end of an old, northern continent. But Gobarí, Old Town, the *sierra*... Billions of years ago, when the then continents separated, this bit of land had ended up on the right side of the divide. They belonged there by mere chance; they were so much farther south, so much at the edge of the world, that they could as easily have been part of the next continent, and left unsaved.

I did not like these southern people. Or at least, I hadn't before my trip. Now, I was getting to know my new companion. After our encounter on the shore of the pond, we had dinner together every night, by the light of the candles. Sometimes moths as huge as bats would enter through the open window, although I had to revise my out-of-date taxonomies: when I saw a jungle bat they turned out to be much bigger. The ampleness of what we ate was another exercise in excess, but I wasn't complaining. I enjoyed the aloe and vanilla hot-pot, the jackfruit salad, the mango spread... Even the cold durian soup, which smelled like rotten flesh.

After the copious meals we would retire together; we were now sharing the same bedroom. We would read one of the two books in the house, salvaged from a time now gone, sometimes out loud to each other: *When* jeré, *men, have a bad, violent death, they sometimes come back transformed into* mullos, *or* alive-dead, *and take with them someone they loved deeply, to keep them company for all eternity inside the forest.* We nursed our cups of camomile to settle our stomachs, our sips of infusion punctuated by long kisses. When the boiled water was cool enough to drink in one gulp, we had already exhausted our explorations; we could be together several times each night, for neither of us knew how to stop, it felt so wrong to stop. So much else was not right out there, in the world, and this felt different. We hardly ever heard about the emerging problems in Old Town that followed the attack on the Barrier: several short uprisings that had been promptly contained. Nothing I carried within me worked in Gobarí, and the only way we had of listening to digests was inside my HoveLight300 when I switched on its communication panel; but we soon stopped this daily routine, immersed as we were in each other. I started to think that I could be happy like this, in this place, that there was a kind of bliss in a surface life.

But I had other reasons to be here, reasons of my own. I had readily agreed to make the journey, as soon as it was suggested by Father. I had already decided that I would do anything not to be a burden to my family. My family. Who knew what their wishes were, their hopes? Did they have any? I had been an oddity to them, a bookish child born in the middle of a tribe of people who never seemed to display any interest in anything, who seemed to go through life without thinking. No one knew how to nurture my inclination for learning, and I remember that my parents only took me to see the collections kept in the ring on one occasion, they themselves having no taste for looking at things or reading digital scrolls on portable electronic books. Therefore, I would always feel a sense of dread when faced with repositories, which almost maimed my studies. Left to my own devices, given no direction or attention, I was forced to find my own way. I became interested in Pan-Inuit culture, submerging myself in its study, even travelling up to the one remaining northern hamlet, the first time that I ventured outside of the Settlement. It was customary to descend to the planet for at least part of one year for our studies. Of course, my family resented me for this: why was I not interested in 'our' culture instead? I was denying my 'roots', they claimed. My father, who had never written a HiveMessage to me in living memory, sent this when a picture of myself among the remaining Pre-Inuits appeared once on his screen, as part of an information digest. He, who had never written to me, saw fit to express his frustration in this manner. I could not formulate a reply. What roots? What culture? He and my mother, and to some extent my older brother, only involved themselves with scenarios and fictions that implied as little thinking as possible. I doubt they had given a moment of their time to try to understand why I was interested in learning. Still, they saw fit to recriminate me for my interest in 'foreign' traditions, and demanded that I abandon them by their crude actions and reprimands. They had, however, no alternative to offer. They had never offered a tradition themselves. Not even as a family did we have 'roots'. Other families were known for this or that trait, or some story or anecdote, or even some achievement. My own tribe was a blank. Was it then so strange that I had felt the need to try and go looking for an identity? With time they became more demanding, of my attention, of my time, but I truly did not understand what exactly they were offering in return. My brother, for example, had always lived a parallel existence, uninterested in my parents or even me. He never included anyone in his jealously guarded privacy. This privacy extended to everything, even friends; even when those had first been *my* friends. But he arrived one day and claimed them for himself, in the process leaving me behind. At home he was silent, surly, always a sly smile on his face as if he knew something we didn't, as if he pitied us. But there was never an indication that I could participate in this knowledge. In short: he had never, to my recollection, behaved as an older brother should. My surprise when he started demanding some of my time in a couple of unexpected HiveMessages was acute. Busy with other things, fighting my deep-seated anxieties, I did not reply immediately to them. This was a source of anger for him, and when he saw me next he reprimanded me. I could not understand: he had shown no interest in me in the past, and therefore, as an adult, my life was organised around other things and people. Carving out time and space for him now would be extremely problematic; some of the things I had fought so hard to obtain would have to be left behind.

I was uninterested in this version of a tribe, or a 'family', in which some had to swear allegiance to others without getting anything in return. I did not desire to have a family at any cost to my sanity: for I imagined there should be some reciprocity in the basic traits of respect and understanding. What I was eager for was to start a family of my own.

I should have realised the impossibility of this, how much I was lying to myself. I was hoping to form a bond with someone who viewed me with mistrust, who belonged to the world of the surface, with all the difficulties this implied. I had not been entirely honest with Pearl, either; for there was some truth in the suggestion that, at times, we 'staged' assaults by the forest in order to move settlements and people. This, however, was only done to my knowledge in areas that our prediction algorithms told us were at risk, and so they were an exercise in protection, in adaptation to our environment, a necessary cull.

Would she believe me if I explained this to her? I truly did not know.

None of this was shown to me more clearly than on the day when a letter was delivered to her by hand. Why that woman decided to write I would never understand; for the shock of coming to see her would have resonated much further. But a letter she wrote.

Pearl vanished for most of the afternoon, and only later I realised this absence must have been connected with the unexpected arrival of the post.

When I noticed Pearl's absence, I asked the servant girl if she had seen her. She said no.

'Can you please ask Savina?'

'Why don't you ask her yourself? Savina is leaving.'

I went looking for the woman. She was in the process of gathering her few possessions.

'Why are you leaving?'

She looked at me with disgust. Eventually, she spoke.

'I don't like you, and you don't like me; and I don't like what you do to the little bird every night.'

At first I did not discern her meaning. I still had not got used to the way they spoke down here. Then it suddenly hit me, and I felt my cheeks reddening in anger and shame. Pearl had told me that her family called her little blue bird when she was a child on account of her dyed hair. How this woman had the insolence to refer to our intimate life was beyond me, but I had no intention to remain silent.

'She is my chosen companion. I am her chosen companion. And it is none of your business.'

She looked at me, smiling oddly. I knew it would kill Pearl to see her go, and I had gone to find her with the idea of asking her not to; but now I could not wait until I saw her disappear: from the house, from our lives. It was true that she had brought Pearl up; it was also true that she had made her scared about so many things as well, presumably to keep her under her power.

'Lie down, lie, little *jeré*; enjoy your days and your nights. But the *murí* will never be yours, for this is her house! The *bengué* will come to find you, and prevent you from taking her up to that place of death!'

I left that horrid place, and went into the forest, deep, deep into it, until I thought I recognised the way to the pond. I walked alone for a while in that hostile place, a reckless thing to do, no doubt; not finding anything, not finding my way, not finding Pearl either.

Eventually, I found myself back on the path to the house; I have no idea how I managed it. Dusk was falling. Soon it would be our dinnertime. I got in, and was surprised to see that the table hadn't been set. I could not smell any food being cooked, so I went out into the kitchen shack. The fires were out, and everything was packed away. I started panicking a little. I went back into the house, and everything was so quiet, so still; the dark was getting inside now, and the wooden furniture was getting lost in its shadows. Where were the servants? The smiling girl, the old man? Had they left with Savina?

Had Pearl left as well?

I remembered the letter then. What did it contain?

I went into her bedroom, and I found her sitting there, in front of the heaviest piece of furniture in the whole house, a very old looking-glass. This had been her mother's room, and I knew it made her sad. She looked at me through the mirror's reflection but did not turn to greet me. Her face was a serious mask.

'Pearl, whatever is the matter? Where are the servants?'

'I told them to leave,' she said. Then she got up slowly, walked past me and, without saying anything, put a piece of paper in my hand: the letter she had received that morning. My first reaction was that someone must be sick, perhaps Mr Vanlow, perhaps her school friend, Laurel, who had been at our wedding.

'Is everyone all right?' I asked. But she did not reply, and went and sat on the bed instead.

I read the letter, I read it as quickly as I could; and then I had to start reading it again. For I could not make out its meaning the first time. It was very hot, and I had no light. I moved towards the window; but dusk was falling quickly now, so quickly...

Little Death, little Death, what have you done to me... What was happening? Everything felt so unreal in that moment: the *sierra*, the Upper Settlement. Perhaps everything was an illusion, and we had been lied to from the beginning of time, from the green winter itself.

'I need more light...' I mumbled.

'No need,' she said, and got up, came down to me, and took the letter from my hands. She started reading it out loud, in the darkness. I realised she knew its contents by heart.

It was signed by someone called Eli, someone who asked Pearl to come to find her at once, to go to somewhere called Benguele and join her and others. It asked her to leave me behind, not to tell me where she was going, or to kill me if she had to. And I realised that, if she was sharing it all with me, perhaps that was what she intended to do.

Was it true, everything that the letter said? She would come with me, and would give me a child, and then another. And then, when she could not give me more, I would put her to sleep forever, and I would come down again, and claim another bride, and then another, and then another. Or even better, she would end up inside a vessel, and I would make sure she disappeared up into the ether, never to come back. *Up and up we go, high into the sky*, like the children's lullaby.

Was that true? I had come looking for a family, wishing for a family; a family of my own.

But I had seen the other things as well, I had seen them.

'Is it true?' she asked.

And I really could not tell her if it was. I was standing next to the window, and I saw the mountains in the semi-darkness, with a purple light hovering above them, and an ominous, dark sky. I truly did not know at that moment if I was imagining it all, if the mountains, Gobarí, the Settlement, were false things, and we were all living in a nightmare.

'Pearl...' I started. She was looking at me and shaking her head right and left, her mouth pressed into a thin line, her eyes rolling in disbelief. I had to say something, anything. 'Pearl. Please. There are things that I need to explain. But this is not one of them, I can assure you that.'

She looked at me again, let the letter drop onto the bed. Crossed her arms over her chest.

'You asked if we move you, on purpose. It is not exactly that. Sometimes, the data suggests it is safest if we let some areas go...'

'Let some areas go?' she shouted back.

'I've used the wrong words, it is not that, not exactly... We... The energy surge, you have to understand that, at the beginning, it was a tricky thing to use.'

'The energy surge? What energy surge?' she looked at me quizzically. Did she really not understand? Did she really not know?

'The blue light.'

'The blue light?'

'Yes, Pearl. You see it as a blue light, every time we action the terraforming technology; but it has taken us generations to do it properly, and we are still learning.'

That was it, a proper explanation.

So she could forget about the other thing.

It did not seem to have the reaction I had expected. She went silent now, and sat on the bed. She wasn't looking at me, but at the floor.

'Pearl...'

'Terraforming. You just said *terraforming*,' she interrupted.

'Yes, terraforming.'

'What does that mean, exactly?'

And I told her what that meant. How the technology
had got out of hand in the past, when it was thought that
it could save us from the mutation of Earth into a desertic
planet, and how overusing it in the earlier days created
the current ecosystem; and how even now we used it
sometimes, but only, I was careful to add, whenever we felt
it was the right thing to do, in order to prevent a worse
outcome elsewhere, as we can control it better.

She did not reply, and sat there in silence for what felt
like a long time. Eventually, she got up, and left the room,
and the house.

Why did I not go after her in that moment? I was
conscious of my actions, knew that I needed to run after
her. But something kept me glued to the floor. Through
the window, I saw her entering the forest, going, perhaps,
in the direction of the pond.

Eventually, I left the house and went after her, straight
into the forest, but I ended up walking without direction,
deeper and deeper within its dark embrace. I walked until
I passed all the tame marked spots the people from the
house used to orientate themselves; I walked past the signs

that directed me to the pond; I walked past the farthest point where I had been; and then I continued walking. But I couldn't find Pearl anywhere. My face was hot, the heat turning my tears into a warm, sticky liquid, not unlike the *milbao* I had so despised at the beginning, and had only later grown to love. For I was changing, I hoped, like the forest changed, every day, every hour. But it was too late for me or for us, and walking deep into my death was the only thing left for me to do.

I realised at some point that the darkness had changed, but I continued walking. We had all known the truth about marrying surface girls, but no one would speak it out loud; not my father, not Mr Vanlow. Only the girl that I had married.

For a moment I could see the bright orb, fighting to get down among the leaves; it was a strange colour, not yellow, not white, but bluish. Odd, strange, unnatural light.

I had that same feeling again, that we were all props put on a toy model by some cruel God. I realised then: this place, the surface, was no pleasure garden, and it never had been.

I was lost, and kept stumbling and falling in the dark. I kept cutting myself as well, my hands, my face. I knew that spending the night out there would kill me. The hostile trees formed a jungle around me, and I felt that I could fall asleep in its embrace. Die, I said to myself. Lie down to sleep and die. For how was I going to show myself anywhere, now that everything was in the open? That horrid truth? For now I understood, she must be right. Now, my father's insistence that I would accept Mr Vanlow's proposal, and marry his stepdaughter, made some kind of sick sense. And, if that was true, I could not show myself again, not to her, not to Mr Vanlow; but equally, I could not go back anymore to that place, to my father and my brother. If I accepted this truth, its knowledge would force me into exile, but I didn't belong here either. I had nowhere to go.

I must have fallen asleep at some point. Somehow I crawled next to the vast roots of a tree, twisting over each other, thicker than my arms, forming strange cradles that embraced me. It looked like a peaceful place to end it all. Then darkness proper must have engulfed me. But it got light, somehow, eventually. It is hard to know if it surprised me, the new day. I was suffering from a strong fever, I was panting and covered in frozen sweat; but somehow, miraculously, I came out at the other end of those lonely hours. I was shivering, alternating between hot and cold. My body was about to give up. Through the shadows, unreal, only living in my own eyes, I saw them coming: the *mullos*, who surely had come to take me to Benguele, to Hell, and this was right and proper. *When* jeré, *men, have a bad, violent death, they sometimes come back transformed into* mullos, *or alive-dead, and take with them someone they loved deeply, to keep them company for all eternity.* But who could love me?

It wasn't the *mullos*, of course; it was the old man and some other beanie that Pearl had entrusted to look for me. They were not happy to see me. They put together a makeshift stretcher from two oversized leaves, and carried me back, complaining all the way, to the house. We got to Gobarí, eventually; I was told I was truly lucky to make it. I was very ill after that, until the fever broke, days later.

As soon as it did, I saw that Pearl had left me, and I was alone in the strange house.

15

Everybody knows about the monstrous beings that live in the ocean. It is not our fault, it was not our intention. But monsters would happen, and did happen. We were trying to help, we had the best intentions. Now, it is a nightmare, a mismanagement. Every time they saw a blue, fluorescent sky, it was us up there, trying to fix the unfixable. Terraforming Earth, after we had destroyed it, after everything had been destroyed.

The swimmers did not offer themselves to the waters, as Pearl was fond of explaining. The reality was different. They got entangled within the remnants of plastic and drowned, the thick layer of debris on the surface blocking them from reaching the air again. They sacrificed them-selves, that is true; but to a very different God. No doubt some of the leviathans that populated the Three Oceans had a feast now and again; but the leviathans live much further away, in deeper waters, and if they got to eat the rebels it was only their carcasses. When I was a small boy, in school, we were shown satellite videos of them, those trespassers. Their beliefs had been decreed heretical only for this reason: to prevent more senseless deaths.

None of these were things that I could say or explain to her, none of these myths could be debunked. She lived and died for them. Like the myth of a blue horizon, a blue sky, a blue ocean. Carbon, hydrogen, and other elements had conspired to make its chemical structure this colour and no other. However, this waste has changed this chemical formula. The detritus is non-biodegradable; hence, waste is now the central component of the ocean. I doubt Pearl was aware of that.

Perhaps we should not have persevered, should not have generated life, experimented with it in situations where we knew our excesses were likely to compromise or alter the chemical properties of the given milieu. That was our fault, and ours only.

What other environments had we compromised? Impossible to know.

Alone, abandoned, I found solace in putting together some notes for my report. I remained in Gobarí as my base, and decided that I could not summarise my findings on the coarse paper provided for my use, so every afternoon I would write my thoughts and findings on the little screen of the HoveLight300. It wasn't ideal, but was slightly less uncomfortable than writing by hand, when I cramped up after only a few sentences.

The mornings I spent visiting the beanie and *shuvani* dwellings in the area, populated by the people who had provided some kind of service to the house; I also went to a nearby beanie town Pearl had not mentioned. It wasn't difficult to locate a couple of families willing to let me observe their daily routines at a distance, and who did not mind answering my questions. While women tended their hearths and men went out into the forest, I took notes and interested myself in everything I saw them do. None of them seemed to mind, and in a matter of days I had a substantial number of paragraphs that could be moulded into a coherent narrative, albeit one that was unexpected, utterly alien to what I had learnt about these people up home.

The final draft of the report started by noting that, contrary to my previous experience with the Pan-Inuits, the changes proposed from the Settlement—those interactions with the environment that undermined the landscape and damaged livelihoods—did not result in the expected erosion of the people's sense of place. Emotions run high in that southern part of the world that comprised Gobarí, Old Town, the narrow stretch of ocean coast. Emotions electrified the air, as surface inhabitants resisted losing their sense of belonging, their connection to a small stretch of land. They did struggle to survive, and still they persevered, even at the expense of their basic human traits.

The *shuvanies* took pride in their ability to bend flora and fauna to their will; but they were also weary of our meddling, an almost uncanny intuition allowed them to see that the changes and the mutations that their habitat experienced could not be the mere product of the natural upheavals that the human race had endured in recent centuries.

I noted in my file that issues of social justice and human rights still marred what could be sensibly done down here. This was happening, even if, for the first time in generations, we were meting out the fundamental principles of sustainability. We were using the resources our environment provided in a way that didn't compromise the ability of future generations to meet their own needs. What was threatening livelihoods, then? People of different castes remained enslaved one way or another, even after the Act was successfully passed. Social networks of reciprocity and local knowledge were not harnessed for the common good, but for a twisted idea of self-preservation. This extended to tribes, clans, families. Strange alliances and loyalties prevailed. The end result was that overexploitation, of resources, of people, remained a constant threat; not immediately visible, but hovering just around the corner. For those who knew how to benefit, all they had to do was attune themselves to the new order of things, the fittest adapting for survival.

The problem with women seemed to me of a greater order, and infinitely more worrying. Onto their shoulders fell the responsibility for every single strategy that was needed by their family or tribe for everyday survival. Every time something stopped working, and an alternative solution had to be found, they were the ones in charge of providing their communities with the basics. In some cases, I noted, it seemed that their partners did not simply have no inclination to help, but refused even to acknowledge that alternative provisions needed to be made: to put it bluntly, the men expected their home comforts whatever the weather, and weren't remotely interested in helping out or even finding out how water, or food, or other precious resources, had been obtained. This order of things placed a massive pressure on the women's shoulders.

Observing the women was by far the most interesting thing that I did with my time over those weeks. Men seemed to be guided by very automatic thinking, they lacked the creativity and resourcefulness of their female counterparts. I noticed the women invariably engaged with the jungle in a very particular way that was almost animistic, an odd religious thread running through a great number of their actions. They had little chants, or perhaps prayers, to aid different everyday processes. They took care to provide offerings to certain areas or places, and in exchange collected plants for cooking and medicinal purposes from those same areas. The women also appeared to be responsible for providing clean water to their communities. In Gobarí, a very sophisticated system allowed for rainwater to be collected. However, this was destroyed in the last flash flooding disaster, a few years back. Access to fresh water, and the constant worry that this caused, contrasted sharply with the tension that existed in their mythological relationship with the Three Oceans, and that down in the Gobarí-jungle area I could experience at its fullest. The *sierra* wasn't far away from the coast. In my HoveLight300, the trip would not take more than forty minutes. However, there was a clear psychological distance to it. These jungle communities were certainly inland communities, saw themselves as such, identified as such. They did not like the idea of the open water; rather, they feared it. This was partly due to the leviathans and other creatures that lurked beneath, and this idea of not seeing what was going on below the surface, of believing in the existence of the monsters or not believing, weighed heavily on them. There were factions, I noticed, who agreed or disagree with their existence.

They also had their own water monster to placate, in the form of the pond's basilisk, which I am sure was no more than a legend. Fresh water was in a completely different category; I noticed how they sourced it in a different way— never, for example, drinking from the pond which, due to the existence of the basilisk, an *alicanta* in their language, was 'tainted'. If they ever saw themselves forced somehow to use this water for washing their pans or their clothes, I noticed how they always used different containers than those in which they would receive the drinking rainwater, which for them was a 'pure' variation of the liquid. They never mixed those containers, which I found interesting. And rain-pure drinking water was, at times, difficult to obtain. In the times when it didn't rain at all, the women were forced to barter with the more affluent members of their own communities, those who had managed to build huge containers where this water was kept to last many months. The fact that the burden of procuring these basic needs fell disproportionately on women, I concluded, forced us to reconsider the impact of our actions down here, not just on the environmental, but also on the social processes and among genders. I wasn't sure my readers in the Settlement would cherish this notion.

—

In truth, I was not prepared for any of these findings. The knowledge in the Upper Settlement of what our strategies were affecting down here was patchy, scarce. We also lived by our own myths. That we brought some 'order' to the chaos below was one of them. At least, that was what always was impressed upon us. We would be sitting in our orderly rows, dressed in the regulated white of the gymnasium. Image after image would appear on the screenboard: graphs, statistics. From an early age, we were encouraged into the chamber in which the energy surge was enacted. We entered the round chamber in orderly rows, and stood behind a glass partition, usually accompanied by a teacher from the gymnasium. The beam of light would move towards the planet below, and a change in the surface would subsequently be visible from above. We did not see the energy as a blue light, as they did down there; but we knew what was being enacted, what we were trying to achieve. From that distance, orbiting the world, it was sufficient to understand that we were doing a good thing, and we questioned ourselves no further. We did not see the cities as more than dots, scattered here and there. We gave no thought to the people who inhabited them.

Equally, we would analyse the Jump, bit by bit, but without looking deeper than its superficial tenets. The ceremonial covering of the streets with green leaves and branches, the elaborated constellations reproduced with flowers of many colours. The parade in which those about to be sent were treated like heroes. Their long white clothing, their tunics and long-sleeved robes that surely could not be of much use inside the vessels. It all had a particular meaning attached, a reason. It created an illusion, the elevated illusion of control, of highly regimented rules with a purpose, when in fact they were nothing other than arbitrary options, designed to make the onlookers feel some sort of reverence towards the proceedings, some sort of inevitability. The iconography of that ceremony created the idea that sending those children up to the sky was something that had to be done, in that specific way and no other. Hence, getting the right kind of flower to reproduce a Kingfisher constellation accurately on the floor became more important, more relevant, than the fact that the young person, whose constellation the Kingfisher was, was about to be slaughtered.

(We were never told in as many words that this is what happened, but we all knew it, somehow. You could smell it, in the fact that the programme had stopped, that no vessel had gone up in decades. That nothing, ever, had come back from those ships that were sent.)

Hence, for the people down here, venturing into the forest was the main adventure of the day, made you a hero of sorts. Pearl had explained to me that she had grown up in fear and awe of the forest.

'Don't get me wrong; I love Gobarí. I think Mother felt we would be protected here, somehow.'

'Protected? What did she need to protect you from?'

I could not tie the notion of protection with that ever-changing, unpredictable space, an uncertain refuge where one day you could be swallowed up by the extreme green, or taken away by some unknown giant birdlike creature, or simply devoured by a carnivorous plant you had no time to flee. Pearl was acutely aware of living like this:

'Some days, I was constantly on alert; Savina would know when the forest was hungry, or was about to change. Those days were terrifying,' she explained. It all sounded as if she was explaining how she had survived, rather than lived.

And then she told me about her father.

'I think he was trying to save me.'

'From what?'

But she could not formulate a reply. I did not tell her that I already knew the story, and that, like her, I could sense holes in it, parts that did not add up.

'My father was innocent.'

'How do you know that?'

'I found the report in the Registry. He never confessed to killing the girl.'

'Is that all your proof?'

She said nothing else.

In the gymnasium, we would write long convoluted essays about the meaning of some minor ornament, of that or this thing, tracing back its historical and anthropological origins up till before the Green Event, or, as it was called down here, the 'green winter'. Our research included reading some of the fables that moulded their beliefs. I knew the tale of the white lady, the tale of the three sisters, the tale of Alira. Those were Pearl's favourites, we read them together in Gobarí, at night, under the light of an oil-tin candle. Or rather, she read them to me, as I found it hard to read under that peculiar light. I craved the immaculate, clean and crisp white light of the Settlement. The pristine row of tables on which we did our work. The screenboard surface where the text would appear, and there we would read them, make sense of them, memorise them, form our own theories. At the time, I was not interested in this part of the world, and I learnt more about the northern regions. Now, I regretted that.

I had only been selected to write this report because I was coming here to marry Pearl, under my father's orders. I didn't see us up there as saviours, I didn't see us as anything. I believed in very little; certainly, not in myself. Nor the Jump, the vessels, or the false hope they brought to an exhausted world. I know we were not supposed to 'believe', that wasn't our role. But, at least, I should have believed that the current status quo would bring some solace to those below us, that everything was done for a reason.

Unfortunately, I could not find any evidence of that down here.

Up in the Settlement, I would go running on the upper deck quite often. To my right, the transport lines carried citizens from one section of the Settlement to another. To my left, I could enjoy the oval garden, my favourite place, with its invented trees and its strange birds, none of them belonging here, there, or anywhere, a figment of our imaginations that, somehow, we had managed to bring to life. From time to time, an oversized dragonfly would fly to me, and accompany me for a while, her colours bio-engineered to shine with many different shades. She was expecting some of the sweet lumps of energy-sugar that we runners usually carried with us; I, however, chose not to pollute my body with any of those additives. Above me, the dark sky, some stars, and the occasional old satellite, still orbiting after all this time, sending empty messages back to nowhere. Sometimes I would push myself, tire myself out, strive further, and the effort would make me giddy. At those times, I would always look at the glass ceiling dome, and consider the sky. And wish I could fly, just like Alira did in that children's fable; Alira, or the lady in white, our founder. She had separated herself from what went on down below, from the ideas of the old men who took it upon themselves to run the planet when everything changed irrevocably. It was she, as well, who sought a way for more of us to be up in the sky with her. It was she who decided that some of us would be here, and some of them would be down there. She, in her infinite wisdom, had decreed these separations so we could survive, and we ought to thank her daily, for survive we had.

But I would look at the open space, visible through the massive windows in the oval garden, and would want to go further, further up. Did I want to Jump? I would have been the first starborn to do so. I do not think so, I was not so brave. I think I just wanted an escape. And I had found it somehow, but by heading down instead.

The Fable of the Lady in White

There was a boy who had grown up next to a desert. Over there, a little mountain range. Past that, another village. A girl who he was fond of lived in that village beyond the mountains. One day, he travelled there, and asked the girl to unite with him. The girl refused. She was promised to another.

He returned to his village, angry to be rejected. That night, he could not sleep for the anger and the jealousy he felt.

'I wish,' he said to himself, 'that a terrible tragedy might befall both of them!'

No sooner had he said those words than a lady in white descended from the sky, and stood in front of him.

'Boy,' she called. 'Boy, is that what you want?'

He had to cover his eyes to look at her. She was shining like a star, her whole body luminescent. Her clothes were immaculate, pristine. She walked on the earth floor of his house, and her feet did not get dirty. Her silver bracelets shone reflections here and there.

'I can help you,' she insisted. 'But you need to be sure. Once it has all started, there will be no turning back.'

The boy agreed. He was resentful of the lovers; jealousy was eating him up.

'Very well.' Then the lady in white did something strange. She caressed one of her silver bracelets, and a little man made of light appeared and posed himself on her hand. She talked to this little man made of light, and whispered for him to do something for her. Then the man disappeared. The lady smiled kindly at the boy, and flew away into the clouds.

That night, later on, there was a blue explosion of light up in the sky. The light danced over the horizon, forming the shape of animals, playing with one another, hunting each other. At some point, the light went out.

The boy went to sleep. He did not know what the lady would do; he suspected it had all been a dream, and nothing would come of it.

In the morning he was woken up by a commotion. There was a lot of noise outside his hut, a rattle of people talking to each other. He went out to see what had happened.

The little mountain range ahead of them had changed colour and turned completely green overnight. But the transformation wasn't the most incredible thing of all. People were saying that the green that now covered the little promontories was moving in the wind, rippling like fur does.

How could a mountain grow green fur overnight?

People moved away as the eldest member of the community advanced slowly to see the marvel. 'That is not fur,' the eldest said.

And then he explained.

The word stirred some memories: forest. A forest that had appeared overnight. There was no surprise at this: most of the members of the community had not known anything called forest in their lifetimes, and so they did not recall how they were made, or came to be.

Then the elder spoke again. What about the village on the other side of the mountain? Rangers were dispatched. They returned at night. The village did not exist any longer. It had disappeared. It might still be there in theory, invisible, buried deep under the green that had emerged seemingly out of nowhere to gobble it up.

The strange thing was, the members of the community did not seem to react. Even when trees and bushes—all new words that their mouths had to rehearse carefully—had grown overnight, until they covered it all, the little dwellings, the parked wagons, the people. Even when there were no survivors. It had happened somewhere else, to other folk. Even when the rangers spoke of vines growing through the empty carcasses of carts, discarded rubble, children and their parents… The villagers had been spared those images, so they did not mind the fate of their neighbours.

It had happened to others, they said. We are lucky.

Soon, however, there were reports coming from other places, other occurrences. The apparent repetition of the phenomenon, in which the green mantle gobbled up a human settlement in its entirety, could simply not be ignored any longer. Nor could the fact that it was obvious another similar event would eventually happen. It was anybody's guess where, or when, it would happen. And it did happen. Again, the same song: it did not happen to us! It happened further away, over there!

The final realisation struck at last: their turn would come eventually. As if the message that someone had been sending had not been loud enough, until finally, suddenly, it had been picked up with a loud bang. Humanity's final awakening, though not before going through the normal cycle of denial, negotiation, and acceptance.

The night finally arrived, when the blue light shone directly over their heads, over their houses, over their tame desert animals and over their dirty children. There was no place to hide. When they saw the green rushing down the mountain, advancing in their direction, they understood it was their turn to disappear.

PEARL

16

On the surface, every pregnancy was cause for rejoicing. There was a sense that it made everybody involved a better person. Me, I dreaded it all, except what was bound to happen.

They took Alira, and brought me here, one of the inner docks, filled to the brim with other refugees. It is a strange limbo-life, sleeping in a dark section, with gritty blue-fluorescent lighting alongside the grey walls. Every morning, a knocker-up comes and, for a small fee, wakes me up, so I can be on time at my place of work, several levels up.

I am a cleaner now, up in the ring.

The dock where I sleep and dream of my daughter is at least six levels down from the white and pristine sections inhabited by the ringers, their promenades and boulevards infused with the benign light of their fake sun. They walk up and down, drink and eat delicious looking food, attend theatrical events in little, intimate venues, and,

215

once a week, they congregate around the Forum, a circular piazza; on some days, by virtue of the citizens occupying its round steps, it transforms into a theatre. Those days are my favourites. The storyteller appears, and delivers the news, and explains the latest scientific advances, and relates the deaths and the births, and creates new myths for us all to follow.

I am no more than a shadow, moving around collecting discarded things, and taking them back to the incinerator. I wear the required working attire, made of a fabric that makes me almost invisible to passers-by, so as not to be in the way. I actually prefer this arrangement, as I imagine these garments will also help me one day to look for her. At night I return to my dock, eat a protein pouch, and go to sleep in a room with twenty strangers.

I am finally here.

Do I think about the surface? I think about Arlo; about Eli's letter that took me back to her. Those days, which were so painful, are now also the happiest ones of my life. I close my eyes, and think about the forest, and about Eli, and about the green.

We usually went into the forest led by Eli, our main task to collect a huge number of plants. It was a massive effort.

I wasn't used to working with the machetes, and the procuring of the branches, all covered in wavy leaves and hard to manoeuvre. At some point, I was trying to take a long one, overgrown with endless smaller branches, back to the place where we were collecting them, and, not looking behind me, I almost hit somebody on the head with the wood.

'Careful!' a voice shouted behind me. Then, patiently, this person showed me how to drag the fallen branch to the place where it had been cut, which ensured that I could control where the crown, spilling widely in every direction, stayed on the floor instead.

It was a long time since I had felt so useless.

We had spent the past two days pruning the path towards Benguele, cutting and cutting again—it always felt such a useless endeavour there, it felt as if the next day it would look exactly as it was—and we had started covering all the paths into the house, and then the patio, and the porch. Nothing remained 'humanised' except for the walls themselves.

Those green-covered paths were decorated with intricate flower patterns, representing the constellations of those we were honouring. We were mimicking the ceremony of the Jump, mocking it perhaps, to send our own heroes into action. Some of the outer walls were also decorated with

MARIAN WOMACK

bunches of flowers, and after the festivities some people would weave long, thick plaits out of the greenery lying on the floor to hang on their doors and from thresholds. They would be burnt in another festivity or kept for a year for luck.

There were also other rituals, connected with fertility, reproduction. I preferred not to think or hear about them.

Benguele wasn't simply a house whose only purpose was to demonstrate the techies' dominance. It had also been a proper farm, long ago. Some rooms were lavish, white granite and marble formed the shapes of what we thought were trees and animals in the epoch before the green winter. I knew the name of some; others had been lost now from history.

At first my stepfather had rented it for a while, and, even if he had abandoned it after he got Gobarí, he had managed to do some repairs. A fire had only destroyed some of the outer barns, and the main house was intact. But what mattered now to its occupants were the fields. Eli's people were getting them working once again. The fields were cut-out squares in the middle of the jungle; the trees thinned so that they could not grow into a light-blocking canopy. These vast expanses, miraculously, received direct light from the sun. That simple fact changed everything: different things could be grown here than in our little temporary patches, things that required more space to breathe, more time to mature. It took huge amounts of effort to keep those fields free of the forest's embrace. A large battalion of men had this as their only job: keeping the forest from encroaching on them. There were things growing, so many things. Things I had never seen before, tasted before; they were not new species, but old species, some predating the green winter itself.

Eli's older sister had worked in town for a couple of years, in the house of a high-ranking vessel-building engineer connected with the farm—his sister had first built it. That was how she had known about the place. None of us had known a Jump in our lives; the last one had occurred nearly twenty years ago, when I was a very little girl. I still remembered that image of the vessel going up. Up and up we go.

The vessels were sent by NEST, a now-defunct programme to look for an alternative to our planet. For our parents' generation, it had been a common sight to see a couple of the massive structures climbing into the sky each decade. It was never made clear to us how the children were selected, but it had to be children, in order to maximise the time they would have to explore outer space. I gather the selection had to do with connections, as everything else did; who you knew where, as your family was set up for life in exchange of the sacrifice. Still, the child's natural skills and abilities also counted for something. The ones with potential to become curators and storytellers were especially sought after. They could both document their findings, and report back, or even achieve communication with cultures outside the planet if this was needed. It wasn't a punishment to be sent into the vessels, but a high honour, and the children chosen lived in the programme's complexes surrounded by luxuries untold, copious food, and plenty of knowledge and instruction for the last few years before they were sent up. The young people who mounted those machines were very sophisticated members of our society. I do not know if children from the ring could take part in this, but I imagine that it wasn't the case.

The number of vessels sent simply reflected the amount of time that was required to build them. But my generation had not seen this happening: the same two vessels that I had seen from the coast with my father the last time we were together still languished abandoned at the end of Old Town, beyond the Registry. There were different theories as to why this had happened. Some believed that the NEST programme had run out of money; some said that an alternative planet had already been found. And some believed that the Jump was no more than an illusion to keep us sane. The vessels were sent into the infinite void of space, never to return, never to find anything; at some point, people had become tired of sacrificing their youth to this monstrous lie.

The one thing that had surprised me most from my findings in the Registry: Verity, my little friend, the girl my father had supposedly killed, had been earmarked for a Jump.

Before my father did what he did, our family fortunes had not been in danger. We lived in Old Town. We had servants to look after us. We wanted for nothing. The vessels had been parked for so long by then that they were already in disrepair. If someone were going to decide to send them now, several years would be needed to make them fit for purpose. By the time they would be ready, I would have been too old to go: nineteen was the age limit to perform a Jump. I was lucky: I would never have that fate. Now, it did not look like those vessels were going anywhere.

When they Jumped, the children carried seeds with them, the building blocks of our civilisation.

Before the green winter, a few visionaries had an idea: to store in a repository—a building similar to the Registry, except they were called libraries, museums, *bibliothecas*, treasuries, vaults, archives, menageries, and other innocent names—the building blocks of an old custom that had defined their existence for over twelve thousand years: agriculture.

Until then, humanity had been weighed down by its past, trapped into interpreting collections and repositories put together many generations before them; but some saw through this mistake. They had the technology to do it, armed with new tools that transformed their repositories into monstrous centres for data-mining, collections destined to last forever. The seeds were an afterthought; they started by archiving the DNA of half the lifeforms on Earth. As always, they built a centre of untold knowledge, but they did so without asking themselves the right questions: where would these animals live, if they were to be replicated one day? Who would have access to their DNA? Who could use these resources in the future, if indeed there was a future ahead for humanity?

It was these very seeds on which Eli was building her own version of civilisation.

Eli and her sister had worked inside the wall, for the engineer in charge of preparing those seeds for their interstellar journeys inside the vessels. The men from the past had built the vault to store them deep within something called the permafrost; an iced strata of soil, I think, meant to last forever.

Unfortunately for them, this eternal permafrost melted. They rebuilt the vault.

The team in charge of this treasure travelled to the northernmost point of the planet every year, where they met with colleagues from other NEST programs scattered around the globe, in order to check on the status of this eternal vault. Eli's master had followed the usual protocol on his last ever trip to the north, many years back. He had collected the seeds, placed them into the little sorting pods, and brought them back to his compound. Once in town, he stored them in specially created conservation freezers installed in his chambers until they were needed. And there they stayed, for no trip happened, no Jump had been performed for decades. And there they still were, long after Eli's master had died, just waiting for her and her friends.

From this story, what surprised me most wasn't the forgotten seeds, or the first vault disappearing into the melted permafrost, or the fact that Eli had a life of her own while I attended the Registry school. What surprised me was that she lived inside the wall, all those years, long enough that she knew her way in and out of the place undetected. After Savina, she was the only other person I have ever met that had been inside the Barrier. Perhaps my stepfather. I had never asked; but this tallied with my knowledge of him, of his comings and goings, his business and his associates.

Eli was filling me in on all this information while she stroked her pet coypu. It was a large specimen, only a baby and already weighing around thirty kilos. She expected him to reach sixty-five, and maybe to ride him one day.

'We do not intend to farm animals here, plants only,' she said, as she played with his muzzle.

'Why not?' I asked.

'Rearing animals for their meat was also one of the ways in which they warmed the atmosphere. Besides, it happens to be the most unproductive way of using land known to man.'

'Where did you learn all this?'

'My techie master, he taught me these things.'

Eli explained that right before the green winter, millions of people were starving; but the remaining millions, apparently, went on undeterred, had not given up their frenzy of meat consumption. Only the poor had been affected by the shortages of water and food, the bad air, the forced migration, malnutrition and death.

'The ultra-rich continued evolving their technology as if nothing that was going on was their problem. First, they had escaped into exclusive compounds; then into orbiting houses; and lastly, into the ring itself. With time, half of us had been abandoned here.'

'But I thought the ring was created for the good of all humanity, and whoever went there earned it somehow, by pleasing the lady in white...'

She laughed at this.

'Of course, that is what they want you to think! That there is a predetermined order in what they did, that whoever ended up there deserved it more than us. The lady in white? Do you really believe all those children's stories? Let's face it, Pearl, they abandoned us here.'

All this made me think: was Arlo right when he said there were more people already in the ring and its satellites than down here? What did that say about humanity, what did that say about us? We had evolved separately for so long, two sides of the same coin, that it was as if two different kinds of human beings now sat awkwardly opposite each other: the ringers on one side, and the rest of us on the other.

Some of Eli's followers lived in the various barns, whereas she and the others, mostly from the first group who had fixed the farm with her and her sister, had claimed the main farmhouse for their use. It was decided that I would stay there, as Eli's guest. Her wife, Unity, also lived in the main house. Her name told me she was a techie, and she hadn't come alone. Some techie whizz-kids had followed her here from Old Town, perhaps with genuinely good intentions, perhaps attracted by this kind of easy activism they could abandon at any point to return to their comfortable existences. They occupied one of the barns, and worked endlessly over HivePods, punching commands on old-fashioned keyboards, dictating them orally to the machines, or drawing them directly onto the screens with their fingers. I saw them only once, but they were dextrous, worked fast. It was obvious they knew what they were doing, although it did not occur to me to ask what their task was, what they could possibly be doing holed up on a farm.

Eli had grown, not much taller, but definitely stronger. The years had given her a muscled body, toned and dark from working in the fields. She wore her hair cropped now, and her arms and upper torso were covered in images and writing and little *shuvani* protection spells. Three tiny luminescent sparrows floated over her collarbone. The heroes we were honouring in our ceremony were all going to the ocean. But not to swim, Eli wasn't a dreamer. And the farm needed something that could only be found inside the Barrier, inside the wall, at the end of the short half-moon of salty water available to the elegant oldtowners.

'It's suicidal!' I protested. But I knew better than to ask what it was: there were certain things Eli did for the good of her community that I felt she preferred to keep discreet, and ought to be illegal. I did not press her; I was a guest there, after all, and knew nothing, understood nothing. They had gone many times back to Old Town, taken what they needed from those who weren't sharing with others.

'Besides, if it really was dangerous, what do we have to lose? We are left to rot out here, we are left to die. It is different for you.'

'Why is it different for me?'

She laughed at this.

'Because you have a choice. You can go and live in Old Town, and become a storyteller, or a curator, or anything you want to do.'

I said nothing. It wasn't so easy, even for me, to do anything. No one could simply do anything. But it would be difficult to explain this to Eli. To my surprise, she added:

'And, now that you are married to a ringer, you know that you can go up there as well.'

'You know I could not do that; I would never do that.'

But I had thought about it, so many times since my

stepfather mentioned the possibility of my union. And I had married for that reason, had I not? I could not deny it. What did that say about me? I had been ready to unite myself with someone I didn't know in order to get away from the surface, following the stupid dream of becoming somebody, doing something.

'I looked out for you many times, in Old Town. But once I knew you were in the Registry school I gave up. It's impossible to get inside.'

'How did you know I was back in Gobarí?'

She laughed.

'Savina,' she said simply. 'What took you so long, little blue bird?' she laughed.

I had so many questions for Eli. When she left, the pond had lost some of its charm. It was almost as if I resented the water. I avoided my reflection in its quiet surface: it was as if the water was showing me something that I didn't want to see. Was the basilisk lurking down there, perhaps? I listened for the water, hoping to understand its ripples. And I knew that it hid more than it showed, there was more life unseen than seen there. And, in the process of this understanding, of transforming myself into one with the pond, I knew that other things also took place in the adult world, equally, under the surface.

I was alone now. I would sit on its deceptive little shore,

the tide ebbing. If I dipped my toes, I could sense its rippling, all the undisturbed life that hid down there. After Eli left, I started questioning everything. As always, jumping into the water forced me to confront myself, be attentive at the dark secrets within the water, the unexpected undercurrents, the unrequited embrace of the overgrown seaweed, the risk of staying too long, getting too cold, for sometimes the water was cold somehow, even if the forest was heaving. I was an explorer, discovering a new realm, where normal rules didn't apply. That's why Eli and I could make it ours.

I had many questions. How had she survived without it? How had she survived away from the *sierra*? She was a true believer now, of her own religion, her own myths; she had created the way of life I saw in front of me, and recruited all these people. But what I wanted to ask her more was this: why had my mother chosen to initiate her, and not me? For it was an initiation of sorts, I knew that.

This was the only question I could not pose. However, I could see in what she had achieved here the ending of a lineage that started then and there, at that precise moment, surrounded by young and old women, chanting and hiding and meddling on the shores of Kon-il. I could almost trace it. And, perhaps, I thought, I could have been this person, I could have led all these people that have gathered here, of all places, an abandoned farm, semi-destroyed by fire, in the middle of nowhere.

She had asked me to come to the farm to become their storyteller.

'We need one on our side, someone to give us hope, not overburden us with predictions of a new apocalypse; but, also, someone who can learn to narrate our side to others. None of this matters,' she said, pointing at the fields through the window, 'if we cannot tell it to others! You know that better than anyone. We need someone to show them how to dream, show them what this place can offer, to inform our opinions, establish our truths.'

'Why you think I can do this? I am not a storyteller; I have only trained as a curator, which is a much lesser form of knowledge-making.'

She dismissed my words with another wave of her hand.

'You are the closest I have, little bird. Out of everyone that I, or anybody here, knows, you are the only one who has seen inside the vaults.'

Eli's faith worried me: I had seen what storytellers could do, back in Old Town. Masters of imaginative thinking, curators of our thoughts, moving us into action. I did not have that kind of power within me. As a curator, my studies had concentrated on the act of organising, describing, storing and preserving information. The act of collecting itself fell on other, more experienced individuals, with years of curating under their belts. The art of storytelling was left for the truly exceptional. I assumed I had not been good enough to become a storyteller. I still had not even processed the different episodes of my life, how who I was and where I came from had conspired against me from the beginning, how those circumstances had determined to some extent what I could expect from my life.

In truth, I had gone to find Eli because I was lost, still. If I did not understand my own story yet, how could I communicate anything to anyone?

I had seen storytellers in Old Town, sipping *milbao* surrounded by their entourages. They seemed so confident, so sure of themselves. I had always wished I could feel like that about anything, only once. But, in truth, I was not sure about anything; I guess I had never been. The certainties that we were meant to infer from the Registry's collections had only generated more doubt and confusion within me. Eli's faith in me, however, was clear:

'Pearl, all those stories you told me, back in Gobarí! I learnt all the constellations listening to your stories! Their meaning, and where they come from, and what we could do with them. You brought them to life in front of my eyes! You taught them to me, and I was able to see through their lies.'

The word 'lies' threw me. Were they lies? And had I managed to convey this idea to Eli? If I had done so, it had been completely unintended. Yes, she was right, they were only stories, designed to make us comply. But I had not realised they were until that moment, in Benguele, when she told me.

Now, those first experiences with the storyteller observances felt frankly naïve. If I think of my younger self, I can only see myself in relation to how my body reacted, in feelings and emotions borrowed from the narrative, perhaps initiated inside myself, but ultimately provoked by others. The observance would start with some musical notes, which would always brush at the back of my neck, while the words of the narrative would fly around me, forming strange geometric shapes. And then there would be the taste of the weaving, or the interlocking of sounds, the union of music and words. For some it was a sour taste; to me, it was as sweet as *milbao*. Could I do those things? Could I produce a weaving that people were capable of understanding, empathising with? It was true; I had seen the collections. But my contact with them had only generated more questions, given me more uncertainties. Perhaps this was a good thing, not a bad thing: after my years in the Registry I could now interpret certain elements of our society, perhaps the ones that Eli was more interested in transmitting. Perhaps I could now reflect and create narratives that would communicate this to others. I only understood now, for example, that the vastness of the collection had made the teaching and storytelling of the collections themselves problematic. I was bothered by a number of ethical problems—what to collect, how to teach it, to whom—all of which had been left unanswered in our training as mere managers of information storage and preservation. I also felt uncomfortable with the amount of power that the storytellers accumulated: ultimately, what was told, and when, and to whom, was their decision. The incessant collecting was as problematic as the question of providing access to the information, deciding who would have access to it and who would not.

These vast collections, their duplicated robins and ospreys *ad nauseam* in the vaults we had inherited and adapted, only served as metaphors for the power that those people, mostly old men, accumulated. Were the problems posed by its colossal size an excuse for its secretiveness, for keeping the decision-making limited to a few individuals, calling upon the complications that would be posed by opening something so limitless to the public? I could see the shadow of my worry cast over the furtive acts of de-accessioning I had performed. I thought often of that person, risking so much by walking over the wall with her stolen stuffed animals, little flint objects, or the carcasses of crude centuries-old versions of HivePods. I see her deft movements throwing them out into the deep; I see her dodging other passers-by, elegant promenaders showing off their latest fashionable outfits, speaking loudly into their latest HivePod model, flaunting their wealth. Perhaps, some of them were even followed by an array of servants—paid servants, that is—a luxury that, after the Act, only the extremely wealthy could afford. These men and women and children would always walk a couple of steps behind their masters, carrying something for them: a picnic basket, an extra coat, a closed parasol. Nothing that they could not carry themselves. Lastly, I see me, always managing at last to find a secluded corner, a less visible spot, a solitary moment with no one in view, where I would perform my secret ritual. Only once did I miscalculate, and a little servant girl caught me in this act of treason; but she said nothing, and I said nothing. In her eyes, I was doing the most heinous thing: polluting the ocean waters, a crime paid for with life imprisonment. What I was throwing did not matter to her, but I knew only too well that what I was throwing *did* matter; it would make the charges worse were I to be caught red-handed. I went rigid but, to my surprise, she just smiled a little, and said *orí* to me, the *shuvani* word for goodbye.

Remembering these little acts of sedition, I knew I did not possess the right tools to do what Eli had asked of me. But I had to try. And I would start by recalling what I knew, what I understood.

17

Eli took me to an outer building, round like a little dome planted on the Earth. She opened its doors by entering a number and letter code on a pad, and made a gesture that I should go in. Upon my entering, a few lights turned themselves on automatically, following their ancient settings. I looked around me for a second, and was speechless.

The room was made up of round walls with round shelves fitted to measure, and on top a glass dome that allowed light in at any point of the day. In order to preserve the items from the light, the shelves were covered with a high-tech self-tinting glass, of the kind that reacted by darkening itself when exposed to radiation. A dedicated, carefully rendered space, equipped with the more sophisticated preservation methods. It reminded me of similar places in the Registry: telescopes, orreries, astrolabes. Three-century-old tech. Miniature paintings, drawings on preservation boxes. Manuscripts, scrolls, and as many books as I had seen anywhere outside an institution. It seemed that the Benguele woman who had first built the house had also participated in these small acts of treachery, insignificant on their own, impossible to ignore when superimposed together, one over another. I was in the middle of an illegal cabinet of stolen things.

Until that moment, I thought I knew everything that I needed to know, everything there was to know, about the Benguele siblings. I had even seen them sometimes, had some faint memories of them. As our closest neighbours, they had visited us in Gobarí, at least while my father was alive. After he was gone, we lost everyone connected to us, slowly at first, then with ruthless certainty. Everybody was gone, and our return to Gobarí, now as our permanent home, was built with the taste of solitude in our mouths.

Inside the round chamber there were pictures of the Benguele woman and her brother, printed in that old-fashioned way on paper, and pinned to the wall in the manner of decorations. In some of them were Urania, and even my father. I swallowed hard, struggling to order the narrative in my head. So, the Benguele woman had a brother, who was also a high-ranking official. This was Eli's master; that was why she had known about the farm. And they both had known my mother, Urania; that was how Eli and her sister got their positions. My thoughts were interrupted by Eli, who was still trying to explain the place to me.

'This around us,' Eli said, waving her hand at the unexpected myriad of objects and mementos, 'is quite likely why your stepfather got rid of the farm so quickly, after spending so much money on it. He must have been shit-scared when he found it.'

I knew what she meant. If this had been discovered on his property, he would have been accused of treason, perhaps even put in jail.

Eli explained that it would be my job to make sense of this madness. I soon realised that I would need to spend a few days, perhaps weeks, alone inside the chamber, visualising it all so as to try to make sense of how it was set out. She left me alone. However, despite my training, I couldn't find any obvious key to the organisation method. I made notes on some repurposed paper I found. I looked in vain for the acquisition ledger; there wasn't one. All these were indisputable signs of a secret collection, an illegal collection. The lack of order also made my task potentially more difficult on two accounts: the collection would probably have no thematic thread, no narrative of its own, but would be a haphazard selection of whichever items the Benguele woman had managed to pilfer at different chance moments. This would make the building of a catalogue, one that a storyteller could use later on for something coherent, much more difficult. Even worse: it was clear that, if I were going to put some order into the place, I would have to do so from scratch.

The Benguele woman, Eli explained, had been a traitor indeed. It had been revealed at the end that she was also a swimmer. For many years, perhaps her whole life, she had managed to keep her faith hidden from the rest of the world. At the end, she had not been able to resist—a swimmer is always a swimmer.

I did not reply that I knew this already, for she had been the older woman who had danced with my mother at Eli's initiation.

I did not know how to interpret my findings, how to interpret *her*. Had those things been de-accessioned, liberated out of a much larger repository, rather than stolen? Were they proof that I wasn't alone in my anxieties? Had I found a twin soul in the deceased swimmer? That was the answer I wanted to read in those shelves and drawers, the little wooden doors that, when opened, overflowed with detritus that spilled out onto the floor. I started looking underneath the tables, behind the little reading sofas, inside every cupboard door. Everywhere I looked I saw the anxiety revealed by the little mountains of things, displayed without purpose. The act of taking something for the simple sake of taking it. She wasn't liberating artefacts from somewhere else; she was bringing them here for herself, a senseless accumulation for its own sake.

I unhooked one of the pictures of my parents with the Benguele siblings, such a strange image, oddly discomforting, and looked deep into it. My parents were so young, smiling so broadly, that I felt unsettled. Who were those people? I could not recognise them at all. The background of palm trees and oddly-shaped yellow flowers I did recognise: a little meadow that used to exist in the direction of the pond, now overgrown and disappeared. The four adults were brandishing hiking sticks—my mother, hiking? I turned the strange object around; it was a sort of wooden square conceived to hold the image behind glass, possibly inspired by an old design I had seen in the Registry. There was something strange at the back, as if something too bulky was about to burst it open. I fiddled with some little metal flaps, and the wooden square at the back gave way. What fell to the floor wasn't the picture only, but a group of them. Already, as I knelt down to get them, my heart was fluttering wildly inside me.

There were images of me and my brother, as little children, holding bouquets of flowers and smiling. There were also crowns of flowers sitting on our heads, and we were both wearing costumes for the Jump, the dressing-up kind that children sometimes play in, or wear during actual ceremonies. The pictures could in fact have been taken during the last Jump in Old Town, which I knew we had attended. My brother and I weren't alone in the pictures: the little beanie girl, Verity, was also in them. Why did the Benguele woman have a picture of me and my brother and the beanie girl in Jump costumes, hidden away? It probably meant nothing, but looking at it sent a shiver up my spine.

I found something then, moving some stand-alone shelves, following an intuition.

Die now, little bird. Die now.

The pigeon, a small specimen, no larger than my forearm, was rotting behind one of the shelves, a gluey patch of green and pink feathers and little white moving things. Her two heads were turned in opposite directions, as if she was pointing around the room at the mess. She must have got into the building through some flap in the air-preservation system that had opened at the worst moment for her, become trapped inside this room nobody ever went into, and died here.

I remembered the osprey, and its nest, and its parasites. And this absurd idea of keeping all the pieces of the puzzle; what was there to do, except put the puzzle together again?

And that, I knew, would take time, would consume time. And, in the process, the person dealing with the puzzle would forget their real purpose: what they were meant to do with the artefact in the first place.

Already, while in training, I had understood something: we were as blind as ever. We were dooming ourselves to the same nonsensical repetition of the same nonsensical mistakes that the pre-Winter men had made. We were weighed down by things that had come to us centuries ago, for which we now had a crude sort of responsibility. No future awaited us, none at all. Our epoch, without a name, was slowly exhausting itself to a point of no return. No matter how much we had been told not to repeat the past, we were already replicating its mistakes. Our forefathers had also been weighed down by their ancestors' previous collecting, and that had made them unable to interpret their own epoch, to see what was coming. And now we were again weighed down, intensively cataloguing and interpreting the past, unable even to articulate our present.

Perhaps they saw something of what was coming, out of the corner of their eye. And they did what humans do: they looked the other way. Or, perhaps, they simply thought themselves eternal. For it was the idea of time itself that disappeared somehow for them, that they made disappear. They saw time as a continuum in which they were the highlight, the most enlightened women and men ever to walk the planet.

Their love of the digital was a sign of their strange relationship with time. There was no need to spend time going from place to place anymore, to invest months, years, in accessing culture, learning how to read, to look, to understand. One of their most successful digital inventions was still in use in the Registry. The tool in question reunited in digital form several parts of a given manuscript, fileted at some point in the past, and now divided between several repositories, scattered all over the planet. Over the screen, the pages would virtually recover their places, appearing as they had been before the volume had been destroyed, as if by magic. Before, some researcher had to go from one bibliotheca to another bibliotheca to see how the tome had been put together, and now everything was at their fingertips, without the need to leave their compounds. Of course, for this invention to be needed, it was necessary for someone previously to destroy these manuscripts, steal and sell their illuminations. It is ironic that the pre-Winter men themselves both destroyed the manuscripts and invented a way—digital, unreal—to put them back together. It is also symptomatic of their epoch: the destruction and the guilt;

first the ruination of everything and then the hurried, superficial repair. And they believed the fallacy that the digital would be eternal. Even after the rebooting of the systems that made their crude HiveCulture possible, the digital society, the connectivity that was lost after the Winter, lost in a moment, our painstaking work as archaeologists of the digital has shown us that not all that was in their own Hive had remained there forever. There are no forevers. They created a sphere that was meant to last an eternity; there are no more eternities.

If the woman of Benguele had been a collector of anything, it was of these digital archives, files and documents. She seemed to have been fascinated by them. It was clear that she had enjoyed exclusive access to the ARACNet, the web of satellites that had retained some use, even after energy was too scarce to power most web-spaces. She had access, therefore, to some documents that I had never seen, that I had never expected to see.

When I entered the cabinet room, I did not see the digital reading pods immediately. Eventually, I would find several of them, scattered here and there; they would prove the key, the real treasures of the collection.

I did not want to tell anyone what I had learnt in her private cabinet; I had to storytell it to everyone. I remember it well, the conflicting feelings of that day, numbing my senses a little: I was scared of what I had found, of course. But I was also relieved, as if I had always known, as if I had always suspected. Perhaps I had. A feeling as if the world didn't make sense somehow, a strange feeling of déjà vu. As if suddenly I had to reorganise all my knowledge of the world, what was good and what was bad, who to trust and who to mistrust.

There was nothing here for us. There was nothing left, nothing at all…

It was an account—secret, perhaps forbidden, maybe heresy—of what had happened, of the green winter itself. And it made sense, and at the same time it didn't. And this indeterminacy was so scary, so scary…

Die, die, now, my little blue bird…

I was mixing my childhood songs, I was mixing memories, I was mixing memories with dreams. What was reality transforming itself into? I was tackling the digital reading pods, her own personal archive of web-spaces. There was order here, there was purpose: there was a running theme. She had seemed to want to collect items on this topic and this topic only.

I knew the story of how the green winter had come to be, we all knew it. But all stories are half-made. And there is always another story behind, a different one, a slightly darker shade. And the green winter had not happened because of some strange animistic reaction by the planet, although it was a living thing, oh yes. It must be, after all. But that wasn't what happened, not really. Now I understood completely, utterly, what Arlo had said to me. I felt sick.

It happened then, another episode. Everything became too much, and all the objects seemed to whizz around me, turning and turning, making me dizzy. Everything became black, like the water at the bottom of the pond, and I lost consciousness. Eventually, Eli found me, crunched up against a wall. She had come looking for me because I had not been seen in two days.

I had found my story, a story worth telling. Now I needed to decide how I was going to tell it. Perhaps, if I forced everyone to dream a future, to imagine a future, we would have one after all.

18

They were all looking at me, so many eyes, so many faces. I could almost taste their displeasure as the seconds became one minute, two minutes, and still I had yet to speak.

The ring, I said at last, the ring. It had not been built during my parents' lives; I am not sure why I started by thinking that. Or was I speaking? I visualised the images that I had seen in the digital reader, and willed them to those around me; I wanted them to see them, I needed them to see them. And they all exploded at that moment, those images, triggering a series of emotions, my words, suspended on air in full form, painted in many different colours, the ideas I was convoking for them, forming pointy geometric shapes, difficult to swallow, to accept.

It was happening: somehow I was syncing the ideas and the words and the senses, exactly as I had seen story-tellers do. Perhaps I had a natural gift.

I got bolder. I showed them the ring being built slowly, many centuries back; the first hovering abodes perfected by the wealthy, and the ring taking shape slowly, slowly. And I showed them the other earlier versions, the places where scientists had orbited the planet before.

I showed them the first relocation process, less than one per cent of the population, the wealthiest families. I triggered the idea: they combined more wealth together, these families, than the rest of the people on the planet.

I was waving, I was syncing. I was enraged, they were enraged. I was telling, they were understanding. I was storytelling, or at least trying.

It was now or never. Arid earth. No green in sight. I had the notions inside me, the images inside me. I tried to sync again; this alternative reality resisted my audience, it almost resisted me; I myself had problems believing it.

The syncing started to fail. I was losing them.

Desperate, I thought of the Three Sisters, of those words in their fable, so difficult for us to understand, 'arid', 'desertic'; I tasted the words in my mouth, the hotness I knew well how to feel. I built around them the straight lines of their shapes: I was wowing again!

Earth had not been green. Next, the blue light. I knew what had happened, for Arlo had told me, for I had seen it, preserved in the secret digital pods. Then I hadn't been able to believe, or rather I could not understand what he meant. Now, I understood. The Benguele repository had finally helped me to do so. And emotions were triggered in many colours, an explosion of them, and the blue surge appeared in my tale, as always directed from the ring onto us, onto the planet, mismanaged, misused, by some who didn't care about us, why would they? We were nothing more than ants to them. The energy was released, with the idea of reforesting, at the same time from the five Upper Settlements onto us who remained below. I showed them how the energy surge worked, provoking the massive over-growth of some areas, overgrowth that showed no signs of abating.

I showed them the ring-dwellers' mistake. Now, every time they saw the bluish-tainted fluorescent sky, they would know: regular explosions of energy were still poured over the surface at intervals to stop the progression of the green, or to try to manage some areas, exactly as Arlo had explained.

Everything made sense now. And, as the pieces in the story made sense to me, so they also made sense for my audience.

Thinking of Arlo, of the ringers' lies, I felt a strong surge of love within me. Thinking of Arlo I saw other old men, all ringers, and other images started appearing when

I closed my eyes. I did not know if only I could see them, or if everyone around me could, too.

There was no lady in white in those images, only old, decrepit men, spinning her fable to the others. I opened my eyes and these images and ideas, spinning out of my field of vision, filled the air, running free. What was happening now? Was I storytelling, or having a vision? I had not read this anywhere, but I knew it to be true.

It was Arlo, and his love for me; he was guiding me to that knowledge.

I felt sorry for me, I felt sorry for Arlo.

The triggering sensation again, the surge of green, red, multicolour emotions, and the tinkering sounds, they all combined only one meaning: my story.

I fell on the floor exhausted, but relieved.

19

I miss my LivePod as much as I miss having her inside me.

Once a week, I hide behind the crowds and attend the storytelling observance. Well, not attend exactly, for I am a cleaner, a dirty surface immigrant. But I see it all, spy it all. The storytellers here are so much more imposing than down on the surface, there is no comparison. Down there they are no more than a cheap copy of what goes on up here. Even as I am seeing them performing, I am learning things: I study their light hand movements, the impossible colours they convoke, the neatness of their syncing.

I am not really allowed to do this, to be here, to experience these emotions, but somehow I feel I am owed this. I am still in pain where they cut me to take her out, and I ran out of illegally obtained painkillers weeks ago. The observances help me manage this pain, offer me some solace. Surely no one could deny me this.

This is the plan: I have to rescue my daughter.

I have found out some things: she has been named Alira. A new friend helps me buy some more information from a paying source: she is in the NEST nursery.

I shiver at the implications of this. Why a NEST nursery? I thought ringers did not send their children up in the vessels. I thought there were no more vessels. The paid informant offers some more, free of charge: the programme is being resurrected, and ringers will also make the numbers now. Only then do I realise something: we are a dying breed down there. Population is dwindling rapidly. And they are not counting on our survival.

I have to get in, get her out.

In the room where I sleep with twenty strangers, people start knowing my story, pitying my story, and they want to help somehow, although they have nothing themselves to give.

But if I ask for some *milbao* I am given *milbao*. If I ask for a different flavour *milbao* I am given a different flavour *milbao*. I was as huge as a whale; now, I am nothing, a deflated balloon. And they all bring the *milbao* to fill this absence. I cling to those little acts that pity me, mistaking them for power.

Where is she? Where is the NEST nursery? On which level? I need to start cleaning there, as soon as possible.

Soon, I cannot eat anything else except the *milbao* of the same make I had while I was inside the LivePod, waiting; everything else tastes of nothing, everything they grow here tastes of nothing, of the eternal void of space.

After my storytelling I went to see Savina.

She had decided to celebrate my visit, and the table between us was laid with an impressive assortment of delicacies. I could also see a steaming jug of pure green herbal drink. While I looked at it, the delicately moving liquid turned turquoise, yellow, back to green. Rainbow leaves. Precious, expensive, delicious. I could feel my mouth watering already.

'Please, Pearl, eat! I cleaned your *bú* when you were a baby, and still you are waiting to be told to serve yourself some food at my table!' Was she mocking me? It certainly felt that way.

'I'm sorry,' I replied, while serving myself some mango-bread and spreading grease over it.

'No, please, no need to apologise. Not to me, child.'

I looked confusedly at the scene, as if from the outside. What was I really doing here? Why had I sought out Savina, of all people?

My findings at the cabinet room had affected me

deeply. I had acted as a vessel, I had communicated. I was obviously better suited for storytelling than I had anticipated. However, immediately after the observance I had suffered one of my episodes; and, together with the one in the repository, that meant I had suffered two in rapid succession. I hoped this was normal: the effort of performing, and doing so for the first time, had to be accounted for. Everything felt so strange, so unreal. I needed someone to ground me again, and Savina was the closest thing I had to a family.

'It is good to see you, child,' she said, pouring some herbal drink into my mug.

'Tell me about my parents.' It wasn't a question; I didn't frame it as a question. It was a statement. It came out of my mouth without me thinking. The pictures in the Benguele house.

Silence cut through the room, and I started cleaning my fingers, sticky from the mango-bread, with one of the white napkins, in preparation to leave. Just as I was getting up, Savina spoke.

'What exactly do you want to know?'

What kind of question was that? She knew exactly what I wanted to know: everything. It was difficult to explain this to her, or anybody. Those images, the hiking sticks, the Jump dresses, kept dancing inside my brain, creating a narrative that I needed to order. But I could not do this without her help. There was no one else left. I said:

'Why did Mother take us to Gobarí? She must have known it was dangerous to live up there.'

Savina's mouth twisted as she rolled her eyes, a sign of her displeasure with me that took me back many years, down into the dark well of childhood. She got up slowly, and went towards her makeshift sink. Savina's house had no running water, but a clever system of pipes brought some in from a nearby well that belonged to a neighbour. I wondered if the arrangement was legal.

'How are things up on the farm?'

She didn't answer my question, but asked one of her own. I wasn't sure how much she knew about Eli's plans, if she knew anything. I decided that the best approach was to be as vague as possible.

'Everything is good. They have been successful with some crops, and are working hard to develop others.'

'Good! Let them do that.'

What could she possibly mean? It sounded as if Savina was dismissing Eli, and all her efforts. She resumed chopping some herbs that had been on the counter, and I said nothing. Suddenly, the display of food was not so appetising anymore. I sipped my drink; it burnt my mouth. She turned back to face me, the little knife still in her hand.

'I am their storyteller now,' I announced proudly. To my dismay, she snorted. I had expected her to be a little bit more impressed.

'You know nothing, all of you. You are children playing houses. What is Eli doing? She is bringing back to life the same things that caused it in the first place!'

'What do you mean?'

'Those crops! Those vegetables! Growing them was partly responsible, child, growing them without thinking, growing them in oversized proportions,' she resumed chopping furiously, 'putting things on them so they would grow faster and faster.'

Not so long ago I would have believed every word that came out of her mouth; now I knew a different reality, a new reality. If she ever knew what the green winter meant, how it had come about.

'Why are you chopping that?' I asked, hoping to make amends. 'Are you going to do some magiks? Can I help?'

Her eyes opened wide and she stared at me as if had gone mad. For one second I imagined this was possible.

'Magiks?' she said. '*Magiks?*' she repeated, obviously alarmed at the idea.

'I'm sorry, I thought that…'

'You thought what, child? What do you think I am about to do? Tell me, tell me right now, what you think I am going to do.'

I was confused; what exactly had I said to make her so mad at me? I tried to explain myself:

'Well, sometimes you chopped herbs for our recipes…'

'And?'

'Our *shuvani* recipes…' Was my meaning not clear?

After I said this, Savina held the kitchen counter with both hands, and let out a long sigh.

'Oh, child. Oh, child,' was all she kept repeating.

I felt worried now; she suddenly looked old to me, as if she were shrinking before my eyes. I got up and went to comfort her.

'Savina, whatever is the matter?'

She looked up at me, and she looked so tired.

'Who told you that I was doing magiks? Who said such nonsense?'

'We, you and me, did some, when I was younger…'

She shook her head, left and right.

'And why did you think that was magiks? Why do you call it magiks? They are recipes! They are cures! They are ways of extracting the properties from the plants around us! There are no magiks here, child!'

I waited, until the notion sank in. No magiks? The mixing of herbs and other things had been simply medicine? I remembered now her big, oversized stone mortar, where she would turn everything to dust.

'But,' I started, 'you used to sing while you put things in the mortar, and said words while you crunched them...'

'That is only to "help" the process, old wives' tales, superstitions my mother used to have. I repeat the same things she did because that makes me feel closer to her. But those words are not magiks of any kind! They are simply said to pass the time!'

'And the cards, the reading of the cards? You taught me to read them!'

'That is a game, child! You cannot possibly believe that people look at the cards for guidance! Everyone knows it is a game!'

'Some *shuvani* do not take it as a game, I'm sure of that!' I childishly protested; to which she replied, making me blush:

'And some techies give their babies to the ringers, don't they? But that doesn't mean that all of you do! Do you not think that there could be many kinds of *shuvani*? Some who believe in the cards, some who don't; some who will be good cooks, some who aren't? We are exactly like you! You understand nothing! You are looking at us with the same glasses as everyone else! And you, with your *shuvani* blood and all!'

I sat there quietly, my head bent. But I had to ask again.

'And what about *mullos*? Are they not real either?'

'Pearl, really? Those are only stories to frighten children.'

I had grown up so terrified of them, of my father, coming back to get me.

'Very well,' I said coldly. 'Thank you for clearing all this up.' If I sounded ironic, I could not help it. 'Now, could you please tell me about my father?'

She sighed again, and looked at me with much eye-rolling and head-shaking. But eventually she left the knife on the counter, and came back dragging her feet on the earth floor to sit down again. She considered the herbal tea, and said:

'We are going to need something a bit stronger.' She got up and produced from somewhere cranberry liquor and two glasses. She drank her first glass in one long swig, and served herself some more before starting to speak.

My father was scared of my mother, of what she could do to me. He feared that she would send me on a Jump.

He knew she was friends with the Benguele woman; she had enough contacts to put me in a vessel if she so wanted.

I state all of this, again, not a question in sight. To my surprise, Savina simply replies:

'No, child. Nothing like that.'

I realise I am still looking for reasons for my father to have protected me, for I *feel* that he intended to do so. But protect me from what, exactly?

'No,' she is saying. 'No one was going to send you up.'

Savina starts talking, and I am transported to another country, the past. I am playing with my little brother on the floor. I vaguely recollect that carpet, beige and brown, orange, with striking geometric patterns. My parents are shouting upstairs, and I try to get my brother to concentrate on the game. I am protecting him from the shouts, and the slamming doors, with all the ease of a person who does this regularly.

My parents are arguing about me.

It is difficult to follow, and I don't really want to follow the conversation, perhaps because I know what it is about, I have already sensed what this is about another time, perhaps before I was born, while I was inside Mother's belly, and she tried to swim away with me.

'She felt responsible, or as if she had done something wrong.'

'Very well. But that didn't necessarily mean that she was going to hurt me. Or that he had to take me away. Because that is what he did, right? He could have asked to dissolve the union with my mother.'

'You see, child; things are not always so crystal clear, are they? There was a lot in that union that wasn't right, although nobody knew at the time… Oh, but I knew. I was there. Your father did terrible things, terrible.'

'Like what, exactly?'

'Nothing that can be put into words… Things that he did again and again.'

'Did he beat Mother up? Did he hurt her?'

'No, nothing like that…'

'Then what?'

'Nothing exactly like that… But he hurt, oh yes, he hurt her… He knew exactly how to do it.'

Words, actions. Nothing as bad as bruises, nothing as terrible as broken bones. Or were they as bad as bruises, as terrible as broken bones? For those words, those actions, had broken my mother: not her bones, but her spirit. This was the second side to the story, the darker side. The unknown occurrences that take place behind the walls of a house; the privacy of locked doors, the hidden rooms of a union. It was more common than would be expected: more people than cared to admit possessed some 'hidden' *shuvaní* blood, even among the techies it was possible to trace some *shuvaní* descendancy, especially in towns like ours, where Jumps took place, with its long tradition of cultural melting pots. In short, there were more *shuvaní*-related techies than not in Old Town. But these families tended to obscure the fact, subtly, by letting their techie identity be the one covering it all, by carefully avoiding the performance of anything that could be constructed as a *shuvaní* trait. The question of the blood, once revealed, opened a wound within my family.

'Your family needed to trace back their genealogy for three generations, in order to keep Gobarí.'

'Gobarí?' So it had been the house, of course.

'He went to the Registry, did all the necessary research. Hired a curator to dig up the most obscure bits.'

Yes, they could trace the ownership of the house long enough, but other things were also unearthed.

'Your mother always swore she didn't know. It was a cross-marriage, more than a century ago; it was more common then. But, he claimed, it always stays in the blood, a hundred or a thousand years.'

I cringe. 'Yes, you had already told me about this marriage, many years ago, Savina. But I would never have imagined that was the reason behind it all.' She looked at me, raising her eyebrows, as if I was stupid, or as if I should have understood it all much earlier. Should I have? Had I willingly ignored this about my family as well? I hardly ever spoke about my *shuvani* lineage, not even Laurel knew. What did that make me? The *shuvani* caste was, without a doubt, the most hated in the Three Continents, the one that suffered the most. Was that the reason why I had kept quiet about it myself?

More importantly, was my father really so shocked by this, to the extent that it eroded the marriage? I hated what I was beginning to feel now, embarrassment at my own father, at myself. If he had those beliefs, what did that make me?

'He felt deceived,' Savina continued, 'developed his own ways of manipulation: once he drank a whole bottle of alcoholic *milbao* and lay there semiconscious; your mother saw him turn white and blue, thought he was going to die. He did this because she had announced that she was going to leave him. And this went on and on and on: she could not take his behaviour, and every time she said that she was leaving, he would pull some silly stunt like that.'

'I don't understand. She was going to leave him, and he reacted that way? I thought he was disgusted with her, and would have wanted to leave her himself!'

'No, no, no, child. You don't understand. He was not

interested in leaving her. He wanted to punish her. He had no intention of leaving. What he wanted was to make her as unhappy as possible, for as long as possible.'

Those last words were the ones that did it. They opened up the horrid possibility; and, for the first time, I could see—no, not exactly see, but maybe start to glimpse how it may have looked to others, recognising their narrative of what may have happened with me as a possibility.

The father that Savina's words evoked in her kitchen was an alien creature, someone who had fallen from the stars beyond the ring or even farther beyond. I did not recognise him. Then again, I never knew my father, not really.

I feel it then, finally: the waves welling up around me. But they are not taking me up, even if I make it to the horizon, these interstellar waves, ebbing and swerving; they will never help me become one with the cosmos. Instead, they are swallowing me into a big dark mouth that opens beneath me, as I descend into the unknown.

The ocean water beyond the wall must be colder than any I have ever experienced, colder perhaps than I can imagine. But I can intuit how it must feel to swim in it: I know well the refrigerated chambers in the Registry, where some bacteria specimens are kept. I have stayed inside them at times a tiny bit longer than I was expected to, enjoying how the cold chipped away, little by little, all my senses, numbed my fingers, until I was nothing; not Pearl anymore, not the junior curator, but simply a mass of bones and flesh gripping at her existence with desperate fingers. Now, I imagine that must be what ocean-swimming feels like, except that, once numb, surely you stop moving; and, once you stop moving, surely you stop managing your flimsy grip on the water. And, once that happens, all that remains open to you is to allow yourself to be swallowed up whole by the vast immensity of black, where no past, no present, no future, could possible exist. Only the enormity of the ocean and yourself.

'Look, child, the story I am telling you is not special; it is as old as life itself. It is we who pick up the pieces, again and again. As if we weren't already doing enough!'

'Do you mean the beanies?' I asked, not wanting to mention the *shuvanies* again.

'No, child! I mean the *rumi*!' By which she meant us women.

'Is that why he killed Verity, then? Because he wanted to punish Urania? But how were those two things related?'

Savina shook her head.

'No, child, your father did not kill the little girl…' But she would not say more. She got up, turned her back to me, and for a moment I thought she was crying. I had never seen Savina cry before, but I was elated by her answer.

'Savina,' I started, 'do you think they marry us to upper-settlers because they can't have babies up there?'

She pulled one of her faces, eyes wide open, and said:

'Don't get me started on the ringers! Besides, why can't they leave us in peace? Tell me, where do they come from? Are you sure there is a ring, that it is not a drawing they have put up into the sky? Are you sure there are people living up there? Because I am not, child,' she said, her face a sad, angry mask. 'There could be, or there could not be. Perhaps it is only something planted in our heads, and it has been like that all this time.'

Time? What time, exactly, was she referring to? But I could not dispel the similarities with my own conversation with Arlo. Savina did this often, acted as an echo of my own anxieties. It was as if she could read my mind, exactly as Alira might have done.

'Savina, you know why I have come here.'

I said this because she had looked me up and down when I arrived, pausing her eyes on my belly for just a slightly longer second. But, oh, she knew, she knew. Just by looking at me, she knew. She turned to me now and looked at me, frowning, clearly enraged at my words.

'I can't do it, child.'

'Even if it is not a spell, or a potion… Even if it is only medicine: I know you can. For if you can provoke the opposite, and I have seen you do that many times, there must be way of doing this as well. It is the other side of the same coin, is it not?'

'You don't understand me. It is not that I can't. It is that I won't. What you are asking me to do is to poison you.'

'Wouldn't you poison yourself, if you knew the fate that awaited you?'

'Don't ask such blasphemy, child, for I would not do it. How can you ask me such a thing?'

She knew what I wanted and I would not leave until she gave it to me. I decided to try another approach.

'Look, I need to go up there, I need to go into the ring. And I am not asking you only to do that, not exactly.' I touched my belly, an unconscious gesture.

She looked at me, horrified.

'Why?' she asked, her face contorted somewhere between disgust and pity for me. 'No, child, I will not make you infertile.'

I didn't say anything. I was thinking instead: because I must! Because I need to help Eli. Because I need to know what is going on up there. I need to see it, only then will I be able to tell the story as it needs to be told.

Perhaps she had read my mind; for she said nothing for a few seconds, but eventually got up, with much sighing and head-shaking, and went out into her herb garden. I followed her, and looked at what she did from the threshold. Some vine that hadn't been properly cut was spreading to one of the beds, and she took a machete that was stuck in a stump, and cut it with a dextrous movement. Then she collected some herbs. She also took a toad from somewhere and brought it back inside.

'There, child,' she said, instructing me to go into her bedroom.

It was half-dark in there; in a corner I could see some little orange feathers. They made me think of the pigeon that I had found in the cabinet room at Benguele, but also of the hare, so many years back. The sensation of crunching her brains had never left me, the triumph and disgust mixed together. Had Savina used some little orange-feathered animal previously, in some of her recipes? Was she right when she asserted that they were only medicinal? Was there no suggestion of anything unnatural in them? The little orange feathers made me shiver, and I looked the other way.

We both knelt in front of the stove by the wall, and she put a little stone bowl on top with some water. As soon as it started to boil, she threw her ingredients in; the toad she pulled apart with her hands, then and there, and removed its insides, all the while singing her little words, that she had been so sure were not incantations. The concoction inside the bowl smelled fetid. She said:

'To do what you want, you must drink this. I will let you decide. But there is no turning back from this, child.'

And with that she left the room, leaving me alone.

Everything went black then. But when did it go black, exactly?

I am back in the Registry, still have time to go for a walk in the quad before we need to report for the night. I come out and find myself next to the slope at the back of Gobarí, the one you take to go up to the mountain. I walk down the slope, and follow the path until I reach the middle of one of the clearest meadows in the whole of Gobarí. I see machines bringing up the earth with huge metal forks, but I am not sure I understand what they are doing. I see young men and women dressed in ceremonial robes.

The meadow has become a yellow expanse of wheat, one of the crops that Eli is growing, until it ends abruptly in rocky formations, small ranges, as it gives way to the beach.

Until that moment I thought I knew that spot well.

If I turn, a brief ante-forest, pine mostly, and Venus flytraps, and other things as well. At that end, the eucalyptus bushes.

I have been here on countless occasions, normally to harvest a little from the eucalyptus. I am familiar with the landscape. But now I cannot see exactly where the meadow ends.

I realise that I need to orientate myself a bit better, and look around. Where is the slope? Where can a mountain range, even a little one like ours, hide itself? The light has changed suddenly, as if the dark was gathering slowly, slowly, picking up consistency.

I set off, and walk for a moment. I had decided which way to go. But then I see, all of a sudden, that I could be going the wrong way despite my careful efforts. I turn round, and look for something, anything. After recognising the shape of a rock, I walk there, never quite reaching it. The *sierra* looms over me. So it is there, after all. An eerie sense of dread, the anxiety of looking into an abyss. I start drowning in that anxiety, in that fear. A fat white cloud passes by, revealing a sky of pale blue, burnt blue that is almost white. The sun threatening to burn it all, and the light changing once more.

Far away, the little red dot that I suddenly, urgently, know is Eli, flutters and shakes like a little firefly. She is perched on a rock, looking at me. Any moment now she will wave her hand at me in recognition. One, two, three... Any moment now.

Behind her, the hare appears, looms over her figure; and I know, painfully, urgently, that I will not get there to save her in time

I run towards her, but I find that I cannot climb the rocks and gradients as easily as I should. As if something were paralysing me.

When I look back she is gone. There is no one there. I still run, up and up, falling, stumbling, bleeding from the palms of my hands, fiercely running over dangerous rock formations and gradients, until I get there. Once up, I have to remind myself to breathe, and I double over, hands on my knees, exhausted by the effort.

There is a girl lying on the floor. Not Eli. Someone else. I crouch at her side: Verity, pale and beautiful at first, suddenly becoming grey and swallowed, as my brother had been. I take a branch, and I nudge her in the head. I know, at once, that she is already dead.

20

I notice I am being followed, oddly, by a bio-engineered bird, an old model with red, bionic eyes. The first time I see it, the bird is fluttering around me as I clean a section of benches in the piazza. At first I dismiss it with my hands, and continue working. Nothing makes me think that the bird is here for me.

But it reappears, and I worry.

I am on my ten-minute lunch break, and see it again while I hide in a darker corner, sucking avidly on a protein pouch. I haven't had real food in so long, I dream often of Savina's cooking. Postpartum pains come and go still, but this is the only time of day when I feel them, this and at night, when I am lying for a few hours trying to sleep among the coughs and the snores and the breathing sounds of my roommates. The rest of the time I am moving, moving, moving; working furiously in order to complete my allocated section on time. While I move, I have no time to think about any pain.

Now, the bird reappears. And once it even scans me with its bionic eyes.

I start shaking all over.

It is probably time to pay for one of my many old crimes: the acts of de-accessioning, or, more probably, my connection to Eli. I will have to disappear into the hidden levels for weeks, find another job. And this one has been very hard to come by.

After I drank what Savina gave me, I woke up alone in my bed, back in Gobarí.

I was in Savina's home, now I was here.

I took something, but I could not know if it had worked or not; or even worse, if Savina had tricked me. Whatever she gave me, it seemed to have given me strange dreams, nothing more for now.

But why did she bring me here?

That was not all she had done. She brought me here, to the last person I wanted to see. Why would she do that? Was this some obscene form of torture, of revenge? Next to me, Arlo sat in the semidarkness.

I looked up and I saw his blue-eyed face with his soft flaxen hair and his curly beard.

'Please leave,' I said.

Arlo moved backwards, his hands up in a gesture of surrender:

'We need to talk. Please.'

Why was he here? What did he possibly want to talk about with me? The end of time had finally caught up with us, signalled, among other things, by infertility up in the ring. Perhaps there were other things that went on that we were unaware of, even more terrible things.

Just looking at his face made me gag with disgust. I wanted to hurt him, I wanted to hit him; but I had no energy left in me.

'You are so sure of yourself, Arlo; all of you, up there. But don't you see? Nothing lasts forever. What if the ring falls eventually?' My words surprised even myself, for I had never thought of this possibility. But as soon as I blurted them out, I realised it was possible. Nothing was eternal, I had learnt that now. 'What then? Everyone you love, everyone who means something to you, will die.'

'Everyone I love is down here,' he simply said.

I was breathing with difficulty; recently I had felt so tired. It was probably what was growing in my belly, even then, after seeing Savina. As soon as I woke up I knew it: it was still inside me.

'The ring cannot be destroyed anyway,' he continued. 'It is connected to the axis of the planet by gravitational geo-engineering; if the ring falls, or if it is destroyed, the planet will also be destroyed.'

I considered this.

'Well, perhaps that's what should happen. Perhaps everyone should die. There is no point to us, to humanity, any longer.'

'We are all equally guilty, all of us up there. Your friend is right.'

'My friend?'

'Eli. That letter she wrote. She was right. But, don't you see it, Pearl? She and her friends, they were the ones that put that bomb on the Barrier, the week before our union.'

'You are being ridiculous.'

I saw his face drop then. It was clear that he had expected another reaction to his big revelation; perhaps gasps of horror, screams of anger, and me telling him to take me away from there, to save me. But I wasn't going to give him that satisfaction. I knew well how the narratives of our world worked, I had seen the truth so clearly; and no, I didn't want to give him that satisfaction. Besides, he was wrong. Eli might be a swimmer, but she wasn't part of those acts of terrorism. She and her followers were growing food, not murdering people.

Arlo sat back in the old wooden rocking chair. I felt

momentarily sorry for him, for us, for what was growing inside me.

But I loved Arlo as well, of course I did. I had fallen for him on the shores of the pond, as we read fragments from Gobari's remaining mildewed books to each other, books that had not been deemed important enough to be sold to the Registry, abandoned and untreated by any conservation machine, dearer to me exactly for that reason. I loved Arlo, a bit like I loved those books. I loved him because below his pristine ringer looks he was faulty, imperfect. He was real, somehow, even if he came from a place that I wasn't sure was. I loved him, but I didn't know if I would be able to love him forever, or even if I had space left for that love. He would not come with me where I wanted to go, where I needed to go. What was growing inside me... He must never know.

'The ring, your beloved Upper Settlement, is an abomination.'

'This place is no better, for all that you love it so dearly.'

He was wrong: I hated it too. I thought I understood the surface, but I didn't, not anymore. For me, it was filled with sorrow. I had lost everybody; I missed my mother and my brother terribly. And after finding out as much as I could about my father's crime, things were still not clear. Murderer or not, I also missed him.

Arlo approached the window, his back to me. Was he looking at the mountain range? Or at the sky, perhaps?

'What are you going to do now?'

'I am going to create prophecies. I am going to find things out and tell them. I am going to tell the story.'

He looked at me, surprised.

'Little Alira is going to fly up to the sky at last...'

'Don't call me that, it's not my name.'

Eventually, Arlo got up and left; left the room, the house, and I thought my life as well.

I was alone once more in Gobarí, exactly as I had been years ago, before departing for the Registry. I had taken from Benguele the images of my parents and my brother and me, and I was looking at us. The strange child, Verity, who had been my closest friend, and whom I hardly remembered, was also in them. I thought of the strange dream that Savina's fake potion had provoked, instead of doing what it was meant to. Verity... Why could I not remember her?

I knew then, with a strange finality, that my dream held the last key to the puzzle. For I should believe in my dreams, as Savina had said. In it, I had seen myself as if from above, attacking her. Had I hurt Verity, somehow, and that was what my father had been trying to cover up? The implications were horrible; but it certainly fitted the puzzle. Had there been an accident while we played together, in Kon-il, perhaps? Was her death my fault? And then my father had tried to cover it up, and was trying to escape the authorities with me, to keep me safe? And then, when we had been caught, had he tried to take the blame for whatever had happened? But what had happened, exactly? Why could I not remember?

I fell into an uneasy sleep, and woke up feeling heavy-limbed and unrested. For the first time, I rejoiced in the child inside me; but only a little. I had no intention of growing very attached to something that would be born to this world to suffer.

I decided it there and then, though. If it was a girl, I would call her Verity.

The Fable of the Three Sisters

There was once an old man who had three daughters: Vertina, Analetta and Florica, the smallest, and the one he loved the most. Their father was jealous of the sun, whose rays might burn their beautiful white skins, so he built them a house underground, spacious and luxurious, and so the old man kept his daughters imprisoned in a golden coffin. In these magnificent rooms they received the visits of suitors from all over the land, who came to them attracted by the legends of their pallid beauty. The visitors were all scorched, their skins dry and dark and red, thick and coarse, and all without exception brought news of the marvels of that desert world just outside their door.

One day, their elderly father fell ill, but only Florica looked after him. Her two older sisters spent their time daydreaming about their suitors.

When he was about to depart for the final desert, the old man called them to his bedside, and he made them promise him that they would never venture into the dangerous outside world. The two elder daughters agreed unwillingly; only Florica was true in her promise. That same night, the old man died, and the three sisters stayed sitting next to his corpse all night, although Florica was the only one who cried, for Vertina and Analetta only desired their underground penance to finish as soon as possible.

And so it happened that one morning the two elder sisters decided they would go out into the garden outside of the entrance to their underground world, just to the garden. They did not wake their little sister, for they knew that she would not approve of the idea. So Vertina and Analetta tiptoed up the round excavated stairs, and eventually they opened the heavy door into the garden. The sun blinded them for a few minutes. Little by little they got used to that infinite light, and with tentative steps they inspected the garden; only, there was no garden. Outside, the desert stretched, impossibly hot under the sun. The two sisters were dressed in heavy drapes and skirts, and, for a moment, they had to struggle not to faint there and then.

But the sisters did not know that their father, before he died, had asked the godmother of all, the lady in white, to look out for his daughters. So the lady in white, who knows it all, came flying down from the sky, and produced such a strong storm that the two girls disappeared in its blue light.

When Florica woke and did not see her two sisters, she knew instinctively that they had escaped into the outside world while she was asleep. But Florica was pure of heart, and she hated to have to disobey the promise she had given her father. Eventually, with a heavy heart, she decided she needed to go out to find them.

Outside, the lady in white who knows it all was waiting for her.

'You, as well? How dare you break the promise you gave your father on his deathbed?'

Florica said that she only wanted to find her sisters, and that she was very worried about them. The lady in white told her she must be punished for breaking her word.

'You will come to my house, and you will work for me until I decide your punishment.'

The lady in white made her climb into her magic, egg-shaped chariot, and they both went up and up until they reached the clouds. Finally, the chariot came down again in the middle of a grey and craggy moorland, where the lady in white lived.

A whole year passed, while poor little Florica worked as a slave day and night for the lady in white. She got up early every morning and lit the fire, swept the floors, scrubbed the table, collected twigs for the evening fire, looked after the kitchen garden, mended her nice clothes; she had time for nothing else. But, given that Florica accepted her fate without ever complaining, after one year the white lady said to her:

'I thought I would keep you here ten years; but you have been very hard-working and I must let you go now.'

The lady in white gave her a red velvet bag with three magikal stones: one would provide her with nutritious food every time she needed it; another had the power to open a magikal door wherever she asked for this to be done; as for the third one, the lady in white said that she could not remember what it did. Then she told her that once she left the wood, she should cross the steppe to the east, without losing view of a dark and tall mountain. At her peak, among the clouds, she would reach the place where Vertina was held.

Florica walked for a whole day, and another, and another, and it seemed that she could never reach the mountain. The magiks of the first stone kept her provided with food every time she was hungry. One night, when she was especially tired, at the end of the first week of walking, she thought about using her magikal stone to transport her to the mountain; but something went wrong, and the door opened on the arid mountain slope. She went ahead.

To give herself strength, Florica tried to remember happier days with her sisters, reading books to one another. Florica remembered one of her favourite stories, the adventures of a just and brave fighter who travels the land trying to avenge the murder of his beloved, until he himself dies, an old man. She wondered if this would be her fate.

Everything was silent. She stepped over some particularly crunchy thing. Shells? Bones? Of little animals. Babies. Broken pieces of flint. Where was she now? An ossuary? A graveyard?

'What are you doing here?' A voice, ahead of her, hidden in the fog. Eventually, the figure of a wrinkled old woman with yellow teeth emerged.

'Careful where you put your feet, child! If you break them any more, I won't get any money for them!'

'I'm sorry. I'm looking for my sisters. I need to get to the fortress on top of the mountain.'

'Really? Is that so?' The old lady broke out laughing, laughter that soon mutated into coughing. 'Don't you know that if you cross this desert to get there, you never come back? It's always been like this, and it will remain like this forever!' she decreed. Then, to Florica's surprise, she started singing: 'Crossing the desert to get to the fortress. Crossing the desert to get to the fortress. One by one we all die...'

'What is that? What did you say?'

The old woman ignored her.

'There is only death in that fortress, child! Don't be mistaken for a minute.'

The wolves wailed in the distance. Florica shivered. The old woman felt sorry for her.

'Wait, don't go so fast, let me tell you something that may help you. I ignore why you can see the fortress, for not everyone can. It is there, but at the same time it is not. It is really above us, among the stars. I am afraid that the door is not through the mountain; that is an illusion. It is a round, white fortress, with only one door. And you can only get there if you can fly.'

Florica thought for a moment. Even if the old woman was telling the truth, she had an advantage: the three magikal stones. She replied:

'Many thanks for your help, old woman. You have shared your knowledge with me, and I want to reward you.'

After saying this, she placed the first stone on the floor, took a step back, and suddenly there was bread and cheese and fruit and wine. She was going to offer this bounty to the old woman, who stood speechless before the miracle. But, thinking it better, she gave the old lady the stone.

'You will not be hungry again, or ever feel the need to come to this place to collect bones to sell.'

The old lady didn't reply; her cynical eloquence seemed to have disappeared, but Florica could see her eyes shining, and a thick tear rolling down her cheek.

All of a sudden, the old lady changed into the lady in white. 'Florica, you have proven to be hard-working, brave and generous, and I want to reward you.'

It got darker, and a cold breeze started floating in the air.

'Think of your sisters,' the lady in white instructed.

Florica thought very strongly of Vertina. A rift appeared in front of her, a tear in mid-air. She advanced a foot towards it, and crossed towards the unknown. Her surprise was genuine when she found herself on the other side, floating over the ground, travelling up and up and up. So high she travelled that she left the planet, and still she had not reached the round white fortress. And she found herself swimming among the stars, and still she had not reached the white fortress.

Eventually she arrived, and her floating took her directly to a window, behind which was her sister. Not knowing what to do, floating in the sky on the other side of the window, Florica looked in her velvet bag for the third stone. And then something else happened. A blue fluorescent light erupted everywhere, blinding her. Florica passed out. When she woke, she was lying by the mountain slope, but the mountain was now covered in a deep velvety substance. It was cool to the touch, fresh and covered in drops of water. The colours were impossible, a colour she had never seen before. Next to her were her two sisters, both asleep.

'Vertina! Analetta!'

Beside them there was the lady in white.

'Well, well, well.'

'Leave us in peace!' Vertina and Analetta cried out.

'No,' Florica explained to her sisters. 'She has helped me find you.' She knew of the immense power of the lady in white and realised that they would only stay together if it was her will.

The lady in white continued, 'You must love your sisters very much. You certainly deserve some reward for your bravery and perseverance. However, the three of you still need some sort of punishment for not fulfilling your promise to your father on his deathbed.' The three sisters held their breath, awaiting the worst. 'I will take Analetta to the white-ringed fortress to live with me.'

'No! Why?'

'Because you all need to remember the meaning of the word "duty"; for living up in the fortress will be a sacrifice that only a few will need to make in order to save us all. Vertina will need to apply herself to her books, and, if she wants to stay down here, she needs to become a more productive member of society. And you, Florica. You, the youngest and most beloved of all daughters. You have shown that you are capable of enduring great suffering and sacrificing yourself for others. So be it, then. Put to good use everything you learnt in your time with me, all the knowledge about herbs and remedies, and help Vertina to achieve her goal.'

And that was how the sisters were given their tasks, and how the three castes of the world came to be.

ARLO

21

I could have told her about the bacteria, then and there. I should have. But I didn't. Now, she was gone from my life. It had been discovered by accident: some thought it was a mutation that had occurred spontaneously, due to the fact that, in some large sections of the planet, plastic was its only available food source. In any case, Ideonella sakaiensis 202-F5 was a plastic-eating bacteria; unfortunately, it did not eat every single kind of plastic that our ecosystem had inherited as debris. It was clear that there was a possible future solution if we continued researching the micro-organism; it was also clear that the Settlement did not intend to do this at all. In fact, the project was bound tight with the highest level of secrecy, and nothing could pass down here. When I had come down from the ring, I had signed NDAs to this effect, as well as for many other things. At the time, I had not seen any reason not to do so. I was happy to comply with what was required of me.

Now, even after so little time down on Gobarí, I wasn't so sure anymore that I didn't want this to be revealed to the world: I could not find any other reason for the secrecy than the Settlement's insistence on keeping power over the surface. At least, I thought, she ought to know.

But, how to reveal it? Who to tell apart from Pearl? I did not have a sample with me. And I doubted there would be sophisticated enough labs down here to help us understand if the Three Oceans could be cleaned for future generations as a result of this research. No, down here there were no labs, not really. The surface was a place for the repositories, the curators, the objects, all of which kept their inhabitants entertained, so they did not have to think too deeply. The truth was, the ringers were not interested in Earth anymore; nothing called them here, they were not going to come back down to this mess. And, if they did not need the bacteria themselves, they would do nothing about its existence simply to help those below. And I was part of that. How could I live with myself?

So we said our goodbyes. I knew she would go back to the farm, for Eli. It was a sad goodbye; somehow I knew that eventually she would find a way of going up to the ring, without me.

I found a small hut to rent in one of the settlements that I had used for my research. Days passed; my solitude was unbearable. I felt as if all the trees and all the leaves and all the flowers were laughing at me. I felt so lonely, I even started missing my family's bio-engineered bird, a hybrid of pre-Winter bird types, which always kept me company whenever I escaped to read a book in the solitude of the deeper rooms of our little compound.

Eventually, I couldn't endure it any longer. I packed a few belongings and started walking. Once I was on the road, I turned in the direction of Benguele, almost without thinking what I was doing or where I was going. I had lost Pearl for good this time, that was clear. But, equally, I felt that we were not done yet, that our destinies were still interlocked, our story had not yet run its final course. I reached Benguele, but of course I didn't see her: on arrival, my allocated quarters were placed in the barns, together with the rest of the volunteer land workers that had come to join Eli's revolution.

I was quickly allocated a set of daily tasks. There was some beauty in the simplicity of this life: hard work, rest, and eating all together around a fire at night. Other workers seemed bemused to find a starborn among them, but I never felt excluded, or in danger. Sometimes I would be surprised to see a woman looking in my direction; this happened more and more regularly, but I kept my distance. One day, we were picking mushrooms, and I teamed up with Vania and Dika, brother and sister. When we were done, everyone collected the different tools and took them back to the shed, and I caught Dika advancing in my direction, waiting, slowing down.

'Hey,' she said.

'Hey,' I answered.

'Look!' and she opened her palm, slowly like a flower, and showed me some mushrooms she had kept. 'Do you want to come and have some?'

The way she was looking at me, I wondered if hallucinating mushrooms was all that she had in mind. I followed her behind the shed, and she put the little mushrooms onto her stuck-out tongue, and put her arms around me. I kissed her, deeply, partaking of her offering.

I woke up, as if from a dream without images, or as if someone had cut out the intervening hours between our kiss and this. I was in the middle of a crowd, the sky above me a furious blue. People were chanting my name, 'Arlo! Arlo!' as well as the names of others. The yellow sandy paths had disappeared, covered by leaves and flowers, making strange patterns, the constellations now formed on the Earth as well as above. Other ornaments were there, woven with sedge.

It was that strange time of the year, when the colder months give way to a bursting spring. And the spring would make way for summer, and temperatures would soar, higher and higher, or so I had been told. Heat, heat, and more heat. The oleander flowers would die. For nature was meant to have its cycles, even now, even after all we have done, and all that had happened. I had been warned that the smell of carcasses would conquer all during those hellish months, those months when the cork sheets would pull easily from the trees. Their harvest would have begun then, exactly like every year. But not anymore… The cork was used to furnish the insides of the vessels, and no one was building vessels anymore.

There would be no ascension, no Jump.

Sitting at the table, we were enjoying an elaborate feast. What am I doing here? I was thinking. It became clear that Pearl was not in Benguele; or, if she had come here, she had not stayed long. She wasn't at the feast, a feast partly in my honour. Those who marched were being celebrated like heroes. And that mimicking of the other ceremony, the Jump ceremony, was playing with my head, I know. Perhaps it was the feast, or the mushrooms I had eaten. We were wearing imitations of ceremonial robes, the women in the long white skirts and those crude woven garlands on their heads. Where were we sent? What was the mission? What had I done, or agreed to do? It hardly mattered. Recovering this or that or the other, something needed for the community, a missing piece in their never-ending puzzle of beating the end times.

I felt sick, made sick by the wine, by the meal, by the mushrooms that I had taken. It would be time soon. The procession approached wearing their animal masks, like distorted creatures from Hell.

When I was a boy, up in the ring, far away from here, so far away, the fashion for nostalgia reached new heights one season, and the cloned pets of extinct animals became the craze. Cats and dogs and even rats. Not our versions, of course, bio-engineered to be as clean as little birds.

Little bird, little bird. Where have you gone, my little blue bird?

Our own evolved species, the orange hare of Pearl's childhood nightmares, those she had told me about on our afternoons by the pond, were very different. She was right to fear animals, for they were unpredictable, and all of them raged with hatred for us. The hares she feared so much were huge creatures, covered with yellow stripes as a kind of war paint; thankfully, they only lasted one summer, and disappeared as silently as they emerged.

Or those wild horses that ate human beings; and all the birds, of course, huge and hairy and beautiful, that they now called abominations, unnatural; as if we had not done that to nature ourselves, as if she had chosen an uncanny path to spite us. All those species we did not care about up there, for we would not have to suffer them. We were clean of them, our pristine-tamed sections of generation-old exemplars, well-tended, well-kept.

The same happened with the gardens of my childhood. It is absurd to say that they felt unreal, for they *were* unreal, of course. There were also, for a long time, the most real thing to me. Imitations of century-old gardens, they were, they are, with their geometrical designs and their lack of excess. Everything exactly as it ought to be, not in reality, but in somebody's dream. Those images were the picture postcards of my childhood, and still I knew that the nightmare down here *was* the reality.

The feast had finished, and I had yet to understand why I was being honoured with the others. The wine and the heat forced me not to mind in the slightest. Whatever was happening, I would submit to it, I would accept it.

It was that hour I liked so much, when the light looked very alien to me, now bluish, now green; *turquoise*, someone had called it. Neither the colour of the ocean in the olden days, nor the colour the sky should ever be; but rather, I had understood, the colour of the atmosphere as it only looked in dreams. At the back of the field, the *macheteros* were still working hard, preventing the green from reaching the edge. With every thrust, a fresh smell of recently cut grass reached me, such a pure smell, exactly as real grass ought to smell. Above the house, the peaks of the mountain range shone indigo, cut against the now purple sky. I knew that I would say yes to anything, to everything.

I volunteered. Once I understood what the new mission consisted of. There were many reasons for doing this, or at least that was what I kept telling myself. There were many reasons, but only one that mattered: Pearl. I wanted to explain, I needed to explain. But I couldn't, of course, for she wasn't there.

Although it wasn't exactly true that I hadn't seen her: that day of celebration passed as if in a dream. The procession, the paths decorated with green, the feast. And, to top it all, the woman on the newly built wooden stage.

She looked as if she was made of fire itself, as if she breathed fire, a bluish-reddish fire. And, out of this fire, a symphony of colours and sounds that weaved her tale.

Through her storytelling, I saw the Kingfisher resolving itself into a Fox; and I understood this to be a bad omen for the days to come.

I saw a group of warriors fighting a round metal

monster; and I saw inside my mind's eye all the injustices ever committed against beanies, techies.

I saw an old building, with an egg-shaped dome, floating slowly into the stratosphere; I knew deep inside that the warriors were going to a certain death.

I saw that they all knew, had known; or perhaps they didn't but she was telling them now, then, at that moment: for I saw the ring circling over us, and sending the blue light into the sky, and the plants moving and covering all, farm, fields, machinery; men, women, children. Another settlement annihilated from above.

It was only when I saw that I knew her, as the crowd dissolved, but Pearl looked at me.

Alira, Alira, and how will we know if you are the one?

There was an instant of recognition, perhaps; no, she was looking over me, at something behind me. I turned around, following her eyes, and saw nothing there.

Still I am not sure if I lived through this scene, or if it was a dream after all.

I could not sleep for days. I was scared; of her being right, the baby farms and all of that. I had never seen it happening, but, somehow, I knew it to be possible.

Do you want to know the truth, little bird? Can you handle the truth?

Up there, we had always known: those blue skies after

each surge of energy sent from above, trying to 'manage' what cannot be managed, to recover what had been lost. Perhaps, I thought, when I come back, I will tell her. And perhaps, only perhaps, she will forgive me. It was a nice lie to tell myself.

22

Try as I might, I could not do it, I could not leave without speaking to Pearl. I appeared at Savina's house unannounced, but she did not seem surprised to see me. There was a mocking smile on her face, dancing there. She hardly acknowledged my presence, and continued chopping her herbs, an acute acidic smell filling my nostrils with each one of her movements.

'She is not here, *jeré,*' she said. So she knew what I was doing at her door, of course. She said nothing for a few seconds; I said nothing for a few seconds. I felt lost, exhausted, out of my depth. But I did not want to give her the satisfaction of realising.

Eventually, she took pity on me.

'Do you know the coast well? I bet you look at us all the time from up there.'

She was walking in my direction while she said this, slowly, moving like a snake. Of course, that part of the coast was engraved inside my brain, a circle curving upwards, and the blue sea pushing into it from one end, and the hellish green enclosing it from the other. The coast was a white curve there, minimal. I had not told anyone about this, but up there we all knew: that coast was going to vanish one day.

'I think I do.'

She smiled again. Her sly smile scared me.

'There is a place up north, following the coast,' she said.

'North?'

'It is between here and Old Town. There is a spot her family was fond of when Pearl was little. An alcove of rocks, a little beach like a half-moon, from which you can see the vessels sitting quietly in the distance.'

'Is she there?'

'She is there.'

She said nothing else, and went back to her cutting and dicing and chopping. I thanked her and took my leave.

It was called Kon-il. Once back in the house, I entered the coordinates in my HoveLight300, and saw that it was no more than forty minutes' flight. If Pearl had gone by foot, it had probably taken her a morning to get there. I climbed into the machine, pressed the automatic, and let myself be taken.

The sky was a strange violet colour, unusual. Horribly, I understood what was happening, although I wish I didn't: up there, in the ring, someone had pushed a button. I remembered my childhood days, when I first asked about the strange lights and what they meant.

'They are nothing, an optical effect, very much like the Aurora,' my teacher had explained.

'The Aurora?'

'The Aurora Borealis.'

And so, I had been fed this lie: that the surges of coloured lightning were a natural effect, not man-made. Hearing about the Aurora had fascinated me, starting my interest in the life and culture and nature of the Northern Hemisphere, or what was left of it. The day I realised those lights were nothing like that, I felt strangely humiliated, as if I should have known instinctively what had a natural origin and what was man-made. But no one could anymore. Eventually, when I was older and attending the gymnasium, we had been encouraged to attend the energy surge sessions, and it was explained to us what they were. It was then confirmed to me, the lie. And still, we had been expected to feel proud of what we were doing.

I followed Savina's directions to the beach, where I found her: Pearl. In fact, the little half-moon of white sand was almost empty, but I saw her immediately, splashing about the ocean water. I wondered idly about perching myself on a rock, but thought better of it. They had sharp edges, and I worried I would cut my feet. I could see the two phantom vessels in the distance, unfinished, translucent and imposing, and the wall at the end of the water. But the wall looked much farther here than in town. It was nothing but a thin line, out on the horizon. I wondered if it would disappear if I closed my eyes.

Not knowing what to do, I entered the water.

The rippling waves caressed my feet.

I jumped in, hands and head first, and emerged re-energised. Suddenly, everything that I had been dreading was a faraway memory; the water had washed away all the fear. I felt that if I spoke to her, she would understand.

She had seen me, and was coming my way, with deep strokes. And I in turn could see her swimming, and felt that if we stayed there, in the water, nothing could touch us, and we could be free.

She reached me but didn't say anything, only my name, softly, and she embraced me. And together as one we twisted and twisted in the water, kissing and embracing and letting go of all our fears.

A feeling overcame me then, of wanting to be free, with her, forever. For a second, I considered what would happen if I pushed her head down and didn't let go. And it was so real, so intense, that I scared myself, and started moving towards the shore. Absurdly, I thought that, if I had stayed close, I would have drowned her.

I was exhausted, lying in the sand. I had not swum for aeons, and up till that moment I had only done so in the pools of the ring and in Pearl's pond. The ocean water was different, heavy over my limbs. She got out eventually, and came to rest by my side. She was wearing a thin white ceremonial dress that clung to her legs and her torso.

'What if we did it?' she asked. 'What if we swam never to return? You and me, Arlo?'

I could not formulate a reply, for I had had the same desire, I had felt the same pull. But then she laughed, and I knew she was teasing me.

'I am going up there,' she said then, pointing at the ring. 'There are things that I need to find out, things that I need to discover, and process, by myself. I am on a journey, Arlo. A journey to learn.'

'To learn what?'

'How to tell stories. Will you come with me?'

'I am going up north, I have volunteered,' I said. What I didn't say was that I wanted to prove to everyone at the farm that I was on their side, because my intention was never to return to the Upper Settlement. I also didn't tell her that up there she would be used and spat out again. I wasn't sure how, I could not articulate how; I had seen it happening too many times to so many who came from down here.

'Will you come back?'

'Yes! Although it may be months, years, before I find what I am looking for.'

This would be the last time that I saw Pearl on the surface.

I should have told her then, another wasted opportunity. About the bacteria, of course, whatever hope it might afford to the people down there. And I should have told her something else, but I chose not to.

It was Dika who had told me. We were lying on the soft yellow floor, hidden behind a hay bale. I liked being with Dika. It lacked all the complications of my union with Pearl, although I was missing her terribly, with a dull ache in my heart. Dika knew Pearl was my partner, my companion, that we had been united.

'It must have been difficult for you, loving her. After what she did.'

'What are you referring to?' I knew that things in

Pearl's life had not been easy at times, but I truly was lost as to what Dika's meaning might be. As a beanie girl in the *sierra*, she had grown up around Benguele and Gobarí, taking up seasonal work whenever it was available. She was a few years older than Pearl, and remembered seeing her around.

'She killed somebody, didn't you know?'

I sat up with a sudden movement to look Dika in the face. She had all my attention.

'Who? Pearl?'

'Yes. She killed a little girl, Verity. They were always together.'

'She killed a girl? When? How?'

'She was little. It was a sort of accident, they were playing at being swimmers.'

'What are you talking about? And how do you know about all this?'

'All of us knew, Arlo! We knew Pearl liked playing dares with beanie children. Verity drowned, they were best friends. Her father tried to conceal it. Everything was hushed up, to protect her. Her mother, and the woman who lived here; they all went along with it.'

Now, things were clearer. The whole horrible meaning of the affair dawned on me, the story taking shape in my mind. Her father must have tried to conceal the body of the girl, and then tried to escape with Pearl, so as to hide her and protect her from the authorities; which is ultimately to say, from us. No doubt he had been seen disposing of the body, and accused of the crime himself; and surely his wife and friends had agreed to his suggestion that he ought to take the blame for it, in order to save Pearl.

'But,' I found myself protesting, 'if the girl drowned, it could have been an accident after all…'

'Someone had hit her on the head before. With a *coquina* stone.'

It could still have been a childish accident, I had no doubt about that. My own brother had once been responsible for one of our classmates losing an eye. They were two kids, fencing with some metallic tools they had found lying around; and next thing you knew, the boy was lying on the floor in pain, his hand trying to keep his bloody eye in place. I knew these things happened, and I was sure that did not mean it had been an intentional act; but what I also knew, with increasing finality, was that Pearl wasn't aware of any of this, and that surely she did not remember the event, perhaps she was not even conscious of it taking place. Or was she?

I could not do much with this new knowledge, at least not for now. I needed to concentrate on other things. If I ever saw Pearl again, perhaps I would try to explain.

Eli and her followers needed something from the vessels, an important component which would help them keep the seeds longer. An incursion into the abandoned vessels in Old Town had taken place, only to find them dead inside, hollowed. What was needed could not be recovered from those abandoned pieces of junk. I found myself offering the solution: there are other vessels. *Where?* they marvelled, as children would. And I in turn marvelled at their innocence; for it was obvious that they could not truly, really, see beyond their forest and their farm and their *sierra*, whereas we could glimpse the magnitude of our task from above, from the stars.

There were other vessels, other NEST programmes operative. The one I knew about was in Pan-Inuit territory. They marvelled again at this piece of information. Did they look more wholesome, those vessels, than the ones here? Oh yes, I confirmed, they do. I did not add that anything, anywhere, would look more wholesome than anything here, in this forgotten southernmost part of this dying continent.

Second problem. How could we go so far? When the ice melted, the Pan-Inuit had to move inland into the

Jutland peninsula, a long way from Benguele. We would have to cross the whole continent. And then I found myself saying to these children: my HoveLight300. *What?* they asked, so I translated for them: my hovering vehicle. Latest available model, with enough power to climb up to the ring itself. Surely it would deposit us there in no time. I calculated the flight at four hours there, and four hours back. That was provided we could do the whole flight in the lower atmosphere. Otherwise, no more than seven hours there, and seven hours back.

I admit that I enjoyed my brief position as saviour.

Third problem: none of us knows how to manoeuvre your hovering vehicle. Solution: I would come as well.

And, as easy as that, it was decided.

That was why I would soon find myself there, flying over the never-ending white expanse.

23

That is why I find myself here now.

Here and there, darker rocks emerge from between the snow, some scattered flaxen shrubs. Far away, I see an arctic hare running away from us. We are now flying very low. It is too far to tell, but I know that it is probably as big as me, perhaps bigger. It is white and grey, with green fluorescent patches. It makes me think of past times, when men hunted seals, whales, and other animals unknown now, or made holes in the ice to find some kind of fish now lost, called, I think, halibut. We follow the hare for a while, and eventually it disappears.

I am not travelling alone. My companions are Vania, Alexander and Bohemas. Children of the south, of the heat and the colours, they have kept quiet in the past few hours of flying over the white. They say nothing, and I say nothing. Back in Benguele, I had explained what kind of clothing would be required, and how to procure it. It soon became obvious that we would need to manufacture everything, an invented uniform of dead animal skin, fur and cotton. When I explained this, and told them we might need to cover ourselves with the animal fur, they looked at me with horror. Surely they had misunderstood. I tried to explain that this was very common among the Pan-Inuit, and that people everywhere did it before the green winter. They did not seem to believe me. I was forced to insist, for I knew there was no other material that would keep us alive.

Now that the cold has permeated even inside the vehicle, and Vania and Alexander and Bohemas have covered themselves with everything they have found, I smile to myself. Luckily, I had insisted on throwing some extra furs inside the vehicle, convinced that they would be useful. The three of them are wearing southern red rabbit faces on their heads as hats, the long floppy purple ears tied up under their chins.

I am too tired to drive; however, I have not dared to use the automatic pilot, in case our course could be seen up in the Settlement, and have resorted to manual. I have been driving for hours and hours. After a while, I notice how they nudge Vania, and he gets up slowly and comes to me, saying that he wants to learn the rudiments of flying my 'machine', as he calls it. I am surprised, touched that they had thought of relieving me of this work, and readily accept. He doesn't look that happy, and I realise that, perhaps, a drawing of lots has decided who will take on this onerous task; I agree nonetheless to go ahead with it. After half an hour, he can control the main features, and once he knows how to programme the basic routes, he is good to go. Grateful, I take a nap.

After thinking that we could perhaps be seen up there, we had also decided to fly as low as possible, and this has meant doubling our time. Once we arrive, we plan to hide the vehicle, so I will need to descend as soon as a pine copse close enough to NEST appears. I have never descended among vegetation; and although I know it is possible, and am trained in all the basics of emergency landings, I have no idea if I will find a suitable clearing between the trees.

I am not sorry to be here, not really; although there is, as always, a doubt nagging at me. I know Vania, Dika's brother. I have often harvested or done some other kind of work with him, or with a group of people that included him. But I have never spoken to Bohemas before this journey. He seems to be a surly man, unusually taciturn, at least for the kind of fierce warrior to the cause that I have been led to believe he is. He is as dark-skinned as Vania, both with the leathery complexion of those who labour long hours on Eli's plantations. The presence of Alexander here baffles me: for he is one of the children of Unity, and I have never seen him unglued from his HivePod, pushing the keyboard, speaking into it, lightly drawing command-instructions with his finger poised on the light blue screen. I am told that we may need him to open the doors to the machines, perhaps to input some light commands needed to retrieve the piece that we are looking for. He is a stout young man, not used to work with his hands and dressed in garments that once were fashionable in Old Town.

And still, and still… Something is not quite right here. Everyone is vague as to what this piece is, what its usefulness would be. Why bring him, a dead weight, someone who may delay us, perhaps get us into trouble?

In Benguele, I had tried to impress on them all the need for bringing some kind of firearm on the journey, but they had insisted on their machetes instead. There were no firearms on the farm. Eli had claimed not to own any, but she had also admitted that she knew where to find some. I saw this as a sort of admission of her connection, even if only a mutual sympathy, with the group that had been wreaking havoc all over Old Town. It was difficult for me to accept that, embedded as we were into our own—Pearl's and my—private drama; we had hardly followed the news. But the explosion in the Barrier had been followed by a couple of smaller attacks. They had poisoned the *milbao* in one of the restaurants in town, one with those signs on the door: 'No beanies. No shuvanies. No exceptions.' They had staged a mass suicide, fifteen of them swimming past the wall into the depths of the unknown.

We get to a snow-covered field that separates us from the compound. Jutland is now an archipelago on uncertain shores, continuously changing—this world has no more certainties, it seems—and circumscribed with unpredictable ice. The snow plains also mutate capriciously: it has been difficult for me to remember which way to come, even with my cartographic training; the geographical features always mutating. I had been assisted in my endeavours by the many screens and panels of my vehicle, the little flickering lights giving me clues as to the locations that I am seeking. The compounds are not kept under a coat of mystery; after all, this one now runs those improvised tourist visits inside the vessels in progress.

My companions have shown caution, mistrust, of their new environment. I know, from reading centuries-old volumes, that when snow was more common, sometimes people who saw it for the first time as adults behaved like children around it, taken by a strange joviality: the white substance, so miraculous, as if from a dream, here today and gone tomorrow, had the strange capacity of quieting the world, submerging it into something closer to a deadly calm. But they have instead taken unsure steps over the ice, which was wet in a particular way that I remember: frozen and refrozen often, perhaps with special machinery. Their feet had completely disappeared in the snow a couple of times, and this they had not understood.

We have not encountered blizzards, and we ought to be thankful for that, for I truly do not know how my companions would handle themselves. I only saw one such blizzard when I was here before, and I saw it from the inside of a construction. I wasn't allowed to go out under any circumstances. Even given my low-ranking status up in the Settlement—the ungrateful child from a lacklustre family—down here I possessed some status. Coming down, I was a sort of little king in waiting for them, and the people who gave me their hospitality truly preoccupied themselves with my well-being. I had imagined back then that, perhaps, they developed some fondness for me; soon I realised with a pang that, most probably, they were frightened of something happening to me down here.

Storms are not rare now, but they are less snowy and more filled with hail, and at the end of them the tundra can become a muddy space, with patches of dirty white here and there, but nothing more. I am therefore surprised at the pristine whiteness surrounding the NEST compound. The snow seems powdery here, with shiny crystal specks of ice. It is luminescent. There are a number of dark constructions, a little tower, and some hovering vehicles parked. At the limits of my vision, only one vessel. The communicating platform for the second lies naked, useless. Were there two here once? I seem to remember so. Has one gone already? It looks like it.

My three companions also grasp this fact at once, and I find myself attacked all of a sudden: how did I know the vessels would still be here, waiting after this long? If both had done the Jump, all this trip would have been for nothing! But I truly did not see why they were bickering: one vessel remained, after all.

Here, I suddenly remember, the celebration to honour the Jumpers is very different from the one down south, perhaps on account of their lack of green. Naked branches, twisted into amorphous imaginary creatures, pine cones, and offerings of berries and nuts featured prominently. No animal heads.

We decide when to make our move. The vessels are much further, closer to an ample expanse of white, and I have not discounted the possibility of crevasses. Behind them, far in the distance is the man-made pykrete glacier, named after its inventor, Geoffrey Pike, with its corresponding snow machine lurching on its top. And then we see them: the pack of bio-engineered mammoths that always accompany these fabrications as standard. They are massive, brown with orange specks, their tusks moving softly in the powdery snow below them; but their presence also gives perspective to the size of the glacier, and to the vessel. For the first time, I feel a strange unease when considering the massive structure. Will it fly, when needed? Will it ever come back with good tidings?

At seven p.m., while I am taking the first watch, and shortly after the sun has fallen, I see shadows around the mammoths, some shape that I cannot understand. It looks like a gigantic floating thing, resting behind the vessels, organic, with a surge of long limbs, unlike plant tendrils, more like tentacles floating down. The mammoths have moved as far away as they possibly can, without making any noise. I do not share this information with my companions, lest it alarm them.

They have learnt a new concept, a new idea: frost. They are complaining, complaining, complaining. My feet are frost, my fingers are frost, my cheeks are frost, they say. As if it were my responsibility, as if I could do something for them. I have become, somehow unofficially, the leader of their mission.

It is clear that we will have to go around the compound:

they complain once more. I point at the open land on which the lonely vessel sits, and suggest that we could not have left the vehicle any closer. But I know, I know. We have been walking for what feels like a long time to me as well, and they are so tired.

I am exhausted too. Again, I look in the direction of the compound, try to concentrate on the task of finding a route. We will have to wait for darkness—it falls earlier here than where we come from. We are covered in all the wrong colours to get close to the vessels undetected. I am concentrating, looking and making some calculations, when I see something on a branch.

A bird—luminous, peculiar, strange—all shades of indigo quivering on his feathers, and so alien to this place, to this landscape, that I gasp, uncomprehending, scared.

What have we done, I wonder?

What am I doing here?

The creature is completely out of place, as much as my three companions, with their raw, coarse skin after endless days labouring in the fields under the sun; with their makeshift uniforms made up of dead animals, and their machetes, useless here. They had not believed me when I told them there would be no jungle, and that the few forest environments that remained had been conveniently and regularly kept in check.

317

A bird. A blue bird. I think of Pearl, and wonder, is she up there now? The ring is no more than a flickering structure, translucent, hard to see in this grey dull light.

Hours later, success! We are testing our step inside the vessel. Alexander has proved his worth, for he is busy with the flickering lights, preventing the alarms from blaring. The interior of the vessel is like an anachronism, one of those we are so fond of at home: the crock-manufactured furniture lends everything a provisional look, the same rundown second-hand feeling that I remember from my arrival in Gobarí. But this is mixed with the dark metal and plastic of the doors, the command chamber, the keypads to open and close the air locks and rooms. It is a strange mixture; I do not recall being taken by it during my tour. Perhaps, as a mere tourist, I did not pay enough attention. Whereas now, now there is so much more at stake; something surely must be at stake, for what would we be doing here otherwise?

I realise I still don't know what we are looking for exactly. What is so important to Eli and her farm that she has sent us on a mission in which we are risking our lives? If we were found here, I imagine we would be shot. I look at my three companions. Only Alexander seems hard at work; the other two are perched next to the entrance and a little window, looking out for any sign that we have been detected. But Alexander carries on, diligently, pushing his commands, speaking orders, and drawing orders onto the bluish screens with his fingers. Only then I get a strange sense of déjà vu, and I wonder: has he been training, all this time, exactly for this moment, to do whatever it is that he needs to do here?

But, even without alarms blaring, giving us away, I am restless. I also feel trapped, all of a sudden. The chambers and compartments are not very large, at least not here, in the downside of the vessel, shaped like a gigantic egg.

'Someone needs to go up, and flare the automatic. Otherwise, the system is not letting me get any closer...'

'I'll do it!' It is Bohemas who has spoken, probably as bored with the waiting as I am.

'No! I will not be able to contain them, if I'm on my own,' Vania says.

'I will go,' I say. 'Just tell me exactly what I need to do.'

It is then that I see it, not for the first time. For I have also seen it during the trip. I have seen it, but I have also ignored that I have, believing I could truly stay, I could make a home down here: Vania and Bohemas exchanging the slightest of looks between them. It is only a second, and I almost miss it. It could mean many things, of course.

But here, this is what it means—that Vania was never happy with me lying with his sister. It means that, while Alexander is busy with the technical part of the mission, he and Bohemas come and push me into one of the vessel's chambers. They come after me, and start punching me in the face and the stomach. Surprised, I fall. They are hitting me hard with their feet now.

I hear Alexander saying something from the other chamber, I cannot catch what, but they stop momentarily, and Vania shouts something back. I take this opportunity to run. Somehow, I get up and scruffle past them to the next chamber. I play with the buttons next to the door until it closes. They both come after me, and smile at me through the window. They are also probing all the buttons on their side. I keep pressing some, trying to keep the door shut.

And, just like that, I seal my fate.

By the time I realise what is happening, it is already too late.

Die, blue bird, die.

Some lights go up. Their faces go pale in comprehension. Some more lights, a purring noise, a massive explosion. In fear, they fly to the exit.

I try to open my door, and find it impossible.

Minutes crawl by, painfully, in which I slowly, slowly,

come to realise what is happening. I cry for Vania, Bohemas, Alexander, anyone. No one comes, of course.

There is another massive explosion. The floor rattles, and suddenly my stomach floats up to my throat, as if I were skydiving faster, faster, as youngsters do with their first hovering cycles. Although I am not going down this time, but up, and up, and up.

And there I go—a worthy sacrifice, I hope—swimming among the stars.

PART II

THE VESSEL

24

They fish for pearls in the depths of the ocean, they say down on the surface. They fish for pearls at the bottom of the sky; and also, it seems, at the end of the Universe, where I am heading.

The vessel is not exactly driving itself, but letting itself go, deep into space, endlessly drifting. The dark is an infinite void of silence, and I embrace it.

I hate to admit to this, but despite my Upper Settlement education, I realise with a pang that I am ignorant of many things: how the automatic systems work, how to manoeuvre this ship, how to turn it around. I did not pay attention in class when I was little. It could never be me, it would always be a child from the surface. Or so I thought. So every hour that passes I am gone a little more, I am gone a little longer, I am forever more gone. And then it hits me, with the shock of panic: this is forever, this is me, gone forever.

The deep advances upon me. And I picture him now, a leviathan that jumps out of the Three Oceans, entering space, where he swims next to me into the unknown. He accompanies me for a while, and afterwards he decides to return to Earth, and I can see him clearly until he dives back into the ocean, a ripple that reaches three different continents.

Perhaps he was never there, perhaps he was nothing but a mirage, of the sort that old explorers had on the ice never-ending.

I am not on the surface, I am not in the ring, I am not on a found star that can house us—I am... nothing. I am weak. I am hungry. I am more alone that anyone has ever been. How long have I been here?

My journey is not into an abyss, it is into myself, into my own consciousness; there and back, the hope against hope of a safe return, and the panic that it repeatedly hits when I dare to say it out loud, to say it to myself: it will not happen. Until the panic stops, and a new realisation dawns on me: I had always wanted this, secretly, I had always hoped for this. There is nothing for me down there. My journey is into a dark sea, and I let myself go into its embrace, like a true swimmer. I am going to die. Not so bad a fate, I think. I have always wanted this, I insist, only to myself, for there is no one else here. I have always wanted to be free.

After what might be hours, days, there is a bird here, with me. She is blue.

The bird flutters around my face, in a repetitive fashion. It wakes me from my slumber, and I find myself lying on a corner, practically hidden below the desk of a control panel. Hiding like a child will hide. There is an alarm blasting and an overpowering red light, that comes and goes and illuminates everything, and the walls seem to be covered in the blood of a slaughtered animal. I think of Pearl, explaining, 'Matanza; but nothing, nothing happened here.' Nothing, nothing, is happening here either, except my own death.

What is a blue bird doing here? Go! Run! Did she

follow us inside when we climbed into our illicit operation and got trapped? Is she even real?

I want to shout to the bird to please let me be, to spare me the annoyance: I am soon to be dead after all. I would like to be left to die in peace. Is that too much to ask?

The blue bird comes and goes through the open door. I try to reach the controls to close that door, without moving from the floor. She quickly returns, attacks me furiously, pecks at my hand.

I cry in fear and in pain.

What do you want, little blue bird? Who has called you here?

I eventually get up, with difficulty; first, I had scrambled to find straps. Now, I have reached zero gravity. I am floating in mid-air, and it is difficult for me to move without propelling myself by holding handles disposed for that purpose on the walls.

The bird is pecking at my hair now; she is insisting now, I see that, as a dog would. She is insisting that I follow her.

We traverse corridors with the same flickering red lights—warning lights—for the vessel is flying erratically, aided only by the emergency protocols. It doesn't bother me; we are ascending without control, and without direction, and that is all fine. I am dead anyway. I propel myself as best I can, but everything takes so much longer in zero gravity. As if I am a swimmer in the ocean.

She stops. There is a door with a small window. She is pecking the small window. Does she want me to peek inside? I peek inside. I look back at the bird, to thank her perhaps? I do not know any longer; I am too stunned to think. She is leaving now, going down the corridor; she is gone. Her mission is complete.

Where are you from, little bird? Are you even here? Are you but a dream?

On the other side of that door there is a short-range shuttle, an evacuation model. I want to cry. And I do.

The little blue bird has saved me.

I am saved.

I didn't want this after all.

I return to the control room, as quickly as I can, which is to say advancing annoyingly slowly. I throw whatever is in my way furiously on the floor until I find it, the guide to the vessels, children's edition. All the codes for all operations are at the back, as an afterthought—never meant to be used, it seems. I also now know where the shuttle can take me, and I am not disappointed.

Only use in case of emergency. Think twice before use! The future of Humankind is in your hands. Ask yourself: do you really need to use the shuttle?

Home. It will be a home, of sorts. I exit the control chamber, again with difficulty—the power is now upping frantically, all systems go, red, but also green, blue, white lights that anticipate the moment of calm before the storm, a crash. Floating, I make my way back towards the short-range shuttle.

But before... *Red flickering lights, green flickering lights.* A sound like a click, the computer furiously beeping, cracking, a static noise in the middle of the rattle. A communication channel that opens. Is it possible? Is someone down there aware of what has happened to me? Am I about to be offered assistance?

I grab the control panel so as not to fall in this erratic flight, and advance towards the comms area. Static. Static. Voice. Static. Longer voice. The message is not coming from the ring. The message is not coming from the surface. I do not know where the message is coming from. The message is coming from what looks like a lifetime away; the message is coming from an impossible distance.

I play the message. I cannot understand the words.

I move quickly back into the shuttle area, holding myself to the walls as I advance. The warnings are becoming more urgent, the alarm even quicker, the lights flicker faster. All systems gone, the vessel powering up towards its unmanned end.

I am going to die, I am not going to die.

No, I am going to vomit.

I cannot stand these lights, this shaking, this crashing. The air is getting hotter around me. I cannot see it, but I can sense it: the vessel is going to disintegrate.

I reach the shuttle, prepare myself to be expelled from Hell, enter the selected destination: the ring. No more fantasies about a surface life for me now. Before the shuttle detaches, as an afterthought, I transfer the message, the coordinates of the message [0 08' 13' / 0 04' 08' QW (M3000)], record them both. I prepare myself for the pain, strap myself in as well as I can. I hold the armrests in fear. I click my acquiescence to this possible death—I have never manned a shuttle, but everything around me reminds me of hovering vehicles, and I am hopeful—feel myself falling into the void.

How far away from home I am? I am farther than anyone has been, at least anyone that has gone with the intention of returning. Luckily, the shuttle remains within range of civilisation.

A thought strikes me then. And I replay the message once more. I think I understand it now, its meaning, for all of us down there. It is simply that I cannot quite believe it.

25

[A click: communication channel operative]

Forgive our silence...

[The cracking voice of an old woman]

The silence of days, months, years...

We have landed.

[Faint static noise]

Explorers, in the old days, chartered their progress with such efficiency, opening new routes to a river's source, to the poles, to the top of mountain ranges. But not the travellers. They had different reasons to want to disappear. They signed their letters 'July, maybe August, 1898', or 'Unknown region. Rocky mountains', hardly distinguishing the solid world from dreams.

On a dream we were sent; we thought we were explorers, but we weren't. We were travellers, allowing the unknown to guide us. We have reached it now, we have landed.

Please, forgive our silence.

[Faint static noise]

Like them, those travellers from aeons ago, we have preferred to chart by getting lost. For they found their way eventually. But they got there making circles, drawing endless spirals, twisting and twisting over each other's steps, endless little islands they were. They got there, eventually; they got there almost by chance.

We are here now, we have found our here.

We are an island.

Please join us.

We need you.

We wait for you.

Crew of Vessel 20003-XN, NEST programme,
Launched from Earth in the year 2346

EPILOGUE

Then

Quickly, quickly, before I forget it all... She had been mixing memories with dreams, with songs and fables. How could she remember now?

> Little blue bird, little blue bird. Where are you going,
>   little blue bird?
> Little blue bird, little blue bird. Where have you gone,
>   my little blue bird?
> Do you want to know the truth, little blue bird?
> There is a star so far away, waiting for you all.
> You may need to die to get there. Not much, just a little
>   death.
> Little death, little death, what have you done to me...
> Die, blue bird, die.
> For the children are waiting in their brown world,
> And they need your blue feathers to survive.

She went backwards, willingly, much further than she had before; only then she would understand what had happened.

It went like this: she and Verity were playing on the coast; it was Kon-il, for there were no rockpools in Old Town, only in Kon-il. Verity had been crying: she had cut her feet on a rock. But she wasn't crying for that reason, she was crying because she was scared of the vessels, quiet and translucent at the edge of their vision.

'I don't want to!' She was saying, or was she? Yes, yes. That was it. She was crying because she didn't want to go up.

Was that what had happened? Was Verity going to be sent in a Jump?

What did Pearl do? How had she comforted her friend?

It all came to her now, like a torrent of images; as if someone had opened a faucet up in the ring, an outpouring of tears. She was crying now, because she had finally remembered.

What was it? What had she done? She had imparted her knowledge, piecemeal and infantile, snippets of conversations dropping from Urania, her father, the lady who visited them often. She had said it: 'Swim! Fly away into the stars!' And Verity had gone, into the water.

She had gone smiling, as Alira had done, all those centuries back; or perhaps she was terrified. But bravely she had walked into the water, farther and farther, until she was no more than a dot upon it, far away from the safety of the shore, but so far away still from the section of the wall which she would never reach. When Pearl's father had got to her and brought her back it was too late already, she was long gone.

Now

The little bionic bird brings its master, and so she is found. She stops what she is doing, feeling that she is being observed. Slowly, she raises her head, and then she sees him, looking in her direction from between the crowd of people. For a moment, neither of them moves.

Pearl fears Arlo may disappear if she does, another hallucination.

He starts advancing in her direction.

Arlo, in the ring. Arlo, wearing rich clothing. Arlo, smiling at her, bionic bird floating at his side.

He stops next to Pearl, and she can see that he is wearing the shiny colours that only the highest officials can display; the contrast between them must be difficult to miss for any passers-by. She hears the gasps of dismay when they embrace and kiss.

Outside of their makeshift house on Kon-il beach, three large white shuttle-labs connect together; the sounds of the ocean and the light of the sun wake Pearl.

Arlo and Verity, their daughter, are already up, collecting samples in the rock-pools to take into the lab. In the distance the Barrier is a gigantic ruin with an open wound in the middle, through which the Three Oceans enter, mixing with the managed portion of water that had been Kon-il. Now, both seas compete in evening each other out, and the colour of the water, that before looked brown and yellow, is now a little more pristine looking; greenish to bluish green, perhaps, a 6 to 9 according to the Forel-Ule Scale. Now, Pearl also understands that the reflection of light off the water is also to blame here, that sometimes the colours are unreal, a mirage of sorts. However, the 6 to 9 mark is a progression of sorts: algae returning, with some dissolved matter still.

Neither Pearl nor Arlo had anticipated this bluish-green, and they are, for now, contented.

Arlo, the Upper Settlement's hero. Arlo, humanity's saviour.

It was not difficult for him to claim Verity back, to convince the scientific elite to let him try the bacteria down on the surface.

Arlo, Pearl and Verity were offered a coveted space in the craft that would depart for the found star. It was only just that they were given this space, as Arlo was the one to bring their message of hope. To everyone's surprise, they declined the offer. Their place was on Earth, on the surface. No one could deny them their wish. The day the vessel departed, this time to a set destination, they did not join the festivities, but they watched it go, climbing up and up into the ether.

In Kon-il, dawn comes quickly. The sky goes purple, more so now that the bluish-green from the ocean is changing the colour and, Pearl maintains, the flavour of everything. There hasn't been a beam of blue light since they got down here, and that is good; no more experiments, at least for now. None of them knows for how long they will be allowed to continue with their work; but for now, this is their life.

It is a good life. There is the lab, and for Pearl her own small repository, where she composes her tales. No excess here, only a few things that matter. Two books, rocks, pine cones, dried flowers, a few images, printed on paper in the old-fashioned way.

Sometimes the night is impossibly eternal, and Pearl understands: she thought she would never see Verity again. She had internalised that pain, and it is hard to let go. Verity's constellation is the Kingfisher, the same as hers. Together, they read the poetic fable:

> Little blue bird, little blue bird. Where are you going,
>   little blue bird?
> Little blue bird, little blue bird. Where have you gone,
>   my little blue bird?
> Do you want to know the truth, little blue bird?

She looks at Arlo, and knows that their union is now blessed, that the tentative cooperation they have installed between the ring and the surface is the key to it all.

Away, in the deep ocean, a leviathan wails: an old song.

ACKNOWLEDGEMENTS

Thanks to the Clarion 2014 crowd; everything I write is still influenced by what I learnt from you, and what I wrote with you. To my PhD supervisory team: Helen Marshall, Una McCormack, Tiffani Angus. To my examiner, Roger Glass. To the Titan dream-team: Sophie Robinson, George Sandison, Polly Grice, Dan Coxon. To my family, James, Oliver and Anita, who allowed me to finish this book under quite difficult circumstances.

There are two works of literature that have inspired me beyond measure to write this novel. One is the Southern Reach trilogy, by Jeff VanderMeer, in particular the first, haunting novella, *Annihilation*. I have spoken and written in many places of the influence of Ann and Jeff VanderMeer's definition of the Weird on my work, and of my admiration for Jeff's body of work. The second is the novel directly responsible for my desire to write in English, Jean Rhys's *Wide Sargasso Sea*. I could never claim to have attempted to re-imagine *Wide Sargasso Sea*, as to do that would be a futile, absurd enterprise: Rhys's novel is a masterpiece, and it would be foolish to tamper with a masterpiece. But I have taken my inspiration closely from the novel. Since I first read it, *Wide Sargasso Sea* has struck me with how closely I could relate to its description of a world in which issues of 'equality' and dominant culture proved that nothing as prosaic as the law could indeed make us equal, and that many other undercurrents decide these things for us. I related intensely to the heroine's navigation of the complex politics of her mixed ethnicity, and saw it a reflection of my own hopes and fears: my own background had seemed to conspire to destine me to some things, had not allowed me to reach other dreams. I hope this has turned out to be a book that proves one thing: no matter who tells you that you cannot do something, there is always a way. Do not let them put you in boxes. Do not listen to them.

Marian Womack,
Cambridge 2020

Marian Womack was born in Andalusia and educated in the UK. Her debut short story collection, *Lost Objects* (Luna Press, 2018) was shortlisted for two BSFA awards and one BFS award. She is a graduate of the Clarion Writers' Workshop, and she holds degrees from Oxford and Cambridge universities. She writes at the intersection between weird and gothic fiction, and her stories normally deal with strange landscapes, ghostly encounters, or uncanny transformations. She is also the author of *The Golden Key*, a Victorian supernatural mystery set on the Norfolk Fens.

Marian lives in Cambridge, at the edge of the Fens, with her husband, their children and two ageing Spanish cats. When she is not writing she can be found working as an academic librarian, or editing books and pamphlets in her indie publishing project, Calque Press.

For more fantastic fiction, author events,
exclusive excerpts, competitions, limited editions and more

VISIT OUR WEBSITE
titanbooks.com

LIKE US ON FACEBOOK
facebook.com/titanbooks

FOLLOW US ON TWITTER AND INSTAGRAM
@TitanBooks

EMAIL US
readerfeedback@titanemail.com